HUNTING THE VA SLAYER
A Bitter Wind Mystery

Also by C. M. Wendelboe

A Bitter Wind Mystery
Hunting the Five Point Killer
Hunting the Saturday Night Strangler

A Manny Tanno Mystery
Death Along the Spirit Road
Death Where the Bad Rocks Live
Death on the Greasy Grass
Death Etched in Stone

A Tucker Ashley Western Adventure
Backed to the Wall
Seeking Justice

A Nelson Lane Frontier Mystery
Marshal and the Moonshiner
The Marshal and the Sinister Still

HUNTING THE VA SLAYER
A Bitter Wind Mystery

C. M. Wendelboe

Encircle Publications, LLC
Farmington, Maine U.S.A.

Editor: Cynthia Brackett-Vincent
Book design: Eddie Vincent
Cover design by Deirdre Wait, High Pines Creative, Inc.
Cover photographs: petroglyphs © Bolo-Photo;
background scenery © Getty Images

Author photograph by Heather M. Wendelboe

Published by: Encircle Publications, LLC
PO Box 187
Farmington, ME 04938

Visit: http://encirclepub.com

Sign up for Encircle Publications newsletter and specials
http://eepurl.com/cs8taP

Printed in U.S.A.

ACKNOWLEDGEMENTS

TO MY WIFE HEATHER FOR taking photos and telling me where to go. To the VA Police in Cheyenne for answering odd ball questions, and for Scott McRae for his modeling panache. To Diedre Wait for her work on the cover design, and for Cynthia Brackett-Vincent and Eddie Vincent for their advice on the telling of this tale.

*To all the women and men in uniform who have sacrificed their lives,
and for those that frequent the VA facilities around our country
with medical issues sustained in the defense of our country.
And for those patching the thankless warriors up.*

"It is foolish and wrong to mourn the men who died. Rather, we should thank God that such men lived."

—George S. Patton Jr.

1

A RN ANDERSON SAT AT THE kitchen table staring at his morning coffee cup like he was reading tea leaves.

"What gives with the hound dog look?" Ana Maria Villarreal asked. She sipped her own coffee between nibbles of an onion bagel. She set her cup down and pulled her bathrobe tightly around her shoulders. "You look like you lost your best friend."

Arn sipped of his coffee and crunched his nose up. Damn if he didn't hate cold coffee as much as he hated what he feared he was about to get sucked into. "*I* didn't lose my best friend—Helen Mosby did."

Ana Maria sat silent waiting for Arn to explain at his own pace. As she always did.

"Helen's husband, Frank, died of a heart attack a few days ago and she wants to talk with me about it."

Ana Maria rested her hand on Arn's arm. "Was he a friend of yours?"

Arn nodded and looked at his piece of toast that he hadn't touched, now colder than his coffee. "Frank's younger brother, Jessup, and I hung together at East High." He pushed his plate away from him. "Frank was the big brother I never had. Thirteen years older than Jessup and me and I looked up to him."

"I'm sorry."

"Me, too. Frank would come sit by Jessup and me when we hung our poles in the water at the Fishing Lake trying to catch some crappie. And now and again he'd let us drive his car, even though we could barely see over the wheel. He even gave us our first sip of beer,

1

warm though it was. Jessup bragged how his big brother was a ground pounder in Vietnam and bragged even more when Frank graduated from Officer Candidate School at the top of his class." Arn forced a smile. "Helen was his high school sweetheart. Married right after he came back from 'Nam, and they were never separated after that. Until a few days ago."

"But now Frank has had a heart attack." Danny Spotted Elk slapped dry wall dust off his jeans before entering the kitchen. He ran his hand through his stringy, gray ponytail and shook dust off onto the floor in the hallway. "Couldn't help but overhear." He refilled Ana Maria's cup and poured himself coffee before washing his hands in the sink. "Must have been some friend," he said over his shoulder, "for you to tear up like you are."

"I'm not tearing up."

Ana Maria leaned across the table and bushed Arn's cheek. Her hand came away damp where tears had cut tiny rivulets in his dusty face. He looked away and grabbed a napkin to dry his eyes. "What makes it so hard is that I talked with Frank just last week. He was practicing for a 5K in the Senior Olympics." Arn smiled as he recalled the way the old Army Major had tried talking Arn into joining him for his daily run. "Frank could be mistaken for a man twenty years younger, he was in *that* good of shape."

"You mentioned his wife wanted to talk to you about his death," Ana Maria said. "Why?"

Arn shrugged. "I can't say." But he did suspect what she wanted. She mentioned his death wasn't *quite right*, and Arn dreaded talking with her. "Maybe she just needs someone… empathetic. A shoulder to lay her head on while she cries," he said with little conviction in his voice.

"No offense," Danny said, "but that ain't you. No offense, but you're not Mister Compassion."

"I know that," Arn said. "That's why I sure would like someone else to go with me," he said as he met Ana Maria's gaze. "Someone who can weep and moan with the best of them."

"Me?" Ana Maria said. "I'm supposed to be taping an animal cruelty story to air next week," she said, holding up her hand. "Sorry. I'll tell

DeAngelo that something has come up, and I'll tape it tomorrow. I'll go with you when you talk to her."

DeAngelo Damos owned the local television station, with Ana Maria as their star reporter. In actuality, she was DeAngelo's *only* reporter with any experience." "I don't want you getting into hot water because I can't... connect," Arn said.

Ana Maria waved the air. "If DeAngelo gives me any grief, I'll tell him I can quit and go back to turning a wrench. Any number of repair shops in Cheyenne would love to have a good mechanic. See how he takes that."

Arn nudged his coffee cup. "I don't know. Maybe I ought to just tell Helen that something's come up." He nodded to Danny. "I did promise that I'd help you hang drywall today."

"Oh pleeease go," Danny said. "Don't feel bad about me doing it by my lonesome. Without your help—as you so generously refer to it—I can get twice as much done with half as many mistakes." Danny was right about that—where Arn lacked any kind of handy-man skills, Danny was the maestro in home remodeling.

"It's settled then." Ana Maria stood from the table. "I'll put on some clean clothes. Where does Helen want to meet?"

"At the funeral home," Arn said. "As if it's not hard enough meeting her at a time like this."

"Then I had better wear my *mourning* clothes," she tapped Arn on the shoulder. "And you do the same. Wear your suit jacket."

"Might as well," Arn said. "The only time I get a chance to wear it is in court and at funerals. And sometimes, it's hard to distinguish what I'm attending at the time."

———

"Go on inside," Arn said. "I need a moment."

"Understood," Ana Maria said and entered the funeral home.

But she couldn't understand, Arn was certain. He didn't need a moment to compose himself because it was Frank Mosby laid to rest—Arn just never cottoned to *anyone* slabbed-up at the front of the parlor under gaudy bouquets of flowers no matter who, no matter how good the mortician-turned-artist had made the dearly departed look. Arn thought back to the many "celebrations of life" he had attended as a lawman, and he had grown to hate funeral homes.

As he stood outside with the funeral music barely audible from inside, Arn's thoughts returned to his father—his send-off had been a doozie. He had passed out on the railroad tracks just in time for a Union Pacific engine to plow into his ratty old Buick, pushing the car all the way before stopping nearly a mile down the tracks, By then, his father had been unrecognizable as a human being inside the crumpled mass of General Motor's iron. That didn't stop the artist-in-residence at the funeral home from trying to make him look presentable.

He had failed miserably.

But then, one could expect no less from a body that had lain inside such a mangled car.

That was one of those times—like now—that he wished he were a smoker. He needed *something* to calm himself. All he could do was take deep, soothing breaths before entering the funeral home.

The wide mahogany door creaked like a warning in an old Bela Lugosi movie as Arn stepped through. The dim lights of the viewing room matched the funeral dirge played in a minor key piped throughout the speakers embedded every few feet in the ceiling, preventing Arn from going anywhere inside the home and escape the depressing music.

A tall Lurch-looking man stood with his hands clasped in front of him. He had an odd way of smiling that turned the corners of his lips up ever so slightly, leaving the rest of his dour face an impassable visage. As if he knew no pleasantries awaited inside. "Please sign the guest book," the man said in a monotone, remaining where he was as if he intended standing there all night to ambush visitors to the parlor.

Arn signed the ledger under Ana Maria's name before placing his Stetson on a bent wooden coat rack and entering the viewing room.

Helen Mosby—a thin black veil covering her face—sobbed even as Ana Maria held the old woman's shaking shoulders. She glanced up for a moment as Arn reverently walked past her to the front of the room where Frank Mosby laid in his plain casket. A U. S. Army flag had been draped over the closed portion of the casket beside an Army 1st Infantry banner. A dozen full bouquets of flowers had been arranged around the casket, leaving a narrow pathway to approach the deceased.

He looked away, remembering his mother's words that people often appeared just like they were alive once the mortician finished working his magic. As Arn looked down at the open casket, he drew in a sharp breath. Frank Mosby looked *exactly* like he did when Arn talked to him this past week. "We'll start easy," Frank chided Arn when he saw the former Army officer stretching his hamstrings against the curb in front of his house. "We can work up to something more strenuous, but for now a nice, easy four-mile lope would do you wonders." Arn had declined, admitting to himself that Frank, being far older than Arn, was in so much better condition. "Clean living," he always told Arn attributed to his longevity. Yet here he was, the youngest seventy-five-year-old man Arn knew dead from a heart attack.

Arn kissed his fingers and touched Frank's forehead. "Rest easy, my friend," he said under his breath and turned to where Ana Maria sat with Helen in the front row.

She looked up at Arn and started to stand when he motioned for her to remain seated. "Silly thing to ask, but how are you holding up, Helen?"

She pulled her veil back from her face and leaned close. Mascara had run down her hollowed cheeks, and her reddened eyes met his. She forced a smile as she took Arn's face in her hands and kissed his cheek. "As good as expected for someone who just lost the only man she ever loved." She looked past Arn to the casket. "He looks so... alive, doesn't he?"

"He does," Arn answered. "Looks just like when I spoke with him last week."

"Frank mentioned you... interrupted his run. But he laughed when he said it. He was always encouraging people to keep in shape."

They sat in silence, then, listening to the filtered music, until Ana Maria broke the quiet of the room. "I talked with Chief Oblanski. He told me someone found your husband on the floor of a restroom at the Veteran's Center here in Cheyenne."

Helen took a silk handkerchief out of her clutch purse and wiped her cheeks. "Another veteran came into the restroom and found Frank. He'd fallen—apparently when he had his... heart attack. He must have hit his neck when he went down, all bruised-up like it was before the mortician hid it so nicely."

A man wearing bib overalls and carrying his Union Pacific hat entered the viewing room. He walked to the casket and stood silent for a few moments before leaving. "Friend of Frank's?" Arn asked.

A slight smile crept over Helen's face. "*Everyone* was Frank's friend. He had that ability to make folks feels special. He was that way before he went into the Army, and it stayed with him through Vietnam." She looked down at her handkerchief stained dark from her makeup, and her smile faded. "That's why it was so hard for me to realize Frank was murdered."

Arn looked to Ana Maria who shrugged. "I thought Frank died of a heart attack."

Helen nodded. "Frank's doctor at the VA thought he died of a heart attack. And the coroner backed him up."

"Is that why Frank was at the VA, being treated for a heart condition?"

Helen looked past Arn again to the casket for a moment before saying, "he always joked that he had a prostate as big as a bagel. That's why he was there—to pick up his meds. And he had to get his annual blood draw." She took Arn's hand and squeezed it. "I need you to look into his murder."

Arn looked to Ana Maria, but she was no help. Even though there had been no autopsy performed on Frank—Arn could tell by the way in which Frank's head appeared undisturbed by any Stryker saw—he just did not understand her suspicions. "Helen," Arn said, "if the doctor said he died of a heart condition and the coroner ruled it as well, what makes you think Frank was murdered?"

Helen sat up straight in the seat and placed her hands in her lap. "Because my brother, Steve, died in the same manner at the Ft. Meade VA Center two months ago. The coroner in South Dakota said Steve died of a heart attack, too, but he was in as good of condition as Frank was. I believe Steve was murdered, too."

"Still doesn't explain why you think their deaths were not natural."

Helen turned red, and Arn could tell she was frustrated that he didn't share her suspicions. "You said many times that few things are coincidental, have you not?"

Arn nodded. "But that was pertaining to investigations I was involved in— ."

"Two men from the same family dying mere months apart of the same thing is just coincidental? Especially when both men were healthy as a horse?"

"Helen, just what do you want me to do? I can hardly argue with doctors and coroners."

Tears started streaming down her cheeks again and she pulled the veil back over her face. "Humor an old woman," she said. "Look into their deaths for me. I need to know if Steve and Frank *did* die naturally."

Arn bent over and kissed Helen's forehead. "Of course, I will." He motioned to Ana Maria. "If there are things that you think of later that might help me, you can be sure Ana Maria will keep it close to her vest."

2

ARN STOOD IN THE LOBBY of the new Public Safety Building in front of the Police Information Desk admiring the vintage photographs adorning the walls on both sides of the desk. The agency had recently moved from the old telephone building, and this was a welcome change from the dingy lobby of the old building. Officer Smith sat in his chair behind the elevated desk overseeing whoever entered with a problem. Right now, Arn had a problem.

"Don't mind if I stick around and watch the action?" Smith said and grinned. "She's on her way down now."

Arn glared at him. Since Gorilla Legs had been relegated to the police chief's *assistant* secretary—pushed out of her position by a *pleasant* lady—she had been on the prod. And right now, Gorilla Legs was stomping down the stairs to confront Arn.

Arn heard her before he saw her descending the stairs, heavy feet clomping on the steps as Arn hastily formulated his strategy of dealing with her. He hoped the secretary and gatekeeper to the Chief of Police had mellowed out since Arn last talked with her. But he doubted it. The woman—a descendent of Vikings she was always fond of telling folks—was as frightening as any usurper who ever sailed a Norse vessel.

"Anderson," a deep voice boomed, echoing off the stairwell leading down to the first floor, "you'd better make your little tete-a-tete with the Chief short. He's got a lot of work to do today, and he don't need your bullshit to distract him."

"Yes, ma'am," Arn said, sizing her up, wondering if he could take her in a fair fight. She would be a handful, with her thick football-player legs and arms any iron worker would be proud of. He finally concluded he would prevail in a battle with the Norse goddess standing in front of him, but he would sustain more injuries than he ever did competing in high school rodeos.

"Follow me," she ordered.

Arn stayed a safe distance behind her as they walked up the steps and she used her security card to open the door to the hallway leading to the chief's office. "Remember," she said as she tapped the watch on her wrist before shutting the door. "Make it damn quick, Anderson."

Chief Oblanski's crew-cut head was just visible above the back of his desk as if he had lost something on the floor. "Safe to come out now, she's gone," Arn said as heavy footsteps faded down the hallway.

"Thank God," he said and stood from his fortress. "That woman is running me to death."

Arn pointed to the stack of paperwork sitting on the corner of Oblanski's desk. "Looks like you got enough *Chief* work to last for years."

"At least until the next budget is in. I'm just damn glad I'm not chief of your old department."

Arn understood where Oblanski was coming from. More than a few times he had walked in his Captain's office at Metro Denver right before budget time to find the poor bastard nearly bawling trying to put figures together.

Oblanski sat and motioned for Arn to do so as well. "As much as I hate seeing you come through the door—because I know you'll be a pain in the butt—you are a welcome distraction from this," he said and slapped the pile of papers. "Want something to drink?"

"Last time I was here, the machine had a mind of its own like something out of a Steven King novel."

"I had Mort down in IT reprogram it."

"Then I'll have a cup," Arn said, "of whatever you're having." He set his hat on the chair beside him while he watched Oblanski swivel in his chair. He punched buttons on the new beverage machine, and it started whirling.

"What brings you here when you ought to be out golfing?"

"I don't golf," Arn said. "Never could get the hang of hitting those little balls on the fly with my .38."

When the machine finished spewing out the liquid, Oblanski handed Arn a cup. "What's this?" he asked, sniffing the hot liquid.

"Green tea," Oblanski said. "You said you were having what I'm having."

"You been talking to Ana Maria?"

Oblanski held up his hands. "Not me. But this does help one's regularity."

"Why the hell is my regularity all of a sudden the object of public scrutiny? You *have* so been talking with Ana Maria."

"Getting back to my question..." Oblanski quickly changed the subject.

"Helen Mosby asked me to look into her husband's death."

"Frank Mosby?"

Arn nodded. "Your department still assists the VA Police?"

"We do," Oblanski answered. "But what's there to look into?"

Arn eyed the trash can on one side of Oblanski's desk, gauging if he could toss the tea in it without being seen. "Helen's brother, Steve, died at a VA Center in South Dakota two months ago of an apparent heart attack as well."

Oblanski sipped his tea and turned up his nose as if regretting going healthy this morning. "I'm still not following you."

"Helen just wants to make sure both men died naturally."

"I can't speak for her brother, but the coroner assured me Frank Mosby died of heart problems." He stopped mid-mouth and set his cup down. "If I'm hearing you correctly, if Helen doesn't think their deaths were natural—."

"They were murdered," Arn said. "At least that's what she is convinced of."

"Well, her suspicions are flat wrong," Oblanski said.

"Based on?"

"The Medical Examiner, I already told you."

"So, the ME performed an autopsy on Frank?" Arn asked.

"If you've been talking with Helen, you know there was no autopsy.

None needed, and she didn't demand one at the time." He nodded to his cup of tea. "Aren't you going to drink it?"

"I'm thinking of tossing it. I'm a coffee guy."

Oblanski grinned. "Coffee doesn't help your condition—."

"What condition?"

"Just trying to nip it in the bud," Oblanski said. "All you old folks have GI issues." He reached around and tossed the rest of his tea in the garbage beside his desk. "Don't blame you, though—I'll make us some coffee."

Oblanski stood and walked to a small cabinet behind where Arn sat before stopping. "Seriously, if we ordered an autopsy on everyone who died an unattended death—natural though it may appear—the department would run out of funds."

Arn understood. When he worked for Metro Denver Homicide, they would get called to all sorts of deaths that were natural—medical complications or weather-related deaths or for folks whose life just plain ran out. Unless there was something pointing to something other than natural, they did not order autopsies, either. "You did take photos, though?"

"Of course, we did," Oblanski said and motioned to Arn's cup. "Want another?"

"I'll wait for the coffee to brew. Wouldn't want my regularity to catch up with me right here in your office."

"Me neither," Oblanski said.

"Can I take a peek at those photos?" Arn asked Oblanski as he was measuring grounds.

Oblanski laughed and turned the pot on. "Are you a member of this department? Of course not. Ergo, you have no right to look at the photos."

"Thought you said Frank's death was natural. If that were true, what harm would it do to show a curious citizen what the scene looked like?"

"Look, Arn, I'd like to show you the pictures and diagrams of the scene—."

"Have you ever meet Helen Mosby?' Arn asked.

Oblanski grabbed a pencil among others stuck in an empty mug on his desk and began chewing the eraser off. Like he often did when he started getting nervous. "I gave her the death notice myself."

"Then you know," Arn said, "that she's just like your sainted mother. Grieving. Wanting answers."

Oblanski dropped his pencil in the garbage and turned to the coffee pot. "She's not like my mother," he said. "My mother was a stripper in Seattle and the only time she grieved was when she got too wasted and fell off the pole during a… performance." He handed Arn a cup of *coffee* and sat with his own behind his desk. He looked out the window of his second-story office at the First Interstate Bank building across the street as if people coming and going had the answers. "I'll ask Gorilla Legs to grab the file," he said at last.

"And not your new secretary?"

"My new secretary, Mary, is busy making people feel welcome to this office. Gorilla Legs still doles out files. When I ask her real nice. Excuse me."

"Good luck," Arn said as Oblanski left the office to grab the files. "If you need backup with that woman, call one of your brutes you have working the street."

Arn felt empathy for Oblanski as he walked out his office to ask Gorilla Legs for the file. Even though Oblanski was Chief, Arn knew she'd just as soon wrestle him to the ground over the file as comply with his request.

After many minutes and as Arn was contemplating calling 911 to rescue Oblanski, he burst through the door and shut it immediately. "She wanted me to remind you that you need to cut our visit short."

"As short as I can," Arn said. "Last thing I want is for her to give me the bum's rush."

Oblanski smiled. "That would be a YouTube moment. Here." He handed Arn the file on Frank Mosby. "While you're looking it over, I'll be working on my budget. Gorilla Legs gave me until the end of the day for my patrol budget requests. Or else."

Arn cringed when he imagined what her *or else* might entail. He opened the file folder across his lap and read the report: a Korean War veteran had walked into the restroom and found Frank lying dead beside the sink. The vet called the VA police who summoned the

Cheyenne Police investigators.

Arn set the VA report aside and flipped to the Cheyenne PD report. After he quickly scanned it, he went back and reread it closer: there was nothing to indicate an unnatural death. The investigating officer had called their crime scene tech to respond to take photographs only because Frank's death was unattended. No witnesses to see him collapse in the restroom.

Arn picked up the stack of photos and donned his reading glasses. He held each photo away from the glare of the overhead lights. Even though it appeared Frank died of medical conditions, the police photographer had done a thorough job of documenting the scene. Frank's body had been photographed from multiple angles, all which combined told a story. When Frank collapsed, his cheek cut from where he hit the stainless-steel paper towel dispenser, slight blood drying on the dispenser.

The bruise on the side of his neck might have been caused when he fell against the sink going down—the investigator had speculated in his report, and a large gash on Frank's forehead matched a blood spot on the floor where he fell, his final resting place.

Arn grabbed the photos and reports and stuffed them back into the folder. He handed it back to Oblanski, hunched over a calculator and eyeballing figures and spreadsheets and request forms. "See anything unusual?"

Arn shook his head. "Looks pretty cut and dry."

"*Pretty* cut and dry?"

"The reports and photos corroborate the coroner's findings—that he went down from a heart attack."

"I hear a *but* in there somewhere."

Arn nodded. "I'll know more when I see the report on Helen's brother."

"So, you're going up to Ft. Meade in the middle of the Sturgis Rally?"

"I have to."

Oblanski held up his coffee cup. "Then I toast the bravest man in Wyoming."

3

"THANKS FOR TAGGING ALONG," ARN said. "I know it's your off-day."

"I needed out of the newsroom for a while anyway," Ana Maria said. She rummaged through Arn's aging selection of eight-tracks in his tape box. "Yanni. Are you serious?"

"Give me a break—it's hard to find eight tracks no matter how many garage sales I go to."

She selected Johnny Cash taped at Folsom Prison. "We are *not* listening to Yanni." She slid the tape into the player mounted under the dash of the old Oldsmobile. "As for being my day off, I wouldn't miss the chance to see a lot of cool bikes."

Arn chuckled. "You just want to see the hot bikers riding them."

They pulled off Interstate 90 and Arn had to slow. Motorcycles cluttered the road four abreast, riding overly slow, wearing the colors of the *Devil's Jokers*. One biker glanced behind at the traffic backed up by the bike and turned back, undeterred. He said something to the others, and they chuckled. "This is my first time here in Sturgis during Bike Week," AnaMaria said, staring wide-eyed out the window. "My God, there are bikes everywhere."

"Last year Sturgis had an estimated six-hundred-thousand attending the rally," Arn said, down shifting into second as the bikers slowed even more.

Ana Maria rolled the window up to shut out the fumes. "Wish you'd get air conditioning for this beast. It's damn near a hundred degrees."

Arn grinned. "You *could* keep your window rolled down."

14

"Not on your life." Ana Maria coughed as she stared at motorcycles headed both ways, most ridden by frightening-looking bikers even Arn wouldn't want to meet in a lit alley, let alone a dark one.

The four bikers turned off into a convenience store, and Arn passed two others, a man wearing a mohawk, and a woman in tube top and assless-chaps. The woman stuck out her tongue at Ana Maria in a crude gesture, and her face turned crimson. "You got your gun I hope?" Ana Maria asked.

"I do," he said, "and—unless you sold the one I loaned you couple months ago—you should have yours with you as well." He laughed nervously. "Not that our two little guns would keep this swarm back for any amount of time."

"Oh, God— ".

"Relax," Arn said. "It's not as bad as it seems. Most bikers who come to Sturgis every year are decent folks just having fun and acting stupid before returning to their ordinary lives." He drove around two others gawking at his car like they never saw a classic Olds before. "It's those one-percenters like those boobs we just passed that give the others a bad name."

At Lazelle Street, they had to wait until an ambulance and two police cars sped by. "Accident?" she asked.

"More like somebody got stupid at the Buffalo Chip."

They headed east and Ana Maria rolled the window down again when the riders had petered out.

"When were you here last?" Arn asked.

"Last year," Ana Maria answered. "I had to pick up a steering column for that '55 Merc I restored. Found one from Jim's Salvage— neat place situated towards the airport. I could hang out there all week they have so many cool parts. But I've never been here during Bike Week."

"And you were never tempted to come here during the rally and get wild and crazy?"

She shook her head. "I was tempted once when I met a dude online who claimed to be a doctor. Said he attended the rally every year— ."

"You're not still on those dating sites," Arn said, "cause you could *probably* find a man with the way you look."

15

"Thanks," she said. "I think."

"And the last time you answered a profile ad on a dating site it damn near got you killed. You forgetting that?"

"How could I," she answered.

When she worked at the television station in Denver, Ana Maria answered an online dating profile. The man sounded ideal—a man Ana Maria's age. Wanting children. A real hunk by his picture. A doctor he said. When she finally met him, he wasn't Ana Maria's age but much older. He didn't want children—it would interfere with his life's work of abducting unsuspecting women. His picture was nothing like he'd posted, nothing that might identify him. And the only thing about Ana Maria's online love that was professional was that he was *professional* killer, intent on making her his next victim. As for a doctor, he called himself one—Doc Henry. He'd kept her prisoner in his ratty, run-down brownstone until Arn rescued her. The dating site was merely how the sociopath had lured Ana Maria and many others. "Thought you would have learned your lesson."

She laid her hand on his shoulder. "Relax. I did. I thoroughly checked this last guy out—he was a groundskeeper at the college and was even older than you, if you can believe that. Besides, I haven't logged onto one of those sites for some time."

They passed the sign announcing they were entering Ft. Meade VA Center, and Arn recalled what he had read about it when he was a youngster in school. The Army had established Ft. Meade in 1876 to protect miners and settlers in the Black Hills from Lakota and Cheyenne Indians bent on driving the white man from their sacred grounds. As they followed the signs to the Administrating Building, Arn thought how they could use the cavalry right about now. A crowd of forty-odd men and women blocked the road, anti-government chants echoing off the buildings, waving signs attacking the VA.

One man—slightly built with the distinct odor of marijuana reeking from his tattered clothing—banged on the front fender and looked in the window when Arn stopped. His greasy and stained arm band matched the logo on the sign he carried—*Righteous Sword of the Lord*. Arn slipped his revolver from his pocket and placed it under his leg. "You here for medical attention?" the man asked. He started leaning into the window when Arn pushed him away. "What the hell's it to you?"

The man fidgeted with dirty silver colonel wings on his lapels as he looked about for backup, but the others were too absorbed in their chants and the waving of their silly signs to pay them any attention. "If you're a veteran, you're part of the problem."

"What problem?"

"The U. S. military, of course," the man said.

"I've never been in the military."

"Then you can drive on through." He circled his hand overhead and the crowd parted to let the Olds through.

Ana Maria turned in her seat and watched the crowd through the back window. "What was that all about?"

"Who the hell knows. Protesting something. None of our business, though."

They drove another two blocks to the admin building and climbed out, the chanting still audible two blocks over here. "You really think these government people will tell us anything about Steve Urchek's death?" Ana Maria asked, as she had several times since they left Cheyenne.

"Bureaucrats are too damned worried about their pensions," Arn answered as he locked the car. "Wouldn't tell me squat on the phone, but I'm hoping you can persuade them."

"It's not like they're going to pity us after a five-hour drive. What makes you think they'll tell us anything about Helen's brother now?"

"By talking to another brother."

"How's that?"

"By talking to a brother in blue—I'm going to talk with the head of their VA police. If he's like other cops, he and I will have solidarity, me being retired law enforcement and all. He'll sneak me the information we're looking for."

17

4

THE *BROTHER IN BLUE* RUNNING the VA Police at Ft. Meade
wasn't a *he* at all. The *sister in blue* was an attractive lady in her mid-
thirties, strawberry blond hair pulled back in a tight bun, wearing just
the proper amount of makeup so as to look the part of a professional.
Lieutenant Misti Waddie smoothed her dark blue uniform shirt
before sitting across from Arn and Ana Maria at the long conference
table. She glared at them for long moments before speaking. "Let
me get this straight—you propose that I allow you to examine all
information on the death two months ago of this Steve Urchek?"

"That's what I'm asking," Arn said. He had tried overcoming her
reluctance to having civilians talking with her about police matters
by cranking up his charm. Apparently, Arn's charm-fairy had taken a
leave of absence for the day because Waddie was not impressed.

"Ridiculous," the lieutenant said. "I can't have civilians waltzing in
here demanding to look at something that is none of their business."

"It's for the family," Arn said, wringing his hands like that funeral
home director back in Cheyenne. "Just so Urchek's sister can get some
closure— ."

"So you've told me already," Waddie said. "I can't let you see the
report. And don't expect the Meade County Sheriff's investigators
to be any more forthcoming to such a notion if you go asking them."

"Lieutenant," Ana Maria said, taking Arn's cue to resume the
request like a good tag team partner. "Please set for a moment and let
me explain our... conundrum."

Waddie remained standing, hands on her hips, glaring at Ana
Maria. "Please sit. For the sake of your government position."

18

Arn saw a micro tic, a slight twitching of an eyelid that told him Waddie had suddenly become nervous. She dropped into a chair across from Ana Maria. "I'm listening."

Ana Maria smiled her toothiest grin. Disarming to most men. Met with cold stares from most women. This one especially. "As Mr. Anderson explained, I am a reporter with a network affiliate in Cheyenne. We have reason… no, we have *good* reason to believe that the deaths at our own VA center is connected with Mr. Urchek's at yours."

"They are not, I can assure you," Waddie said.

"See Misti… I can refer to you as Misti in my broadcast, can't I?"

"What broadcast?"

"The one where I spell out to listeners the connectivity of the deaths of both veterans."

"I told you—."

"I know you said they are unrelated." Ana Maria waved the air as if dismissing Waddie's arguments. "But without proof—without something tangible that Mr. Anderson can compare to refute your argument—I will *have* to speculate on-air that your agency did not conduct a thorough investigation."

Waddie's neck turned crimson, the hot blood flowing into her flushed face. "Steve Urchek's death *was* natural. The man died of a heart attack, for God's sake."

Ana Maria shrugged. "We—Mr. Anderson and I—are not so certain. And without looking at the report, I will have to conclude to my viewership that the Ft. Meade VA Police refused to cooperate. And ask them to reach their own conclusion." Ana Maria's face assumed a hound-dog look, her brows arching, her face slackening. Just like a trainer actor. A transformation Arn had seen many times from Ana Maria when she was extracting information from a reluctant person. "You see how it will end, Misti—that you hid *something*." Ana Maria took a pen from the side of her long notebook. "Is Misti with an *I* or a *Y*?"

The lieutenant slumped in her seat. "What do you need, Mr. Anderson?"

He lowered his voice as if there were others inside the conference room. "The complete file: reports. Photos. Scene diagrams."

Waddie stood and faced Ana Maria. "This better be off the record," she said, her last-ditch effort to save face.

Ana Maria batter her eyes. "Well off the record, Misti."

When Waddie shut the door behind her, Ana Maria breathed a deep sign. "I thought she was going to arrest me for intimidation of a federal officer."

"And have the whole incident broadcast for all of southern Wyoming? I'm just glad the bluff worked."

"What bluff," Ana Maria said. "I think there might be a genuine story here."

"Even without looking at Steve Urchek's file?"

She nodded. "Call it women's intuition. Besides, the big story—one that can be proven—is that RSL group of fanatics. I've heard very little about them."

"Remember, whatever Waddie shows us concerning Steve's death is off the record."

Ana Maria spread her notebook in anticipation of Waddie bringing the report into the room. "That doesn't mean I can't... use information I see in the reports to generate my own contacts. Besides, even if there's no story after I look at Urchek's death investigation, there is surely another story outside right now."

"You mean those fools that are protesting the military?"

"You got it. This Righteous Sword of the Lord have been keeping a low profile."

"Or maybe they've just been laying low until they get enough recruits for their own army to be a serious threat before escalating their protests."

"Either way, I think folks would be fascinated to learn more about them."

Arn checked his watch. Lieutenant Waddie had been gone for better than twenty minutes. Perhaps she was preparing to arrest them for intimidating a federal officer. "I got to admit it was pretty ballsy— generically speaking—for you to push Waddie like you did."

"Wasn't ballsy at all," Ana Maria said. "I tagged her as a career bureaucrat right off the bat, one of those more interested in their pensions and positions, just like you said. As soon as I saw the fifteen-year pin on her lapel, I knew she'd do anything to make it to twenty and to a cushy federal pension."

Arn thought of the brilliance of Ana Maria's reasoning. She was right—the last thing a federal employee wanted was to get the axe—for whatever reason, or for no reason—just *before* they reached their twenty years.

Lieutenant Waddie entered the conference room and dropped the thick case file in front of Arn. "You'll excuse me if I stay right here in the room with that file?"

"I'd have it no other way," Arn said.

Ana Maria scooted her chair closer to Arn as he opened the file and separated photos from officer's reports and began reading. Like Frank Mosby's death investigation from the Cheyenne VA, this one was scant, leading nothing to sustain Helen's suspicions of Steve's connection to Frank's death other than that they were family.

Arn set the officer's report aside and opened the autopsy report. Unlike Helen, Steve's Urchek's wife had requested an autopsy. The medical examiner—a contract pathologist out of Rapid City—had outlined Steve's lung problems—those of a two-pack-a-day smoker, possibly leading to his heart failure. "Guess Steve wasn't as healthy as Helen thought," Ana Maria said.

"She told me Frank had guilt tripped him into quitting smoking five years ago," Arn said, "and to start running. They even did the Run Crazy Horse Marathon last October as part of a five-person relay."

"Too bad he didn't quit sooner," Waddie said. "He might be alive today."

"Might."

"Are you satisfied the man died of heart problems?" she asked.

"Not quite yet," Arn said. "Do you have a laptop I can use?"

"What for?"

"I'd like to look at the death scene photos. They *are* stored on this disc?" he held up the disc that was stuffed in a pocket in the folder.

"So call us frugal," Waddie said. "The government is cutting paper, or haven't you heard."

"Laptop?"

21

Waddie stood abruptly and walked across the room. She reached behind a lectern and came out with a scratched and dented *Dell*. She handed it to Arn who promptly passed it to Ana Maria amid Waddie's snickering. "It's not that I don't know how to use these things," Arn told her. "It's just that Ana Maria is... a bit more proficient than me."

"Think nothing of it," Waddie said. "My dad can't operate those things either."

With the disc loaded, the investigation format popped onto the screen and Ana Maria started scrolling through the scene photos. "Say when."

As she scrolled, Arn saw that the Meade County photographer had taken enough pictures so that Arn got a grasp of where Steve had died. It showed Steve sitting on the commode, pants around his ankles, a copy of *VFW Magazine* lying at his feet. "Did he fall at some point?"

Waddie shook her head. "No. Some other vet got the two-minute warning and burst into the stall to find Steve sitting just like that. Way we figure it, Steve sat down for his constitution and strained a little too much and—*boom*—there went his heart." She looked sternly at Arn. "Man should have drunk something—green tea for example. Keeps a person regular so he don't strain so much."

"I've heard that," Arn said. He pointed to a faint discoloration on Steve's neck. "I ask because it looks like he fell against something in the stall perhaps."

"We wondered about that, too," Lieutenant Waddie said. "Steve had a blood draw and several doctor's appointments that day, but none could identify that mark. Crap!" She keyed the microphone clipped to her lapel and answered her radio call. "I'm needed outside for that damn protest. Be back in a moment, I hope." She jabbed at Arn with her finger. "And make damn sure all of that file is still there when I return."

As soon as Waddie left the room, Arn quickly slid the laptop over to Ana Maria. "I don't know how to do it but send a copy of that disc to my email."

"I can do that," Ana Maria said and started tapping keys.

"Not my regular mail," Arn said. "Waddie might track that if she suspects we've sent the pictures. Use my alternate email."

"Which is?"

Arn sucked in a breath. He had only used that email a few times since Cailee died. "Denverloverboy@AOL.com," he said under his breath.

Ana Maria stopped typing and stared at him. "Say that again."

"You heard me the first time."

She grinned wide and resumed typing. "Okay, Denver lover boy. Where the heck did you come up with *that* handle?"

Arn explained that after his wife, Cailee, died, he tested the waters for potential dating partners. Being a little on the shy side when it came to talking with ladies—actually being rusty and a bit rough around *all* the edges—he figured it was his only chance at a relationship. It had failed miserably when a lady that answered Arn's ad had him by twenty years and forty pounds, and he'd not ventured out into the dating scene since. At least none online, though he still retained the email address. For times than he wished to remain completely anonymous, such as if Waddie found out they had forwarded copies of the photos.

Ana Maria hit the send button. "Done," she said as Waddie came back into the room, panting, her uniform scuffed.

"Problems?" Arn asked when he saw Waddie's *U. S. Navy* pin—previously tacked to her lapel—torn away along with part of her uniform pocket. She wore a dejected look and dropped into a seat at the conference table.

"My guys had to drag six protestors away. One put up a hell of a fight and deputies are transporting the guy to the ER. He'll be resting tonight at the Meade County jail along with the rest of them."

Arn slid his chair back and took off his reading glasses. "I'm not familiar with that group out there."

"You must not be a vet."

"I'm not," Arn answered. "That yahoo that stopped us coming in mentioned something to that effect as well before he stepped aside and let us pass."

"Figures," Waddie said. "They only hate veterans."

Ana Maria closed the laptop and slid it across the table to her. "What do they have against vets?"

"Everything," Waddie answered. She slumped as if exhausted from her contact with the protestors, and Arn hoped she'd make it to her twenty years. "The RSL feels like the country should disband our military. That we are armed invaders when we travel to foreign lands to kill our enemies. All of that horseshit is outlined in their manifesto which you can get online with a donation to that fine bunch of assholes."

Waddie stood and tried tucking her torn pocket into the hole where a protestor had ripped it. "Now if there's nothing else, I have a lengthy report on what just went down out there."

Arn handed Waddie the file. "Just one more thing—I see the toxicology report is not in the autopsy file." Arn knew the medical examiner would draw fluids and send them to the lab for analysis. It was standard procedure for all unattended deaths. "Misplaced?"

Waddie tucked the folder under her arm. "The ME didn't put a high priority order on the tox. She figured with the lung and heart problems Steve Urchek had, there was no need to rush the report."

Arn and Ana Marie followed Waddie out the room and she told them to drive out the east gate to avoid the protestors.

"What are you thinking?" Ana Maria asked as they walked into the parking lot. "'Cause I know that look. You see something you didn't like?"

Arn couldn't put his finger on it just yet. All he knew is that—after looking at the photos—he began thinking of Steve Urchek as a victim. And of the pictures as crime scene photographs.

5

*A*s I sit patiently reading *a year-old copy of* The American Legion, *I wonder if any of the men around me this afternoon has ever been featured in the magazine, or for that matter any of the men I talked with in my own special way. I ran into a Lt. Colonel at the VA Center in Hot Springs last summer right after he returned from Iraq, complaining to me how he had developed medical issues from being close to burn pits. It almost made me laugh—an officer working around burn pits? I doubted it! It's the enlisted men—regardless of what war—who always bear the brunt of the nastiness of combat. It's always the enlisted men tasked with working around the pits who came away with medical complications. An officer working a pit—fat chance!*

A man older than me by some years walks by, and I pick up on the "scrambled eggs" embroidered on the bill of his cap. Unlike many of the veterans walking these hallways at Ft. Meade wearing caps designating their rank—an Army sergeant here, a Navy Master Chief there—his demeanor stands out from the crowd. I can always spot an officer even without them wearing something designating their rank. They swagger like they have more of a right to be in this facility than just enlisted men and women. Officers will elbow their way into an elevator past others, or they'll cut to the front of the line in the cafeteria like they are the protected class of military society. Once—years ago when they were active duty and had control over the lower ranks—they may have gotten by with treating others like dirt. But not now. Not when I'm around to do my small part to rectify their arrogance.

A retired major by his lapel insignia—no doubt living off the government teat—catches my eye as he saunters into the restroom. No one goes in after

25

him. No one has gone into the restroom in the past fifteen minutes, and I set the magazine down. Just as I walk nonchalantly toward the room, another vet—his staff sergeant rank proudly displayed on his Marine cap—follows the officer into the restroom ahead of me.

I pause, the anticipation of educating *the major washes over me, and I catch my breath, finally turning and walking away from the restroom. If I went in now, with the intention of… talking with him, old habits might surface. I might not be able to control my passions. And there I would be, trying to fend off the Marine in my zeal to educate the officer. I have spent too much time honing my hunting techniques to get caught now.*

As I was nearly caught three years ago.

I will not be sloppy again.

There will be other opportunities to deliver retribution to arrogant men!

6

ARN PULLED INTO THE CIRCULAR driveway of the house that Frank and Helen had lived in since they were first married shortly out of high school. The two-story brick affair stood in the historic part of Cheyenne on Carey where—in Cheyenne's infancy—the Cheyenne to Black Hills Stage Line rolled by twice a week on the way to Custer City and Deadwood beyond. Now all that rolled up was an aging former homicide detective who still retained some small amount of justice for those who can't speak for themselves. As Arn climbed out of his car and walked towards the door, he thought of Frank and Steve—both who could never speak for themselves again.

Helen stooped bent over picking up loose pinecones under the bough of a huge evergreen. When she spotted Arn, she used the trunk to stand slowly. She put her hands on the small of her back and arched, stretching, before pulling her wide, floppy hat over her eyes against the bright morning sun. "If you take a seat, I'll bring us some lemonade."

"That would hit the spot." Arn took off his Stetson and ducked low under overhanging pine branches to a wrought-iron wino bench well out of the blistering sun. As he waited for Helen to return with the lemonade, he thought back to the many times he had sat on this very spot whenever he'd come back to Cheyenne to visit his mother before she passed. Towards the end of her life, Arn found himself more and more sitting here talking with Helen. Fearing what lay ahead for her after she died, Arn's mother had practically lived in the Greek Orthodox church that she'd been a member of since he was a youngster. She had tried her best to shame Arn into attending as

27

well, but something about the dedication required to be Orthodox frightened him.

And Jessup. He and his childhood buddy would sit on this bench for hours after they were grown men. Arn would relate his exploits, about gory crime scenes he'd responded to as a Denver Metro cop, while Jessup told Arn of gory details of accidents on the slope when he was a ski bum in Telluride. Before the mountain claimed Jessup in a freak avalanche.

Helen returned balancing a sweaty pitcher in one arm, glasses in the other, and set them atop a small, round glass table in front of the bench. She poured lemonade over ice in both tumblers before sitting next to Arn. "I take it you're here to tell me how stupid it was for this old woman to suspect her husband and brother had been murdered."

Arn sipped his drink, drawing his explanation out slowly. He had rehearsed it on his way over, figuring just what he would tell Helen. He had thought hard about the photos of Frank's *crime scene*—for he had realized after comparing the two deaths it *was* a crime scene. He recalled Frank's body where it had hit the sink in falling down, and Steve's final resting place on the toilet in the Ft. Meade restroom. At first, he reasoned that there was no connection, that he was placing too much stock in his *gut*—a feeling that had served him through thirty years as a lawman. He told himself that common sense would overcome him, and he would be left with explaining to Helen her women's intuition was no more reliable than Arn's gut instinct. Until he compared more closely both crime scenes and determined that he and Helen *were* right. "Frank and Steve were both combat vets— ."

"You know that were," Helen said. She took a neckerchief from around her hat and dabbed the sweat from her forehead.

"And they were officers."

Helen set her hat down and looked at Arn. "Are you trying to tell me there *was* a connection?"

Arn nodded. "I'm thinking there must be something in their war service that is common to them."

"But both served in Vietnam, though at different times and different places." She held up her hand. "I know you're thinking there may be some connection such as a run-in with another soldier who's decided to take revenge after all these years. But Frank was an Army Captain. Military intelligence stationed in Saigon, and Steve was a Marine Lieutenant in charge of an artillery battery at Con Thien. A thousand kilometers apart."

When Arn said nothing, she leaned closer and asked, "you *have* learned something that shows their deaths are connected?"

"I'm just not sure," Arn said. "After looked at photographs of both death scenes, I saw some… commonalities between the two."

"Such as?"

"Both Frank and Steve died in VA restrooms. Both appeared natural, but both had some discoloration on the sides of their necks that no one can explain. I'll know more when I talk to the ME here tomorrow." He refilled their glasses and put the cold, damp goblet against his temple to stem a rising headache as he tried wrapping his brain around what he'd seen in the photos.

About what he *didn't* see that had caused him to lose sleep last night. "How about when they returned from Vietnam—did they have any run-ins with anyone you can recall? Anybody here in Cheyenne?"

Helen stood and walked to a sunflower at the edge of the tree shade and plucked a weed. "Frank worked as an oil field representative after the war. Never had a lick of trouble with anyone."

"And Steve?"

She twirled the weed in her hand for a moment before dropping it into an apron pocket. "When Steve rotated back to the states, he went to the University of Wyoming under the GI Bill. He mentioned a time or two that he got into some heated arguments with the quarterback of the football team—Steve was an offensive end for UW. He said the man—Julie Lang—was arrogant and a bully, but he never mentioned running into the man after graduation." She chuckled. "As big as Steve was, I doubt most men could take him on." She brushed away a pine needle stuck to the side of her glass. "There just was nothing in our family history I could think of to connect them." She brought the glass to her lips when she set it onto the table, her hands shaking, ice clinking in the tumbler. "I hear something in your voice that tells me you found *something* odd when you went to Ft. Meade."

"It's just a small thing. Nothing, I'm sure. I'm certain if I picked up on it the medical examiner did as well— ."

"What did you find, Arnold?"

Like Arn's mother, Helen always called him by his Christian name when she was losing her patience. "Both Steve and Frank had slight—almost imperceptible—bruising on the sides of their necks," he said, indicating the area between the neck and the trapezius muscle.

Helen let out a long sign and slumped back in her chair. "I didn't see Steve's photos, but the police investigator showed me Frank's pictures when I asked to see them…" She looked away for a moment. When she turned back, her eyes were as wet as the side of Arn's lemonade glass and she brushed her hand across her cheek. "Frank had a little bruise on his neck where he had hit the sink when he collapsed. I thought it likely that he would sustain such a bruise."

"But Steve didn't fall *anywhere*," Arn said. "He simply died… sitting on the commode. And he had a bruise identical to the one on Frank's neck."

"What could have possibly made it then," Helen said, "if not from someone else?"

"I don't know," Arn said, but he *did* know. Or at least, he suspected. The bruises were consistent with those made from a brachial stun, a blow police were just beginning to be taught as Arn was retiring from law enforcement. The thought of a lawman who would kill both men repulsed and frightened him. Whoever made the bruise had to know that it would not kill either man, especially someone as big as Steve. They had to have been killed another way. But how?

7

"THAT'S A MIGHTY OUTLANDISH CONCLUSION,"** Danny said. He wore a flowered apron he had found in a dumpster down by the railroad tracks. He stirred sauce on the stove as he had for the last half-hour. "I'm no great fan of cops myself, but even I know they don't go around killing people unnecessarily."

Arn donned his reading glasses and read the side of the tea box. There didn't seem to be any special ingredient that he needed. He was, after all, as regular as the railroad. Most of the time. "I'm not happy thinking that way myself," he told Danny. "I'm clutching at straws I suppose, trying to figure out who besides police would know such a technique."

Arn pushed the box of tea away before walking to the stove and sniffing Danny's spaghetti sauce. He leaned over Danny's shoulder when the old Indian handed Arn a soup spoon. "You're as bad as a kid. Taste a sample, then quit bugging me."

Arn dipped the spoon in and came away with a small portion of the sauce. He let it roll *sloooowly* down his throat, wondering just when Danny was going to patent his recipe. "I just don't know where else to look."

"Has it ever occurred to you that those bruises you described just might be a coincidence?"

Arn sat at the table and cradled the cup of tea, which was becoming cooler the longer he put off drinking it. "I don't believe in coincidences. Especially where deaths occur. No, there is something I'm missing. I thought there might be a connection with their military service, but they were in different branches. Different parts

31

of Vietnam. Different jobs during the war."

The combination of the front door alarm beeped and Arn heard Ana Maria enter. "Wipe your feet!" Danny yelled and put another paper plate on the table.

Ana Maria walked into the kitchen and dropped a folder in the middle of the table. "You'll never guess what I found out in my research this afternoon."

"Oh, gosh," Danny said before Ana Maria could explain. "I can hardly wait. *But*, we will have to wait. I didn't concoct the perfect spaghetti and garlic bread only to eat it cold."

"But—."

"But nothing," the old man said. "It'll keep. Unlike supper. Sit And eat. If you're really good, I made a chocolate mousse for dessert."

———

They brought their desert into the parlor of what used to be Arn's mother's sewing room, where she would sit for hours. Somewhere, Arn had a pair of mittens she had knitted for him. He'd been embarrassed to go out the door on his way to high school winters wearing the pink mittens with so much room for cold to enter they did Arn little good. He'd watched her darn socks in this room, using a wooden egg to make sure the repairs were just right. Only because Arn's father—even though he was a full-time policeman—drank up so much of the family budget they could not afford new socks every time Arn got a hole.

"I'll grab coffee," Danny said and went to the kitchen.

"Ok," Arn said, "let's hear what you're so excited about."

Ana Maria unfolded another TV tray and opened her folder on top of it. "I've been researching VA centers in Wyoming and South Dakota. Know what I found?"

"A lot of sick vets."

"That, too. But I found eight deaths—including Frank's and Steve Urchek's—in the past two years at veteran's hospitals."

Arn took the smallest spoonful of his mousse and rolled it around his tongue. "Don't you think it's possible they died because they were at the VA? I'd bet that if you researched deaths in civilian hospitals, you'd find the same thing. After all, more people die in hospitals than anywhere else."

Danny came back into the room. He had two cups of coffee for himself and Ana Maria, and handed Arn a cup. "What's this?" Arn said as he crunched up his nose.

"It's some of that green tea you bought."

"Well, who said I was ready to start drinking it?"

"Excuse me for exercising my critical thinking skills," Danny said. "I just figured—since you brought home a new box—that you'd be wanting to try some."

"I was going to... ease into it. Wean myself off coffee."

Danny shook his head. "At your age, you might be too *easing*. A man your age gets almighty irregular."

"Can we just talk about regularity and bowel movements another time," Ana Maria said. "I'm trying to tell you about what I found."

"I know what you found," Arn said. "Sick people. You already said that. And we already concluded they die in hospitals all the time."

"They do," Ana Maria said, "But most folks die in their beds. Or on operating tables. All these I found have died in restrooms or unused offices at the VA centers. One died in a part of the hospital that was under construction. With no one there to witness *any* of the deaths."

Arn picked up the internet readouts and the replies Ana Maria had received, all cross referenced for accuracy. Each veteran that died of apparent natural causes had the same discoloration on the side of their necks. Ana Maria had highlighted each bruise with a yellow Sharpie. Arn hadn't told her about the bruising on the victims—she uncovered that on her own. He handed the empty folder back to her. "Have you inquired outside Wyoming or South Dakota?"

" I have not," she answered. "I thought since we... you... were looking into Steve and Frank's deaths that I'd contact hospitals just in those states."

Arn scanned Ana Maria's results more closely. All eight victims—including Steve and Frank—had been found by others stumbling onto the victims. And each—the investigators noted—had odd bruising on their necks.

"What do you think?" Ana Maria said. "They connected or not?"

Suddenly, the chocolate mousse Danny spent so much time making didn't taste so good, replaced by a bitterness in his mouth by what he suddenly realized—all the deaths *may* be connected. "I wasn't one-hundred percent convinced Frank and Steve's deaths *were* related." He handed Ana Maria the folder. "Now I'm not so sure. Now I think I'd better talk with Sgt. Wagner at the VA. Right after I talk with Chief Oblanski again."

8

A RN WAITED OUTSIDE THE TINY VA Police office until Sgt.
Wagner arrived. A towering former Marine Gunnery Sergeant
with close-cropped hair he was—like many security people here at
the VA—retired military who had served combat tours in Iraq, first
as a platoon leader, then a stint in G2—Intelligence. Somewhere in
his three tours, he had picked up a nasty-looking scar that ran down
one cheek that he proudly displayed, like German soldiers picking
up scars from duels with matched rapiers. "My secretary said some
private investigator wanted to talk with me," Wagner said when he
had come around the corner and saw Arn leaning against the wall
beside his office.

Arn took his laptop case from his shoulder and fished into his
pocket, handing Wagner a business card. HAVE OLDS—WILL TRAVEL
was superimposed over a photo of Arn's old 442. Wagner smiled
and pocketed the card.

"I know it's cheesy," Arn said. "It was something my... roommate
came up with to generate business."

"More like drive business away," Wagner said. "What'cha need?"

"A veteran's widow asked me to look into the death of her
husband. Can we talk?"

Wagner looked sideways at Arn. "A death here at the VA?"

Arn nodded.

"All right," Wagner said, "but my office is a bit stuffy. Let's talk in
the courtyard." Arn followed Wagner outside and to a picnic table
next to a planter of blooming flowers. He took his portable from
the belt holder and placed it on the table. "Now which death is it,

35

because if it's that overdose that came in two night ago—."

"It's not." Arn took out his notebook and flipped pages. "I'm talking about Frank Mosby's death."

"Frank Mosby… Frank Mos… sure, that old Army Captain who took a Double Gainer against the sink in the crapper last week. But what is there to look into—the man died of a heart attack."

"I looked at another veteran who died at Ft. Meade—."

"What's that got to do with the facility here?"

Arn explained that Steve Urchek had visited the VA Center in Ft. Meade for a routine blood draw—like Frank had—and had went down of an apparent heart. Like Frank. "Both men had similar bruising on their necks," Arn indicated the area where the photos showed the discoloration.

"Except that they were both family I see no connection," Wagner said as he shook out a Virginia Slim. He lit it with a Zippo bearing the Marine 1st Division insignia on the side. "Heart attacks are common with duffers their age."

Arn took out his laptop and inserted the disc he had pirated from the VA in Ft. Meade. He opened the file and turned it so Wagner could see it. "This is the crime scene photos of Steve Urchek in Ft. Meade."

"How'd you get this?"

"The crime scene fairy," Arn said. "The point is, it looks suspiciously like Frank Mosby's crime scene."

"You are acting like these two deaths were anything but heart attacks. That's just nonsense."

"Indulge me," Arn said. "Look right *here*," he said and pointed to the bruising on Steve's neck and compared it to the side-by-side image Ana Maria had made for him. "I think it might be from a brachial stun." Before talking with Wagner, Arn had researched the technique taught by police agencies around the country, but Arn was unfamiliar if it the VA police learned it. "I talked with Chief Oblanski… the cops here are taught it as are the deputies."

Wagner's hand went instinctively to his neck. "We practice that here in custody and control. It damn sure isn't pleasant, but it never killed anyone."

"Perhaps I could visit with the instructor," Arn said. "Get a better insight into it."

Wagner lit another cigarette on the one in his mouth and dropped the snipe onto the ground. "We have no permanent instructor. We're only twelve officers, but we take updates from a traveling teacher."

"When might he be here?"

Wagner took his phone out of his pocket and ran his fingers down his scheduling app. "He's at the Sioux Falls VA these next two days." He pocketed his phone. "Winger Hays is the guy. He'll be here Thursday to put on a refresher."

"Winger?"

"Steven Hays. He got the nickname Winger in Iraq when he shot a dozen times at an intruder who breached the security fence and only nicked the guy in the arm. Winged him."

Arn flipped a page in his notebook and took out his pen. "What do you know about the Righteous Sword of the Lord? Guess they claim to be some religious zealots."

Wagner snubbed out his cigarette and took a can of Copenhagen from his hip pocket. "Think they're connected with your friend's death?"

Arn shook his head. "Just curious. They were protesting at Ft. Meade when a friend and I were there."

"Where to start," Wagner said as he wiped excess snuff off on the leg of his uniform trousers. "They're just a bunch of idiots that sit around smoking dope in their compound outside Windsor, Colorado. They come out now and again to protest. We've caught some slinking in here trying to recruit for their... cause."

"Compound? So they are some kind of religious sect?"

Wagner chuckled. "They have tax exempt status. Like churches. But they damn sure ain't any church, though to a man—and woman— they are every bit the zealot of any fringe religious groups."

"At Ft. Meade, they specifically asked if I was a veteran."

Wagner nodded and spat a string of tobacco that *smacked* against a rock like a mini-rifle shot. "Their organizational statement says they stand against any American military involvement. Anywhere. They advocate for the disbanding of all armed forces in our country."

"They ever protest here?"

Wagner's radio crackled and he turned his head to answer it. "Get somebody else to help," he said into his radio and set it back down. "Some dude in the ER keeps taking out his catheter, and they want help. Last thing I want is to hold some fella's tally whacker while a nurse shoves it back in.

"But to answer your question, they protested here a couple years ago. We called the Cheyenne PD to help and we stung them pretty good. Hauled nine protestors to the hoosegow, including their leader, Jonah Barb. Calls himself a Colonel. Good news is they haven't been back since, though we've gotten word the RSL is planning a protest here."

"Then I'd watch your back," Arn said. "That bunch we ran into in South Dakota looked ready to drag us from the car and do bad things."

Wagner laughed. "If those boobs we arrested couple years ago are any indication, they'll be too stoned to be much more than an annoyance or block traffic."

Arn handed a copy of Ana Maria's spreadsheet to Sgt. Wagner. "Here are the dates of six more deaths in the last two years at VA centers in the region. Could you check to see if the RSL protested at these facilities these dates?"

Wagner looked at it but left it on the picnic table. "Surely you're not actually thinking these idiots had anything to do with—."

"I'm not thinking anything," Arn said. "I'm just tossing darts to see what sticks." He picked the sheet up and held it out. "Look at the positive side—if anything you uncover about the RSL helps solve what's been happening to those veterans, Ana Maria Villarreal will credit you with it on-air."

"Think so?"

Arn nodded. "Might even include you in her special."

Wagner stood and slipped his portable radio into the belt holster. "Might take me a few days. There's VA centers listed here in two states," he argued to himself, but a broad smile had swept across his tanned face. Like he was imagining jumping a pay grade or two or even getting a promotion. "You really think she'd mention me?"

"I can almost guarantee it," Arn said and left before Wagner could change his mind.

9

"I'LL HAVE THE TWENTY-OUNCE PRIME rib," Arn said and handed the waitress the menu.

Ana Maria leaned closer. "Are you kidding me, a twenty-ounce steak? That's like driving coffin nails into your body. How about a nice…" she studied the menu, "grilled chicken salad."

"Salad? I'm a carnivore."

"Then one of those senior meals—they're smaller portions."

The waitress—a girl a third Arn's age with a nose ring that would sink her in a pool in a heartbeat—put her hands on her thin hips as she waited for Ana Maria and Arn to finish arguing. "But I'm only twenty pounds heavier than when I graduated high school."

"But you're carrying those twenty pounds differently, I'm sure." She looked up at the waitress. "What do you think… he could stand to lose a few, right?"

The waitress looked around nervously for an exit route, finally answering when she saw no way out of it. "He could lose… maybe just a couple pounds."

"See," Arn said. "She said a couple pounds is all."

Ana Maria closed her menu and handed it to the waitress. "Medium prime rib and a dinner salad for me, and an *eight-ounce* rib eye for Man Mountain Mike here. And steamed Brussels sprouts on the side."

"You trying to starve me to death?" Arn asked after the waitress made a hasty retreat.

"You're the one that asked me to help you lose that old gut," Ana Maria said. She squeezed fresh lemon into her water. "I'm just doing you a favor."

40

"Some favor. Eight ounces isn't enough to feed a sparrow, and Brussels sprouts aren't fit for human consumption. Besides, when I asked for help monitoring my diet, I threw it out there more as a conversation piece than a serious request."

Ana Maria had taken Arn literally, lining up a blood draw for the first phase, and a follow-up appointment with a physician next week when the results of the blood work were to be completed. All because he hinted at his regularity issues.

Already he was literally feeling the effects of his new lifestyle Ana Maria had planned for him as he itched his arm under his shirt. After the blood draw, the nurse had slapped on a band aid and threw several layers of Kerlix over that to secure it.

"Don't pick at the Kerlix," And Maria said. "It keeps the bandage on."

She set her glass down and dabbed at her mouth as Arn caught a young feller out of the corner of his eye checking out Ana Maria. But then, she often got looks from men, even though she was as socially-inept as Arn at times. "Let's talk shop," she said. "That's why you invited me to dinner anyway."

Arn nodded.

"I thought as much. Something's bothering you."

Arn sipped the green tea she had ordered for him when he was away at the restroom washing up. As he took another sip, he scolded himself—*this stuff is getting to taste good to me. I am losing my mind.*

"What's been bothering me is that Helen has to be right. Her women's intuition agrees with my gut feeling... don't even say anything."

Ana Maria smiled. "Go on."

"We both believe there has to be a connection between Steve and Frank's deaths. And up until you came up with those other deaths at VA centers, I thought there was a family thing. That maybe someone hated both Frank and Steve for some... history they both had together."

"That was my first thought. So what's bothering you so much?"

"What's bothering me is that I know we're right. In my gut I know it. But I cannot come to grips with what it is. It's like I developed some brain disease and cannot use my thirty-plus years as a lawman

41

to realize just what I'm missing. I was up late last night racking my brain— ."

"I heard you go downstairs a couple times in the middle of the night," Ana Maria said when the waitress had set salads in front of them. "I think I also heard the fridge open both times and the ice cream was gone this morning." She exaggerated a look at Arn's belly. "Almost as if you were sabotaging your desire to lose some of that."

Arn took two bits of salad and pushed the rest away. "What *am* I missing? If there is some link—and I am not certain they *all* are connected—what is the common denominator with them?"

Ana Maria leaned across the table and rested her hand on Arn's arm. "The problem you have is that—when you were a homicide detective—you solved every one of your cases. And now you think there's something wrong with you if you can't solve these. Arn, it is not even your job to solve them. You're supposed to be retired. So, retire."

Arn turned in his seat and looked the restaurant crowd over. "Does a career cop ever really retire? You know what I see when I look these people over—I see potential suspects in everything from shoplifting to assaults to things far worse. Even though there might not be a criminal in the bunch, I am *still* suspicious of people."

"Maybe those suspicious are unfounded with the VA deaths," Ana Maria said. "When I researched those other unattended deaths, I was doing it on a whim. I had just wrapped up a story on the I80 traffic situation during this tourist season, and I had little else to do but sit in front of my 'puter and let my mind wander. I was just tossing it out there. I found nothing—nothing—to connect those deaths to Frank and Steve's— ."

"But the ones you found died unattended— ."

"People die unattended every. Single. Day. Doesn't mean I was on to something." She shook her head. "What I did do was put in your head some notion that there's a grand conspiracy to kill veterans at multiple facilities. Do me a favor. Please. Drop the notion that there was any connection between Frank and Steve and the other six and accept the fact that two old men happened to have heart attacks a couple months apart."

"Drop it?" Arn said. "You were the one got me started."

Ana Maris shook her head. "But this is getting a little . . . dangerous. If there *is* a killer out there, he—or she—might figure you're getting close." She laid her hand on his arm. "I don't want anything to happen to you. Just drop it."

Could Arn drop it? After hard thinking, he concluded Ana Maria was right. It wasn't his job to connect the dots on *any* of the VA deaths. Still, he always spoke for those that could no longer speak for themselves. "You were going to tell me about a special that DeAngelo approved today."

The waitress brought their entrees, and Arn stared at his plate even after she had left. "Look at that," he motioned to the steak. "I'll devour that in about two bites then call Domino's Pizza for a delivery here."

"But you'll walk away tonight a smaller man," she said as she took her first bite of fatty prime rib. She set her fork on the edge of her plate and closed her eyes while she chewed slowly. "Ah... this has got to be the *best* prime rib I've ever eaten." She speared another piece with her fork and stopped when she saw Arn staring at her plate. "You wanted to know what special DeAngelo authorized I go ahead with?"

"I'm more interested in how I'm going to have the strength to even crawl home after this sparse meal. But tell me about it while I drool over your prime rib."

And Maria took another loving bite and dug her reporter's notebook from her purse. She dabbed at her mouth with a napkin as she flipped pages. "DeAngelo gave me the go-ahead to do an investigative series on the Righteous Sword of the Lord. Look." She turned the notebook so Arn could read her hen scratching. "I've been doing some serious study on the RSL. Even though they're registered as a 501 (c) (3), they're sure no religious or charitable group." She picked up the notebook and turned it to the light.

"Getting a little hard to read?" Arn chided. "Like your eyes are growing old. Maybe you need my glasses."

"Never mind me," she said and laid the notebook on the table again. "The group was formed right after the First Gulf War by a man named Waylon Pike. He earned himself a Dishonorable Discharge from the Army for running prostitutes in Saigon."

"From what Frank Mosby told me right after he came back from 'Nam, the military looked the other way when it came to hookers and servicemen."

"Not when the servicemen invariably came up beaten and robbed. Even had a few soldiers MIA that were last seen with Pike's whores."

"Vietnam was a long time ago," Arn said. "How is it we've never heard about the RSL until recently?"

"Because Pike just recently found religion, in a manner of speaking," She took another bite of prime rib. "The religion of money, that is. *General Nehemiah,* as he calls himself now, found enough disgruntled servicemen from the Gulf conflicts to fill his ranks, though until recently they never numbered more than fifteen or twenty. Nehemiah squatted on public lands with his ragtag bunch of misfits—staying until the local law got fed up enough and put the run on them—the forests of Northern California one year. The Sierra Nevada's another. He even set his followers up at the Yellow Thunder Camp in the Black Hills after the American Indian Movement people were cleared out in the '80s."

Ana Maria turned another page and squinted. "After coming back from Vietnam, he made anti-military noise wherever he could. He attracted other vets who—almost to a man—had been drummed out of the military for doing some questionable and illegal things."

"You mentioned General Nehemiah found money?"

Ana Maria nodded. "Certain foreign government that were... in opposition to our country, started courting him. Governments willing to pay money just so that Pike—Nehemiah—could be a thorn in the side of the federal government."

"That's ridiculous, "Arn said. "A few protestors storming VA centers isn't going to alter the country's actions with the military."

Ana Maria finished her prime rib and pushed her plate away. "That was *soooo* good. But back to Nehemiah... he could care less if the RSL has any effect—he's hobnobbing with folks who will pay him to keep his hateful followers spun up and protesting. I found an article that claims that Nehemiah has been visiting Russia for the past eleven months. Before that, he was in Cuba. Hell, he's only been seen in this country once in the past four years."

Arn eyed the porterhouse on the plate of the man in the table next to theirs. He turned back to Ana Maria before he did something foolish. "So Nehemiah is living the high life— ."

"Off donations to the Righteous Sword of the Lord."

"I'm confused," Arn said. "If he's not running the show, who is?"

"That lovely man that reeked of dope and BO we had the run-in at Ft. Meade—Jonah Barb. *Colonel Jonah Barb.* He's running operations while General Nehemiah is away."

"You mentioned Nehemiah's been in the country once in the last four years?"

"He dropped in at the RSL compound in Colorado last summer. Seems like he gave Jonah hell for not staging enough protests. Ordered him to ramp up operations." She shrugged. "Guess the RSL doesn't rake in as much money unless they make a lot of nasty noise."

Arn eyed the Brussels sprouts and picked up his fork. Normally he wouldn't even think about taking a bite of one. But with only an eight-ounce steak in his gullet… "I thought DeAngelo turned you down when you pitched the special? Thought he didn't want to do anything with the RSL?"

"He didn't," Ana Maria said, "until Jonah came into the studio yesterday. He threatened to sue DeAngelo, claiming I have been snooping around, asking too many embarrassing questions about the group." She smiled. "DeAngelo bulled up. Told security to toss Jonah out on his ear and told him to keep a close watch on the evening news. He figured if Jonah Barb made that big a fuss, there must be *something* to the group worth exposing."

The waitress took their plates and replaced them with desert—a type of thick pudding sporting a dab of whipped crème on top. Arn eyed it suspiciously. "Isn't this what they give to old farts in retirement homes to help them swallow their medicine."

"Call it practice for when you *actually* retire."

Arn dipped his spoon in the desert and tasted it. "Damn, this is pretty good. Makes up for the Brussels sprouts." He wiped pudding off the corner of his mouth. "I better ask Oblanski to have his guys swing by the TV station now and again if that fool is threatening— ."

"Don't you dare," Ana Maria said. Her face flushed hot through her swarthy complexion. Her Latino side coming through, Arn thought. "I need space to do my research, and having cops lingering by won't help any."

Arn wanted to argue, but the waitress short circuited it. "Was the meal to your satisfaction?" she asked as Ana Maria grabbed the check.

"That was *the* best prime rib I've ever had."

"We hired a new chef… no, a culinary maestro he calls himself. And it fits."

"I'd like to personally compliment him," Ana Maria said.

The waitress bowed slightly. "I will tell him a grateful diner wishes to see him."

"You gonna put the moves on the cook now?" Arn asked.

"Chef," she said. "He's a chef, not just a cook. And he might be… dateable. I won't know until I speak with him."

"Well, get ready, 'cause here he comes with the waitress…" Arn froze for the briefest moment before putting his hand in his pocket and resting it on the butt of his gun.

Ana Maria followed Arn's gaze and she stiffened. A small man no taller than the waitress walked toward their table. His perfectly-creased and starched tall hat was perched on his head at a rakish angle, and his grin showed perfectly white pearlies. Like he always did when he smiled at Ana Maria in the courtroom.

Doc Henry stopped beside the table. He took off his hat and exaggerated a deep bow. "I thought that was you coming through the door. So glad to see you," he smiled at Ana Maria and his grin faded as he turned to Arn. "I can't say the same for your dining companion."

"Doc Henry," Arn breathed deeply to calm himself. "What the hell are you doing here?"

Doc waved his hat at the other diners. "I am preparing meals for these fine folks, of course."

"I mean here in Cheyenne? I heard you were paroled, but I also heard you're supposed to be in Colorado."

"Keeping track of me?"

"Damn straight," Arn said. "But I still don't know how you were paroled after only six years."

"You might say I impressed the parole board with my... cooperation. But—as you might guess—I was pleased to be transferred out of Florence ADX and to Centennial. Do you know what it's like to be housed between Ramzi Yousef and Ted Kaczynski and not even be able to talk to them about their... exploits."

He slid a chair out and began to sit when Arn said, "don't bother. You're not staying at this table long enough to get comfortable."

Doc smiled and put his hat on. "I see you're a mite flummoxed by my release. Suffice it to say, when I was in Centennial, I was able to study cooking, and expanded my education once I was transferred again, that time to Buena Vista. I became somewhat of a celebrity to the prison staff with my culinary prowess. And it impressed the parole board as well. So naturally when I earned release the Department of Corrections allowed my parole to be transferred to where I could obtain a position worthy of my skills. And, voila! Here I am at Mimi's utilizing my talents. And I have been here for two months now."

Arn started to stand when Doc backed away and grabbed his cell phone from the pocket of his apron. "If you lay even one finger on me, Anderson, I'll call the law. Then I'll own everything you own, including that shack you call a house." He snapped his fingers. "You know, I've always wanted a classic 442 like yours."

Arn stood abruptly and his chair toppled. Diners stared at him as he stepped toward Doc.

"One more step," he waved his hand around the restaurant, "and there'll be about thirty witnesses I can call into court."

10

ARN SAT IN THE SEWING room close to Ana Maria. Waiting. Patiently. As he would any victim who had experienced the horror she had. And tonight at Mimi's—when Doc Henry came prancing out of the kitchen to their table—it all washed over her memories once again. She looked up as Danny entered the room. "The alarm system's working perfectly," he said.

"Didn't you check the deadbolts?" Arn snapped at Danny. "Sorry. I'm just a little frazzled myself at seeing that bastard tonight."

"Understood," Danny said. "I'll grab us some coffee."

When Danny left the room, Arn gently laid his hand on Ana Maria's trembling shoulder. She forced a smile and handed Arn his snotty bandana back.

"Keep it," he said. "No telling when you'll need it again."

Ana Maria looked away and Arn saw fresh tears streaming down her cheeks and her lips quivered as she spoke. "How did Doc ever get his parole transferred up here?"

"That's what I intend checking into," Arn said. "I know a parole officer in Denver who can check discreetly. The main thing is that you're safe now." He gently massaged her shoulder. "I don't think there's anything to worry about. Doc's been working here for two months and this is the first we've encountered him. If he hasn't contacted me by now he won't."

She shrugged his hand off and met Arn's gaze. "Unless he's biding his time to make a move against me. That's what the Arn Anderson I know would be thinking right about now."

Arn had. He just didn't want her turning into a basket case before he found out about Doc.

Danny entered the room carrying three mugs—two hot chocolate and one steaming green tea which he handed to Arn. "For the man with the GI issues."

"I don't have GI issues dammit."

"Stick to that attitude," Danny said, "and before long you'll be wearing a colostomy bag."

Ana Maria picked up the mug of hot chocolate and sipped lightly. Her hand began shaking again and liquid spilled over the side and on to her jeans. She set it down and looked at Danny. "I'll clean it up."

"Don't worry about it," Danny said. "This room needs a good cleaning anyway."

She stood and dabbed at her eyes with the bandana. "I think I'll just turn in a little early."

"Want me to call DeAngelo in the morning and tell him you won't be in to work?" Arn asked.

"Don't you dare!" she said. "If that son-of-a-bitch Doc Henry gets wind that he's rattled me bad enough for me to skip work, he will have won. I'm going to bed early is all. When I wake up in the morning, I'll have all these thoughts about Doc out of my system."

As Arn watched her leave and heard her climb the stairs to her room, he knew Ana Maria would not expel Doc Henry out of her thoughts when she woke up. The intense fear that had overcome her when she saw Doc appear at their table would *not* leave her anytime soon. Hell, she may *never* be free of it, and if Arn had gone through what she had at the hands of Doc Henry he wouldn't have been able to either.

Danny set his mug of hot chocolate on the TV stand and curled his thin legs under him. "I know you and Ana Maria talked about this Doc Henry, but is there something I need to know like reinforcing the locks on the doors and windows? Maybe looking over my shoulder? We don't exactly live in the best neighborhood where folks watch out for one another."

"Maybe it's time I *do* fill you in about that sociopath. Then you can decide if you want to keep living here or leave for safer pastures."

Danny turned his chair so that he could face Arn. "I'm listening."

"Doc got his name," Arn began, fidgeting with the mug in his hand, "while living in southern Colorado. He killed—suspected but never proven—a young veterinarian just outside Trinidad and assumed his practice. He would make his rounds to the local ranches allegedly to drum up business for his new practice. Now and again, the ranch women would be alone while their husbands were in the field or buying stock or just in town at the feed store. Big mistake, 'cause it gave Doc the perfect opportunity to kill them."

"How'd Ana Maria get tied up with him?"

"When she realized two other murders displayed the same pattern—a man claiming to be a vet stopping by the ranches. She got hold of me, even though it was well out of my jurisdiction and we put together the killings—one in Utah, and the two in southern Colorado. But we were too late. Doc had skipped the country. Or so we thought until Ana Maria dug up three more victims in northern Colorado in and around Metro Denver."

"You said once that he abducted her," Danny said.

Arn nodded. "Doc moved to Denver and took on the persona of a professional man—claimed he was a gastrologist."

"An ass doctor."

"I know what it is. Now you want me to tell it?"

Danny waved the air. "Tell away."

"Anyway, Ana Maria was closing in—her research techniques really were something to behold. She knew *everyone* in Denver, and she started connecting Doc to dating sites where he met his victims on-line. Now that the gig was up with his faux veterinarian practice, he had to meet his victims discreetly somehow, and internet dating was it."

Arn stood and began pacing the room, recalling the details that— even that happened so many years ago— sent shivers up his arms. "Ana Maria went live asking the public's help locating the fake veterinarian. Doc knew Ana Maria's broadcasts would eventually lead to him, and he found her profile on a dating site. He passed himself off a doctor and suggested to meet her for a first date."

"Ana Maria's sharp enough," Danny said, "that some alarm bells should have gone off as many first dates turn tragic. She knew that."

Arn shrugged. "She told me later she got bad vibes from the doctor. But she thought she was just bullet proof. Always figured no one could get the better of her. But Doc did. When she went to the Five Points where they were to meet, Doc abducted her. Took her to a run-down place south of there."

"Did he… molest her?"

"Doc's not about rape," Arn said. "He never touched Ana Maria any more than he touched the others… sexually. Doc's all about imposing maximum fear in his victims. Right before he murders them."

"So he did torture her?"

"Psychologically. Every day for the week he held her, he would show her photos of his previous victims, gruesome that they were. He promised to kill her in the slow way he killed the others. But he never got the chance."

"How did you find her?"

Arn fought back tears as he told Danny, "She found me. Or at least she found a cell phone. Doc had taken her phone and purse, but he didn't take her money. When I interviewed him in jail, he said he never thought about taking her money. Thieving—he said—was beneath him."

"My ex-wife used to beat around the bush, too," Danny said. "Will you tell me for Pete's sake how you found her."

"I'm getting to it. She bought a cell phone," Arn explained. "She managed to open a basement window where Doc was keeping her and yell for help, but no one paid her any attention. Shitty neighborhood where everyone minded their own business, especially if it had to do with drugs. Anyway, she caught the attention of one junkie walking by. He wouldn't lift a finger to help her, but he would sell her his cell phone for a bundle of cash. Her bundle that Doc was dumb enough to let her keep. She called me and I figured it out by her description where she was."

Arn sat back down and eyed the cup of tea. "They were gone by the time I got there. Doc had just decided he didn't want her there anymore and took her to a park in Lakewood. Bastard had a thick leather shoelace coiled in his hand ready to kill her when we finally found them."

"Crapola!" Danny said. "I see why she's upset seeing him. But isn't there anything you can do to send him packing out of Cheyenne?"

"I just don't know," Arn said. "I'll check with Colorado Probation tomorrow, but I have my doubts."

"You know," Danny said, "there *is* another way."

Arn looked sideways at Danny. "What way?"

"Take Doc for a one-way ride somewhere. Or rather, pay someone to take him for his last ride."

"If I didn't know better, I'd say you were advocating murder."

"Let's say I'm advocating justice," Danny said. "You give the word, and I'll get hold of one or two of my old American Indian Movement buddies and make sure Doc gets sent to the happy hunting ground."

Arn laid his hand on Danny's thin shoulder. It had been decades since Danny was involved in the often-violent militant AIM, but Arn had no doubt he still kept in contact with many of those in the movement. "If it were only that easy... but thanks. I'll let you know. For the record, I've thought of giving Doc the royal send-off myself a time or two."

"I just don't see how he is out on parole after killing all those women."

Arn thought back to that frustrating day in the courtroom when Doc Henry was sentenced to abducting Ana Maria and killing *one* woman. "Doc is one of those geniuses that think things out methodically. He confounded his crimes so good, we weren't able to lay a glove on him for the southern Colorado murders. But we *knew* he was good for them."

"Pretty clever, meeting women on a dating site," Danny said. "But even I know it's easy to misrepresent yourself. Or someone else misrepresenting themselves."

"Danny," Arn said, "You didn't go on one those sites?"

"I did," Danny said, "Two years ago I wandered into the library downtown and used one of their terminals. I met a lady through *Babes Are Us* site who said she was fifty-three—."

"You would be old enough to be her father. What did she say when you told her your age?"

Danny forced a smile. "I told her I was fifty."

"Fifty! You haven't seen fifty in many moons. Weren't you ashamed of yourself?"

"At first," Danny said. "Until I met her. She had the nicest eagle head walking cane you'd ever imagine. Bad hips, she said. Artificial knee the year before, she said. When I found out she had me by about ten years, I didn't feel so bad fibbing a little. But it still makes no sense that someone as street-smart as Ana Maria got sucked into Doc's trap."

Arn sat, gathering his thoughts. Ana Maria was more like a daughter he didn't have than his friend and roommate. If Doc had been successful back in Denver that night… "Doc was to meet her at a restaurant in Aurora and changed plans at the last minute… claimed a hospital emergency and arranged to meet Ana Maria at an outside bistro in the Five Points. When Doc came up behind her—with not a soul still sitting there by the sidewalk café—she lasted about ten seconds until the chloroform took effect." Arn stood and started for his bedroom. "But before I head for the VA tomorrow, I'll know how Doc made it to Cheyenne."

11

ARN WAITED UNTIL ANA MARIA had left for the TV station and Danny had gone to Home Depot for paint before calling the Colorado Probation and Parole and punching in Sheila Dior's extension. He and Sheila had worked closely many times when Arn was with Metro Homicide, and they even went farther back to when Arn was a street cop. Sheila would tip Arn where he could find someone she wanted to revoke on, and Arn would often tip her off as to activities by parolees under her supervision. Now—ten years after he'd retired—she sounded the same as he remembered. "Thought you had died," Sheila said.

"Not yet."

"Then I might still have to buy flowers one day?"

"Unless you go first," Arn said. "Then I'll pick up a nice six-dollar bouquet at Safeway Grocery for you."

"What a deal," she said. "But what you been doing after all these years?"

Arn gave her the headline version of his stints as a private investigator in Wyoming, and how he was looking into suspicious deaths at VA centers. "But I'm not calling for that. I'm calling to check in as to how the hell Doc Henry made parole out of Florence. People just don't make parole every day from the supermax. Just how his probation could have been transferred up here is beyond me."

"Let me shut the door," Sheila said and returned to the phone in seconds. "Doc Henry was in the federal system, but I'm damn sure familiar enough with that SOB. He managed to sign up for drug treatment as soon as he went to Florence ADX— ."

54

"But he's never been into drugs."

"Florence didn't know that, and he got a year knocked off his sentence right off the bat. For the next three years, he was a model prisoner. Doc was a genius on computers and he helped the staff reconfigure their entire system. That Boy Scout tactic managed to earn him a transfer to Florence High. High security, but sure not the Supermax. While there, Doc studied culinary arts intending to use his new-found skills if he ever got out. He was again transferred, this time to Centennial where he cooked up a storm for the staff."

"Why get into cooking?' Arn asked. "Doc was one of the true geniuses I met concerning computers. I recall how damn hard it was to trace his on-line activity when he was luring women to him."

"A condition of his parole was that he never touch another computer. Ever. And before you ask, the warden got Doc a waiver through the federal judge to reconfigure Florence's system. He studied the culinary arts and became somewhat of a celebrity in prison, and before long, he got a sentence reduction. Of course. And another reduction the next year. Then out the door on parole." Sheila coughed violently. *She was still smoking Camels.* "I understand the warden about cried when Doc was paroled—guess the staff was going to miss his elegant meals. As for how he was transferred to Wyoming... I can only imagine what loophole his PO used to get rid of the son-of-a-bitch." She laughed which turned into a coughing spell lasting half-a-minute. "I would have passed the bastard off myself if he were mine."

—

Arn stopped by the VA Police office, but it was closed. A note telling folks the officers were training in the conference room hung on the door, and Arn walked the long corridor towards the room. Grunts and an occasional scream of pain echoed off the walls, and now and again a veteran walking past the room would flinch when he heard the screams.

He peeked through the tiny window before entering the training room and stood with his back against a wall. Wrestling mats had been placed end-to-end the width of the room, and eight officers were in various stages of throwing one another or slapping handcuffs on their training partner or just inflicting enough pain that Arn was glad he wasn't still in law enforcement. One officer had his larger opponent on the ground, kneeling on the big man's back, his elbow locked when he tapped the mat. When the smaller officer let his partner free, he rolled over and rubbed his shoulder.

Sgt. Wagner bent to his partner when he spotted Arn. He whispered something before standing and walking to where Arn stood. Sweat poured from Wagner's face and down to stain his gray sweatshirt. He stopped and bent over, catching his breath. "I think… we need… another victim," Wagner said, motioning to the officers.

"I'll pass," Arn said. "I did just what you're doing once a year for thirty years. Don't need to work up a sweat thataway."

Wagner swiped his face with the sleeve of his sweatshirt and exaggerated a look up and down Arn. "A ittle sweat wouldn't hurt you none."

Arn laughed. "Nowadays, I work up a sweat hanging drywall."

"Copy that," Wagner said. "I take it you're here to see the instructor."

"I am."

"I'll grab Winger." Wagner walked to the far side of the room and talked with a small man not much bigger than Danny, but about forty years younger. He talked with Winger who looked around Wagner at Arn and called out, "Beak. Twenty-minutes, ladies."

Winger Hays exuded that little-man attitude as he swaggered over to Arn. "Sgt. Wagner said I have to talk to you," Winger said but did not offer his hand.

"And you don't want to."

"For an old dude, you're pretty sharp." His lean face dripped sweat but he let it *drip drip drip* on to the mat. "You're right—I don't want to talk to you after Wagner said you insinuated there was something… dangerous with one of the techniques I teach. But the good sergeant said I had little choice but to answer your questions."

"I didn't say there was *anything* wrong with what you teach," Arn said. "I'm just trying to understand the brachial stun you train your officers on."

"What's to understand? You slap the hell out of them and *boom*, they go down."

"Then look at this for me." Arn opened his laptop onto a table that had been shoved into a corner. When the computer powered up, he scrolled through Steve Urchek's photos. "Look at this one I particular," Arn said, enlarging the image and pointing to the bruise on Steve's neck. "Could a brachial stun cause such a bruise?"

Winger turned the laptop against the glare of the florescent lights. "It could. If it was administered with enough force. But when I teach the technique, I tell the officers they don't have to do it hard enough to permanently injure someone."

"How big would a person have to be to inflict that kind of injury?"

"I don't follow you."

"Steve Urchek was a big man," Arn said. "Nearly as big as me."

Winger laughed. "Size makes no difference. You put the whoop-ass on someone with the stun and they go down."

"Even someone as big as me?"

"It's for guys your size that I teach the technique," Winger said. "It evens the playing field for little guys. Like me."

Arn scoffed, and Winger said, "You want to see what the stun feels like?"

Arn had attended enough custody control classes in his law enforcement career to doubt anything would seriously faze him. "It would help me understand it better. What do I do?"

Arn became aware that the other officers had come back into the room and stood in a half-circle around Arn and Winger. "Take your briefcase off your shoulder and I'll explain."

As Arn set his briefcase onto the table beside his laptop, and took off his hat. He looked around the room and saw—to a man—the officers grinning at him.

"The technique can be used with either hand, with a forehand or a back-hand blow. Makes no difference. And it can be dealt with an open hand like a slap or a fist. But I'm gonna be a real sweetheart and use an open palm on you." He winked at the officers. "Don't want the old dude rushed to the ER." He turned to Arn. "Now get on your knees."

"What for?"

"When you fall, I don't want your hurting yourself."

Arn laughed. "Whatever."

Winger shrugged. "Suit yourself. I'll slap here," Winger said and tapped the muscle between Arn's neck and shoulder. "Ready?"

Arn nodded.

"Say goodnight," Winger said and Arn caught a brief movement, a palm slicing the air, a heartbeat before he felt himself lose consciousness.

———

When Arn came around and his head began to clear, he realized he was seated on the mat. One of the VA officers held him from toppling over while Winger Hays bent over him from the back, massaging Arn's neck and shoulders. As Arn's vision slowly returned to normal, two Winger Hayses emerged into the one instructor. "As you can see, it doesn't take a big man to perform the technique."

Arn struggled to stand as Winger eased him back onto the mat. But within moments, he felt the pain subside, his vision clearing. "Is it normal for the effects to last this long?"

"Long? You've been down and groggy for just a few moments. Thirty seconds tops." Winger and the other officer steadying him grunted as they helped Arn up and into a chair. "Most effects last less than a minute. We like it because it lasts just long enough to slap a set of handcuffs on someone before they recover."

"You've never had any serious injuries in your classes?"

"Never."

"How many classes have you taught?"

Winger pulled up a chair and sat with his arm draped over the back as he looked to the ceiling for an answer. "Hundreds in the last three years since I was hired. I teach in all the VA Centers in South Dakota and Wyoming. Sioux Falls to the VA here in Cheyenne." He laughed. "A real traveling drummer like they had in the old days, except this drummer's a GS-10 with overtime up the wazoo and per diem that pays for keeping my horses in shape and fit when I get the time to ride them."

Arn felt the pain subside, but an ache in his neck still persisted. "*Who* do you teach this to?"

"I teach anyone in the VA system who has to deal with unruly vets—ER personnel for example. Or anyone that has to deal with potentially violent veterans. We are—after all—dealing with men who have killed for a living in whatever war they served." He stood and motioned for the class to form up against one wall.

"If I have any more questions, where can I reach you?"

"I'll be up in Rapid City tomorrow, and from there I can't say— check with my secretary," Winger said. "And if you want to do some more research into the stun, feel free to come back," he smiled. "I'd be happy to show you again."

12

What better way to find *those needing reeducation than at a VA center? Here at Hot Springs facility, the government nearly closed it, but enough folks put up a fuss they had to keep it open. There were just too many people wanting the facility to remain just like it is. Including me. This is the only medical center for veterans in the southern Black Hills, and I truly enjoy the ride through scenic forests and wandering roads. I love seeing the occasional Big Horn ram scaling a granite wall, and now and again I have to slow to allow buffalo to wander across the road in Custer Park. It's almost as if I was on a mini-vacation when I visit here. Almost.*

A light breeze off the creek begins to chill me and I stand, strolling under the porch that runs the full length of the front of the facility. I nod to a nurse bending over an old man in a wheelchair as she tucks his blanket under his legs, and I greet a stooped-over old man with a WWII *insignia on his crumpled ball cap.*

I enter the building and make my way to the waiting room, no one paying me any attention, no one giving me even a second glance.

A middle-aged man bumps against a Navy man, teetering him, nearly knocking him down, not apologizing. Not acknowledging the old man's Korean War service if his cap is any indication. He turns and gives the old vet a sideways glance and nothing more.

An officer!

I can spot them even across a crowded room like this, their arrogance seeping through their very pores—too good for common folks. Too good for the enlisted men and women who helped them during their times of service. My jaw muscles clench and unclench, thinking back to what an officer did to my family. Not this officer. Not like Captain Sims whom I met that cold October day in the restroom at the Sheridan VA Center.

I shudder recalling just how close I came to being caught. I had followed Sims into the head on an impulse and confronted him there. Why no one heard the commotion, why no one came into the restroom as I was choking Sims out I can only attribute to my incredible luck.

God was watching over me.

God knew I had to right a terrible wrong.

I drove back home that morning, checking the rearview mirror, expecting a cop to stop me. But none did. And when I arrived home, I sat alone in the dark room recalling the feeling, the ecstasy that pulsed through me as Sim's tongue—thick and blue and swollen—lolled out of the side of his mouth a moment before he died.

Since then, I have been more measured in my hunting techniques. Since then I have patiently waited—as I wait now—to make sure no one follows me into the restroom after the man who nearly knocked a hero down in passing.

An officer.

I fight to control my anger recalling that first week after returning to the states. The Army had assigned me to an artillery unit... an artillery unit, for God's sakes! I was a Ranger. I didn't want to leave that MOS. I enjoyed it too much. "A change of MOS to field artillery will be a way to transition from your Ranger life," *the executive officer had told me.* "It will be easier for you to get your college degree if you're not away on missions for weeks at a time." *The XO had been right in one regard— artillery allowed me to be available nights to attend college classes.*

I pause at the door to the restroom and glance nonchalantly around, checking one last time before entering. I won't be long inside. My job will take less than a minute.

I am not what happened to me, *Carl Jung once said.* I am what I choose to become. *He was right—I choose to become what I am.*

And I will choose to send that officer to the big induction center in the sky.

13

A RN DID HIS HUNTER'S BEST to sneak past Gorilla Legs, but the woman had some kind of superhuman hearing. Or animalistic hearing. "Where the hell you going, Anderson?" She asked from behind her desk.

"Where's the chief's secretary?"

"Out to lunch. You got the assistant. Now what—."

"I need to talk with Chief Oblanski."

"Got an appointment?"

"I do not. But I figured he'd see me if I just dropped in, since we're pards and all."

Gorilla Legs stood from her desk and walked towards the counter. Arn's gaze froze, and the secretary followed Arn's eyes. "It's casual day, and I chose to wear shorts."

Arn held his tongue. The woman never shaved as long as he had known her, with hair escaping under her blouses from hairy armpits, and the hint of a mustache most men would be proud of. "It's healthier to go au naturelle," she told Arn last summer. But he had never seen her legs... in such a state of hair growth, and she looked like she was wearing a pair of woolly chaps over those powerful legs. "This is a government agency," she said, "not an old-boy's club where you can just drop in and shoot the shit. Now beat it—the chief's got a lot of work to do before budget time."

"That's all right," Oblanski called, presumably from his office. "I phoned Anderson. We need to talk about something."

She glared at Arn so long he thought she'd next throw a punch over the counter when she hit a button on her desk and buzzed him through the door. "Next time, lover boy."

"Loverboy?" Oblanski said when Arn had walked down the hall and into the chief's office. "You and her aren't doing the wild thing by any chance?"

"Hardly," Arn answered and took his hat off. "Just an old... handle, but not sure how she found out about it." He ran his fingers through his wispy blond hair and set his hat on the chair beside him. He'd talk to Ana Maria later about letting his secret dating handle slip. "I don't recall you phoning me for a meeting."

"I didn't." Oblanski propped his foot up on an open desk drawer. "Just couldn't have stood by while that... creature chewed you up and spit you out."

"Then thanks for saving me."

Oblanski chuckled and slapped a pile of papers. "I saved myself from doing this budget stuff the longer you're in here, so it was selfish." He picked up a pencil and began chewing the eraser end. "These No. 2 pencils have been number two for as long as I can recall."

"Your point?"

"If they're that popular, why aren't they number one by now?"

"That and Jimmy Hoffa's disappearance and we'll have all the mysteries solved," Arn said. "Except the mystery of why eight men died at VA centers under suspicious circumstances."

Oblanski put his foot onto the floor and rested his elbows on his desk. "What suspicious deaths?"

Arn handed Oblanski a spreadsheet Ana Maria had made covering the eight deaths. Arn explained that Ana Maria had uncovered six more veterans that had died under similar circumstances as did Steve Urchek and Frank Mosby.

"So you're saying that the six vets besides Frank and Steve died of an apparent heart condition is somehow odd?"

"I am."

"Do you not think it natural that older men would have heart problems leading to their deaths?"

"All died unattended, with no witnesses."

"That certainly doesn't ring any alarm bells for me," He snapped his fingers. "There *was* something that came through the mail a couple years ago. A flyer telling about a veteran's murder…" Oblanski opened each drawer in succession and rummaged through it.

"I bet if you asked her real sweet-like Gorilla Legs would help you find it."

"Bite your tongue," Oblanski said a moment before he came away with a crumpled piece of paper. He unfolded a pair of glasses and scanned the flyer.

"Since when did you start wearing readers?"

"Since my eyes got too damned old. Now you want me to read this for you, 'cause I know your eyes are bad."

"Read away," Arn said as he dug his notebook out of his back pocket.

"A Vietnam Army Captain was murdered at the Sheridan VA—."

"It says specifically 'murdered' and not just unattended?"

"Murdered," Oblanski said. "Strangled. Petrie in the eyes and a crushed windpipe point to murder. Must have been a hell of a fight as the flyer says the restroom was busted up."

"Can I see that?"

Oblanski handed Arn the flyer and he dug his own reading glasses from his pocket. He scooted closer to the window where the light shone into the office. The flyer—sent by the Sheridan County Sheriff's Office and the Wyoming Department of Criminal Investigation three years ago—asked agencies if they had similar deaths as Captain Sims'.

"Could you make a call to Sheridan and see what else they have."

"That," Oblanski said as he pointed to the flyer, "is nothing like the other deaths you described. Besides," he tapped Ana Maria's spreadsheet, "there was a full year between this murder and the unattended ones."

Arn thought better with coffee and he said to Oblanski, "I'll take that cup of coffee now."

"I didn't offer one."

"I could stick my head out the door and yell at Gorilla Legs to fetch us a cup— ."

"I'll make it," Oblanski said and walked to his coffee maker. "Why are you so sure this one and the others are connected?" he asked over his back.

"What do serial killers all have in common?"

Oblanski laughed. "That easy—they kill."

"Besides that, what happens the longer they kill?"

Oblanski turned and handed Arn a steaming cup. The Chief sat behind his desk and put his cup onto a leather coaster, tenting his fingers as he thought. "They get better. They learn. They improve their chosen killing technique."

Arn nodded. "And some even become so proficient they are *never* caught. Can you say Zodiac Killer?"

"Ah," Oblanski said, lightly sipping his coffee. "I see your point. You're thinking one man has perfected his killing so well he flies under our radar?"

"I lost a goodly amount of sleep thinking about this," Arn said. "After that first murder in Sheridan—where it was a homicide to everyone looking at it—the killer learned from that. I had a case once in Denver years ago where a man stabbed his victims to death. There was a lot of blood at his crime scenes, and his victims didn't die easily or quickly. One clawed the hell out of him before she succumbed to her wounds. His MO suddenly went cold, even though we had several more bodies piling up. Victims killed instantly when a blade was shoved into the base of their skulls. When I finally caught the man three murders later, he admitted he needed to be more... discrete. So, he jumped on the internet and found the quickest method to kill a human with a blade, ergo the wounds to the back of the necks. Don Vito Corleone would have been proud of him."

"You're saying these veterans who you *think* were murdered were the product of a killer who perfected his technique—after Sheridan?"

"Perfected and studied and researched until he found the most proficient way to kill and make it look natural."

Oblanski looked around for another victim-pencil. He found one at the bottom of his stack of papers and began chewing the end. "And just how did he evolve, because the others weren't strangled."

"But the ones we looked at—Steve and Frank—had bruising no one can explain. I think the killer incapacitated them with a brachial stun—."

"Nonsense," Oblanski said. "We teach that to our officers, and no one's been incapacitated. Not even any injuries. The technique wouldn't kill *anyone*." He tossed the stub of a pencil in the round file beside his desk. "Drawing your suspicions out, it would have to be someone familiar with the VA system, meaning a vet."

"Or an employee."

Oblanski nodded. "Sure. It could be. That would give the killer opportunity for certain. But how do you square that victims were killed in multiple VA centers?"

"A traveling employee," Arn said. "Here look." He turned Ana Maria's spreadsheet so Oblanski and he could both look at it. "I thought at first it was someone on the move—perhaps they lived in the northern Black Hills and—when they moved to the Cheyenne area—started killing again. But these dates are random. They show someone who moves between facilities, and there is no pattern."

"Back to the manner of their deaths... though I can't speak for those deaths we didn't investigate; the ME has already ruled Frank Mosby's was natural."

Arn waved the air, frustrated that he couldn't quite get his point across to the police chief. "I read the death certificate—mechanism of death was a cardiac arrhythmia." Arn leaned across the desk. "But that was before the tox report came in."

"Arn," Oblanski said, "you know how backed up the crime lab is. When a person dies of natural causes, they don't order a toxicology screen."

"But they have to for unattended deaths."

"They do, but if it's a natural death, the samples the ME submits take a back burner to obvious cases of foul play." Oblanski finished his coffee and pushed the cup aside. "What are you getting at exactly?"

Arn smoothed what wispy blond hair he had left and put his hat on. "I think these men were all killed with some... substance. Maybe something the lab doesn't test for."

"For that, we would have to ask the lab to test for some specific substance."

"You would."

"All right," Oblanski said. "What substance?"

"I don't know," Arn said. "But I'm working on it. In the meantime, could you put a rush on Frank's tox report?"

Oblanski drooped his head. "You are one pain the rear end, but I'll do it, just 'cause you spared me an hour of looking at budget crap."

Arn started for the door when he stopped and turned back.

"Now what?" Oblanski asked.

"Doc Henry."

"That murderer who abducted Ana Maria in Denver? What's he to you now with him being somebody's girlfriend in prison?"

"He's living and working here in Cheyenne."

"What! I thought you said he'd been paroled to Colorado?"

"He was," Arn explained, "though I couldn't believe it, either, that they allowed him to move to the same community where his last victim lives.

"But how—."

"You know the drill. Shit head gets a sentence reduction because he's a model prisoner, then another and before long he's out. To reoffend again."

"We haven't had *any* dealings with him."

Arn knew that law enforcement was reactive—if a crime occurred, the police responded. Oblanski and his department could do nothing until Doc made a move against Ana Maria. But—by then—it might be too late. "Could you fill your officers in about Doc Henry?"

"You know I will."

"And have a patrol cruise by the house and the television station now and again?"

Oblanski nodded.

"Thanks."

Arn turned to leave once again when Oblanski stopped him. "I have a small favor to ask you now."

"Oh?" Arn said, detecting something in Oblanski's voice that told Arn no good would come out of his mouth.

"Yes… Gorilla Legs lost her apartment when the owner sold the building. She has to be out of there by the first of the month."

"I hate to ask—what's that got to do with me?"

"I noticed you are still remodeling your mother's old house… and even with Ana Maria and that old Indian staying with you I'm betting you have an extra room—."

"Not on your life—."

"It would only be temporary," Oblanski argued, "until she could find another crib. Doc Henry wouldn't dare cross your threshold with Gorilla Legs there."

"Ned," Arn said as slowly and sternly as he could, "I would rather French-kiss a rattlesnake than have Gorilla legs living under my roof."

14

A NA MARIA HUDDLED OVER HER plate of tuna casserole. She had eaten little tonight. She had eaten little since learning Doc Henry was in Cheyenne. Even though she tried to present bravado, that it didn't bother her, Arn knew better. He desperately needed for her to get her mind off her tormentor as much as he needed Ana Maria's help if he were ever to connect the dots between Frank and Steve. "Every man who died under these... unusual circumstances were officers?"

She nodded and stabbed a piece of tuna with her fork. "Every man. The only thing I could find linking them all was that they were all Vietnam War vets." She held up her hand. "And before you ask, if my research is correct, none of the eight ever served together. It is like their murders are all random. *If* they were murdered."

"The ninth victim was murdered."

Ana Maria's head snapped up. "There's no ninth name on my list."

"It wouldn't be," Arn said, shaking a bit more salt on his food even as Danny scowled at Arn ruining his dish. "He was killed a year before the other killings began. So, I suppose you could figure him the first."

Ana Maria sat up straight in her chair. "How come I never heard of that one?"

"Because I just learned about the victim—a Captain Sims—from Oblanski today." Arn explained that the chief had called him later in the day when Arn was knee-deep in slapping paint on a spare bedroom wall. "Investigators found no motive for Sims' murder," the chief said. "No reason he was targeted. He had no known enemies and no threats were found in his mail or his computer."

Ana Maria stuffed casserole in her mouth and said between bites, "then we better catch this bastard sooner than later. This might be enough to convince DeAngelo to let me do a special on their deaths."

DeAngelo had reluctantly agreed to Ana Maria's special coverage, dovetailing it into her RSL broadcasts. But when he first heard that Doc Henry was in Cheyenne, he cancelled Ana Maria's reporting on the VA deaths and suspended her coverage of the RSL. He didn't think Doc was connected in any way to her reporting on the veterans. He just didn't want her out there exposed as if taunting Doc with every nightly broadcast. And when she had been relegated to doing pieces on Cheyenne's Botanic Gardens or entertainment at the Depot on Fridays, it had driven her deeper into a depression. Even though Arn knew her nightly coverage of the murders might flush the killer to the surface as it had several other times, he feared for her just as DeAngelo did. "I gave DeAngelo an ultimatum—let me go ahead with the specials or I walk."

"You sure going live with these deaths is a wise idea?" Danny asked. "DeAngelo might be right—it might be too much of the wrong kind of exposure—."

"Don't even talk to me about DeAngelo. I told him I could handle whatever came along. And to hell with Doc Henry!"

Deep down, Arn knew that—if he could keep Ana Maria safe as she did nightly broadcast covering the suspicious deaths—it might draw out the killer.

———

Arn finished his shower and slipped on a pair of sweatpants and a t-shirt. He grabbed his book and settled into his chair in the sewing room. He turned the light just right and opened his copy of *Les Misérables*. Reading only an hour every night had taken him a month to get as far as he did. And the end was nowhere in sight.

He donned his reading glasses, while the sound of Danny's snoring coming from his bedroom two rooms over made Arn smile. He had taken the old man in when he was homeless, when Arn found him squatting in this house after Arn moved back to Cheyenne from

Denver. Arn thought he'd let Danny hang around for a few nights until the old man offered to trade room and board for remodeling Arn's boyhood home. And now it was, more than two years later and still Danny was here. Between the old Indian knowing more about construction than anyone Arn knew to the man's skills as a cook to his insight and being a sounding board often, Arn would have it no other way.

Arn turned to a new chapter and adjusted the reading lamp over his left shoulder when his cell phone rang. He ignored it at the first ring, until that cop-intuition told him he ought not ignore it any longer and flipped it open. "Do you know what time it is?" Arn asked when Chief Oblanski came on-line.

"It's time to get some sleep, but I thought I'd let you know—I called the state lab today and asked them to put a rush on Frank Mosby's tox report. So happens, the lab completed it this afternoon and was just waiting for morning to send it over to the coroner's office."

"I take it you wouldn't have called unless something odd showed up?"

"Sorry."

"Sorry about what? "

"Sorry about your friend Frank—he died of cocaine overdose."

Arn thought he heard wrong, but when Oblanski repeated it asked, "you mean he died shooting up in the restroom?"

"Apparently," Oblanski said.

————

As long as Arn had known Helen Mosby she had gotten up with the chickens, as she put it. No matter how early he stopped by her house through the years, she was always awake. This morning was no exception. When Arn pulled into the circular drive, Helen was just emerging from the house with a gardener's pail in one hand and what was left of a bagel in the other. She set the pail down and polished off the bagel while she walked to Arn's car.

"Can we talk, Helen?"

She craned her neck up at him, and her smile faded as if she knew more bad news was coming her way. Arn declined coffee, and she motioned to the wino bench beneath the pine tree. He had thought about how to ask her on the way over, and none of his approaches seemed right. He'd finally settled on the direct approach and asked, "Helen, Frank didn't die from heart complications. He died from a cocaine overdose."

She stared unblinkingly at Arn for long moments when she said, "That is impossible. Frank never used drugs. Ever. Even when he was in Vietnam, he said he turned down more dope than most people could buy and never touched any of it. How can you say—."

"The state lab finally got the tox report back and they found a lethal dose in his blood."

She stood and walked to where a low-hanging bough brushed against a bird feeder. "The robins and finches were early this year," her voice breaking up. "I suspect they'll be gone early as well…" She faced Arn. "I knew my Frank as well as any person can know another. And I am here to tell you, he did not use drugs."

"Ever?"

"Ever."

"How about that gall bladder operation he had last year?" Arn asked.

"What about it?"

"Wasn't he prescribed oxycodone for his pain?"

"They sent him home with some pills, and I had to get it refilled once, but what's that got to do with him overdosing on cocaine?"

"Perhaps he got… used to taking the drug. Perhaps he built up a tolerance and needed something stronger."

"Like perhaps he bought cocaine on the street like a common druggie? Frank wouldn't even know where—or who—to buy it from. No. If Frank died from an overdose of cocaine, it is because *someone* injected him. I knew my Frank."

———

Ned Oblanski had a city commissioner meeting to go to so he only had a moment to talk over the phone. But that was all Arn needed.

72

"I talked with Helen and she assured me Frank Mosby was no coke head."

"Family is usually the last to know most of the time, you know that."

"I do. What I don't know, though, is how the ME could have missed an injection site. That should have stood out like a sore toe."

"You read the coroner's report—the only injection site Frank had was where he got a blood draw that morning at the VA. That was it."

"Then clarify something for me," Arn said. "When I talked with you last night, you said the dosage in Frank's bloodstream was twice the LD50—twice the lethal dose."

"That's what the lab came back with."

"Then if that were the case, Frank should have been found in the restroom—."

"He was—."

"With a needle stuck in his arm. Or his leg. If he had twice the lethal dose, isn't it safe to believe that the needle would *still* be stuck into a vein? Isn't it safe to assume he wouldn't have been able to get rid of the needle, even if he wanted to?"

"I hate to admit it," Oblanski said, "but you might just have a point there."

"You admit we just might have some psycho targeting veterans running loose out here?"

"Could be."

"Then I'm going to have to talk with a psychiatrist—."

"Arn," Oblanski said, "don't get yourself so worked up you need to seek counseling."

"Not looking for counseling for me," Arn said. "I'm going to find out who among the dead vets ever sought help through the VA. I'm going to see a government shrink."

15

A RN WAITED OUTSIDE PSYCHIATRIC SERVICES Office as veterans walked by, some smirking, others pointing fingers and whispering to their friend or wife walking beside them. Yet others walked by and gave Arn a sad, knowing look, as if to say it's all right for a warrior to seek help. Arn almost felt he *was* a patient seeking help when the door opened, and the receptionist motioned him inside. "Dr. Ames will see you now."

Arn slung his briefcase over his shoulder and followed the lady. He had expected a fainting couch where patients could lie down and tell their troubles to a man trained in classical psychology. Instead, the cramped room sported only a dented gun-metal gray desk and two chairs for office furniture. He took off his hat, but there were no hat racks nor coat racks to hang it, so he held it while he waited for the man behind the desk to acknowledge him.

As he waited, Arn thought back to the many times in his police career where he had been ordered to see a psychiatrist. Every time he had been forced to kill a suspect in the line of duty, every call to an especially gruesome homicide, every action that alerted a supervisor that Arn needed to visit a shrink he did. He had, through the many visits, grown to understand the subtle verbiage of the psychiatrist. And fool them into allowing Arn to return to duty.

The receptionist closed the door, and Arn looked around the tiny room. A framed photograph of the doctor sitting on a palomino was captioned the *Fourth of July Parade, Casper*. Beside it, a photo of Doctor Ames crossing the line at the Boston Marathon. Arn looked closer—the date etched on one corner showed just last year.

Doctor Ames, a fit man, younger by twenty years than Arn and nearly as tall, but smaller—compact came to mind—looked up and smiled. He walked around his desk toward Arn. With close cropped sandy hair and clean shaven, he reminded Arn of an Army recruiting poster. He thrust out his hand, the handshake matching Arn's first impression—firm, yet not crushing. "I am sorry to keep you waiting, but I had a patient session. Sit, please."

Arn sat on a straight-backed chair with an off-color cushion and rested his briefcase on his lap. "Dr. Ames— ."

"Just Ethan," he said. "I have gotten used to my patients called me by my first name. It puts them at ease when we visit. Besides I'm no shrink. I'm no psychiatrist, I'm the VA's psychologist in these parts. At least the one that treats veterans on a daily basis." He sipped from a coffee cup shaped like the U. S. S. Enterprise, and Arn imagined Captain Kirk looking out a window on the observation deck. "My secretary had no idea why you wanted to see me." He laughed easily and set his mug down before it spilled coffee. "Mysterious is what it is. But then, I love a good mystery."

Arn opened his briefcase and took out his notebook and a copy of Ana Maria's spreadsheet listing the deaths of the veterans who had died under similar, suspicious circumstances.

Ethan looked over the spreadsheet. "You say all these deaths were officers?"

Arn nodded. "And all served in Vietnam."

"What is it you want what from me, Mr. Anderson?"

"I thought because you work with veterans exclusively you might have some insight as to who I should be looking for."

"You want my analysis… like Dr. Phil?"

"Something like that."

Ethan looked over the spreadsheet once again, running his hand down the list as if becoming familiar with each victim. "You are absolutely certain these men didn't die naturally?"

"Not one-hundred percent, but I'm going to ask law enforcement in the jurisdictions where they died to examine the bodies."

"But some are two years old. Exhumation," he shuddered, and his hands began trembling thinking about it. "Gruesome. So,

75

you're *not* sure?"

Arn shook his head. "Some of the men's deaths were ruled heart failure. Others the big MI. But right now, I'm just clutching at straws, which is why I'd hoped you could give me some insight into who might have wanted to kill these men."

Ethan walked back around his desk and dropped into his captain's chair missing one arm. He rested his elbows on the table and tented his fingers while he closed his eyes. "The man you're looking for—if in fact these veterans were murdered—would be what you'd call a control freak." Ethan opened his eyes and breathed out a long sigh. "If he managed to evade detection in all eight deaths, he would be a very meticulous man. One not prone to doing anything rash, unless some compelling reason caused him to throw caution to the wind. And," Ethan held up his finger, "he would be the smartest person in the room. Able to fool the inept authorities." He sat back in his chair. "At least in his opinion. But as long as I've interacted with former service members, there is still so much that puzzles me with their mindset."

"Were you ever in the military?"

"Negative." He leaned. "As far as targeting strictly officers and only those who served in Vietnam, it shows an intense hatred for both groups. That he hasn't killed any enlisted man is... fascinating. Have you connected anything between all the victims—work interaction? Perhaps they served in the same units in Vietnam."

"I have found no common denominator among them," Arn said. "Do you read anything into the fact that the murders were committed in two states, and with no particular pattern?"

"That's a little out of my wheelhouse. That would be for the police to determine," Ethan said. "Don't they have some software that can analyze dates and times, find the common theme?"

"I don't think such software exists. I think this case will be solved by LPCs."

"LPCs?"

"Leather Personnel Carriers," Arn said. "Wearing out good old shoe leather talking with just the right person who might have seen or remembered something."

"Understood," Ethan said. "Getting back to your question as to why men might be killed at different facilities, I would wager that it could be someone like me—any given week I see patients in a dozen facilities and two different states." He chuckled. "But as compelling a case as you laid out, Mr. Anderson, I doubt there is any malevolent killer stalking the halls of the VA centers waiting to pounce on unsuspecting vets."

"Let me ask you this, then," Arn said, "since you see so many veterans… have you ever treated anyone that hates officers and Vietnam vets so intently?"

Ethan looked away.

"You have, haven't you?"

Ethan scooted his chair back. He brought the Enterprise to his lips and sipped. "If I did, I could not tell you. Even the government requires strict patient confidentiality."

"Can you at least tell me if you're currently treating anyone who might fit the profile?"

Ethan frowned. "I am currently treating several men with violent histories, but none that fits *that* profile. The ones I am seeing hates *everyone*, not just officers."

"Even though you cannot tell me directly," Arn asked, "you could… steer me in the right direction should you treat such a man?"

Ethan nodded. "I might be able to do that."

Arn stuffed the spreadsheet and notebook into his briefcase and stood. "One other thing—do you treat substance abusers?"

"If they become psychotic, I do."

"Meth heads?"

Ethan nodded.

"Even coke heads?"

"I've treated a few since I entered the VA system four years ago. Why do you ask?"

"Because I suspect when we exhume the bodies of the victims, we might just find high levels of cocaine in each and every one of them."

16

CHIEF OBLANSKI AGREED TO MEET Arn at Starbucks down from the Public Safety building. "I can't take much more of that woman."

"Your wife?"

"Gorilla Legs," Oblanski said. "With the deadline approaching for me to submit my budget, she insists on proofreading everything."

"How about Mary? I would have thought your new secretary would have straightened Gorilla Legs out."

Oblanski shook his head. "I don't think you could straighten her out with a whip and a chair."

"Maybe she *needs* to proof it."

"Hell, I'm not even done with it. I keep getting out of the office for other things. Like your cock-a-mamie request."

"How do you know it's a cock-a-mamie request?" Arn asked.

"Because you're a civilian and you keep sticking your nose into police business."

"It's a good thing I did that a couple times these last couple years, don't you agree?" When Arn first moved back to Cheyenne, DeAngelo Damos at the television station hired him to work with Ana Maria as a consultant, looking into a decades-old series of police deaths. He had helped the police solve that as well as uncovering a serial killer living—and hunting—here in Cheyenne.

"At least you agreed to buy," Oblanski said. He walked to the counter to await the barista completing his order, and Arn turned to the cashier. "How much?"

"Nine-dollars and ten cents."

"What! All I ordered is a small coffee."

The kid at the register toyed with his nose ring. "The chief ordered a Venti Caramel Macchiato with two extra shots. All that gourmet coffee costs money, pops."

"Most meals I eat don't cost that much."

"Just chalk it up to experience," Oblanski said. "Or just figure it's a small price to pay for my pleasant company."

"I hope you have some answers after I shelled out that much."

"Or else?"

"Or else I'll call up Gorilla Legs and ask her to meet you here for coffee."

"I know that's a bluff," Oblanski said.

"How do you know?"

"Would you willingly talk to the woman if you didn't have to?"

"You got a point," Arn said and followed Oblanski outside.

They sat under the shade of the overhang beside two college-age men drinking iced tea. One wore a jean vest with a large marijuana patch sewn on the back, while the other sipped his drink through gnarly teeth ravaged by methamphetamine. They looked Chief Oblanski over for the briefest of moments before leaving. "See you boys sometime soon," Oblanski called after them as they scurried away.

"Just a matter of time," Oblanski said to himself as he sipped his drink through a tall straw. "Now what is it that's so pressing?"

"Ana Maria did some checking on Jonah Barb but didn't find anything matching his name in any of her databases."

"That's because she didn't research under his given name—Quentin. I understand the man has some complex about the name. Hates anyone calling him it."

"Good a name as any."

Oblanski sipped lightly, and Arn thought he herd him *coo* as the caramel-whatever-the-hell-it-is slid down his throat. "From what Brian Gibbs tells me, Quennie—that's what Brian calls Jonah—has always insisted on going by some macho name. And Quennie isn't it."

"Who's Brian Gibbs?"

"Bartender down at the Legion. He served with Quentin—Jonah—in Iraq."

"Same infantry unit?"

"Not infantry," Oblanski said. "Medic unit. Brian got burned out on it and left the Army as soon as he served his twenty. Now, he's just content to tend bar down at the Legion. He says that every time Jonah pops into the Legion for a beer, he harasses the daylight out of him. We got called there last spring for a fight between the two, though it wasn't much of a fight when you see how big Brian is."

"How do you know I'm going to pay Brian a visit?"

Oblanski chuckled. "Because you cannot *not* stick your nose into odd places. And just out of pure curiosity, did your contact at Ft. Meade get back to you about the toxicology report on Steve Urchek?"

Arn had gotten off the phone with Lt. Waddie not an hour ago. She had reluctantly told Arn that Steve had a lethal dose of cocaine in his system. Just like Frank. "Now I have to tell Helen her brother died of an OD like her husband. I just don't see how it could happen."

"It happens because druggies are used to a certain… quality of product. When they get their dope from a new supplier… you know how it goes. I'm sure you've seen druggies who bought a product purer than they're used to. And the moment they shoot up—hell, you've seen druggies OD enough times—."

"Frank wasn't a druggie, and I doubt Steve was."

"Arn," Oblanski said, "don't let emotion cloud your thinking. Coke heads are harder to spot—they can hold down a job. Even be socially viable, with a family. Friends might not even know they use."

Oblanski was right, Arn knew. Both Steve and Frank *could* have been users, leading normal-appearing lives. But damnit, they were both old friends Arn had known through the years, and it was just hard to imagine either man shooting up.

Arn finished his coffee and crunched the cup before standing and tossing it into a trash receptacle. "What else do you know about Q… Jonah?"

"You're still beating that dead dog—believing the Righteous Sword of the Lord has something to do with the veterans' deaths?" Oblanski held up his hand. "I might as well let you have your delusions. After all, you did buy me this," the chief said before sipping his drink like it was a fine, vintage sherry. "Jonah Barb keeps to himself like the rest of those boobs living in their compound in Colorado. He comes to town now and again, though, and hangs around the VA waiting for some disgruntled vet fed up with the system and bureaucracy to recruit to the RSL. And like the fight with Brian Gibbs, Jonah got the dog shit kicked out of him by the VA service officer last summer."

"Did the service officer wind up in the pokey?" Arn asked.

Oblanski shook his head and closed his eyes, waiting for the *thing* he ordered to trickle down his throat. "The service officer did not. Jonah's ego wouldn't allow him to press charges."

"I don't understand."

"Jonah was beaten by a *woman* service officer. If you're lucky you might catch her in her office. She's at the VA on Mondays—Samantha Holder."

———

Arn had just enough time before the VA employees left for the day to stop at the American Legion. When he pulled off Lincolnway, four cars were already parked in the lot. *Regulars.* Arn thought back to his years as a cop, thought about the regulars who would sit at the doorstep of their favorite bar waiting for it to open. Those were the same regulars who—whenever there was a major blizzard forecast— would rush to the bar in the hopes of getting snowed in where they could get sloppy drunk while they ate pickled pig's feet and eggs all night, safe from nagging wives.

Arn was spot on.

When he entered the bar, four men each cradling beers sat pie-eyed watching Arn. Like those regulars on *Cheers* and Arn half-expected Norm and Cliff to raise a toast as Arn walked up to the bar. "What'll you have?" an enormous man behind the bar asked. A white towel was draped over one shoulder, and a stub of a cigar stuck in his mouth. Tattoos rippled on his forearms as he polished glasses, and he scowled when Arn ordered Diet Coke.

"What!" One of the drunks said. He squinted as he tried focusing on Arn. "Your old lady won't let you have a beer?" He nudged the drunk next to him and both men nearly fell off their stools laughing. "Man don't know how to be the boss in his own house."

"That why you're here," Arn asked, "because your wife won't let you drink at home?"

The drunk at the bar set his glass on the counter and started to rise when the bartender stopped him. "Easy, Harlan. By the size of this feller, you couldn't whip him if you were stone sober." He handed Arn a glass of soda. "And I would bet you didn't come in here just to give ol' Harlan grief."

"I'd like to visit for a moment, if you're Brian Gibbs."

"That'd be me, pard'ner. What 'cha wanna talk about?"

"Jonah Barb."

Gibbs tilted his head back and laughed heartedly. "You mean ol' Quennie. I just put the run on him not an hour ago."

"He was here?"

"Stood right where you're standing."

"Problems?"

"Nothing that I couldn't handle," Gibbs said. "Quennie comes in here now and again. Shoots off his mouth about how bad the military is. Dumb ass—the last place he ought to criticize the services is at the legion. I just had to get a mite… physical with him is all."

"That's what the police chief said—that you two got into a scuffle a couple times."

"Weren't much of a scuffle," Harlan said, swiveling on his stool, clutching the bar for support. "Brian here likes to tease Jonah. Like he done today."

Gibbs grabbed a fresh glass, spit on it, and began polishing. "Quennie didn't know I was bartending today, or I'm sure he would not have stopped by. He likes to come in and… recruit for that bogus RSL he *commands*. You two practically brushed into one another. He just left."

"Bad blood between you?' Arn asked, sipping the Diet Coke, lukewarm and flat with the fizzle of a glass of water.

Gibbs filled up another glass with Rolling Block and slid it across the bar to Harlan. "Quennie and me served in Iraq in the same tour.

Medics. We went into the field with the grunts. Or we were supposed to, except that chicken shit little bastard always found some way to stay at base camp. Sometimes it was making coffee for the colonel in Headquarters' Company. Sometimes he'd wrangle an excuse to go to the field hospital for some perceived ailment. It always stuck in my craw, that cowardly A-hole. End game for him was working in the field hospital back at base camp. Why do you want to know about him?"

Arn left out his suspicions about the RSL and Jonah Barb and about the times they had been protesting the dates of the deaths. "I understand Jonah—Quennie—calls himself a colonel in the Righteous Sword of the Lord."

Gibbs smirked. "That's about the only promotion that piece of crap could muster—a self-promotion." He set the glass atop the pyramid of other glasses lined up along the back bar. He bent and grabbed a Budweiser from a cooler and popped the top. "The night after Quennie picked a fight with me and got himself arrested," Gibbs took a long pull of the Bud," three toughs came into the Legion here. They hung around until closing time and were waiting for me outside after I locked up. 'Righteous Sword of the Lord soldiers' they hollered right before they rushed me." He chuckled. "They rushed themselves straight to the ER after I finished kicking the shit outta them."

"Did you report them to the cops?"

"Are you kidding me," Gibbs said, "and risk them not coming back for another ass-whooping?"

17

JUST WHAT THE HELL IS Anderson doing at the Legion at two in the afternoon? He doesn't drink from what I could see. And he sure doesn't hang with those rummies drunked-up in the bar. There can be only one reason he went in there—he's nosing around, trying to figure out a connection between the men I've killed these last couple years.

But why the American Legion?

That'll bug the hell out of me until I can figure it out... Brian Gibbs!

That's got to be the reason Anderson's taking so long inside, talking with that big bastard. But what can Gibbs tell him about me? Nothing incriminating, that's for sure. And Gibbs being the friendly neighborhood bartender everyone wants to pour out their soul to just doesn't fit that grouchy SOB. I think back to my conversations with him, and perhaps he will remember something that points Anderson to me.

Perhaps he already has.

Can I take that chance?

Anderson is leaving in that hot rod of his. I'd follow him and see where he goes but I need to get back to work.

I'll come back to the Legion tonight.

After they close.

And talk with Brian Gibbs once again.

18

ARN DROVE THE THREE MILES to the VA center and parked beside a truck with a Confederate flag on a pole stuck in the bed. An old man slowly climbed out and put his twin canes against the truck before shutting the door. Arn turned to him and reached for the canes when the man sputtered, "I don't need help, asshole!"

Arn shrugged, figuring the old timer didn't need help after all and walked into the center and to the Police Office. Sgt. Wagner sat hunched over his desk writing on a tablet when Arn knocked on the door. Wagner groaned and took off his reading glasses. "You here to let Winger Hays beat on you a little more?"

Arn rubbed his neck. He *thought* it still hurt, though it might be all in his mind, too. "I'm here to see Samantha Holder."

"Ain't we all," Winger said. He entered the police office wearing pressed slacks and a sport coat. He had cleaned up since he beat on Arn, and the man looked like he was going on a dinner date himself. Or to a wedding as dressed as he was. "Don't think less of yourself when she turns you down."

"Pardon?"

Wagner snickered. "Here to see Samantha, you say? Next you'll claim it's official business."

"As a matter of fact," Arn said, "I wanted to talk with her about Jonah Barb."

"And not because you want to line up a dinner date with her or anything?"

"What *are* you rambling about?" Arn said.

"I think you know *just* what I'm talking about. But I'm here to tell

85

you that snagging a date with Sam would be a major coup for an old dude like you."

Arn shook his head, not knowing just what Wagner was inferring. "Just tell me where the Service Office is."

"Second floor," Wagner said. "Just follow the waiting line of other drooling fellers hoping for a date with her."

"And look out for her right," Winger called after him. "She slaps like a mule."

Arn started out of the office when he turned back and asked Wagner, "You have access to military records?"

"Of course. Why?"

Arn jotted down Captain Sims' name and handed it to the sergeant. "I'd like to see his service file—."

"No can do," Wagner said. "Veterans have rights, or didn't you ever hear that?"

"Even dead vets?"

"What?"

"Sims was murdered at the VA in Sheridan three years ago. I doubt that he'll complain to anyone if I have a peek at his file."

When Wagner hesitated, Arn said, "contact the Sheridan County Sheriff's department to verify Sims' death if you don't believe me."

"I'll make some calls," Wagner said at last. "But I can't guarantee anything."

Arn thanked him and walked to the elevator. On the second floor, he read the legend and walked the long corridor towards the Service Officer's room. As he neared, Arn saw Wagner wasn't far off: there were eight men leaning against the wall outside the office waiting their turn to talk to Samantha Holder.

"Take a chunk of wall," one man said. "Sam just now came back from her workout." He nodded to the line. "She's got to hustle through vets pretty quick if she wants to get off work by four."

The line went quick, with each man in the Service Office less than five minutes until the receptionist yelled to him, "Next."

Arn entered the outer office. The receptionist sat behind her desk; half-glasses perched on her ruler-straight nose as she gave Arn the once over. "Vietnam or Korea?"

I like to think I'm a little young for either, he thought. "Neither. I'd like to talk with Samantha Holder about a... personal matter."

A wry smile crept over the woman's face. "Most men would. But you are next in line, so go on in."

Arn started into the office. And stopped. Staring.

"Don't just stand there gawking like a dummy," Samantha Holder said. "Take a seat."

Arn sat slowly, all the while keeping his eyes on her. *Eye candy doesn't do her justice,* he thought. Even sitting at her desk, Samantha projected strength through her muscular frame, her perfectly rounded face accentuated by an angular nose. If her short, brown hair would have been black, it would have reminded Arn of Liz Taylor in *Cleopatra.* She eyed him through eyes only a shade darker behind sequined-rimmed glasses. She wore scant makeup, though she needed none, and she sat straight up in chair which only emphasized her shapely body. "Name and branch of service," she said, pen poised above a notebook.

"I was never in the military."

Samantha took off her glasses and leaned across her desk, eyebrows coming together as she glared at Arn. "Then why are you here wasting my time?"

Arn handed her his business card. "I was hoping you could give me some information."

She doomed her glasses once again and studied his card. "This is kind of tacky—*Have Olds-Will Travel.*"

Arn shrugged. "My roommate came up with it, Ms. Holder."

"Sam," she said. "Folks named me Samantha, but I was always a bit of a tomboy."

"Somehow," Arn said, "I can't picture you as a tomboy."

"And I can't imagine you wasting my time if you're not a vet."

"All I need is a moment." Arn took his notebook from his back pocket, "to talk about Jonah Barb."

Sam leaned back in her seat, the buttons of her blouse threatening to pop off. "What about that weasel—he flapping his gums again? If he is, I'll stomp him like I did last time we met."

Arn smiled. "Chief Oblanski said you made short work of Jonah.

But he never said if you two had a history that started the… fight."

Sam laughed, the smile lines showing through her scant makeup. "We were both in Iraq—he a medic and me a mechanic."

"You were a mechanic in the Army?"

She leaned forward in her seat again, one fist clenching and unclenching, muscles rippling in her forearms. "Are you old fashioned or worse—a sexist? Like maybe a woman can't turn a wrench or something? It was my secondary MOS. Primary was military police, but I never worked in that field. Had too damn many trucks and Humvees to fix. Like my old man when he was in 'Nam—stuck in a motor pool getting greasy every day."

Arn thought of Ana Maria, working her way through college in her father's repair shop. Arn had a hard time picturing Ana Maria elbow-deep in grease and under a car just like it was difficult for him to image someone as beautiful as Sam being there, either. "My good friend… a woman, works on cars in her spare time. So no, I have no problem with it."

Sam's frown faded as if approving of Arn's new attitude. "Fair enough. Now what do you want to know about Jonah?"

"Whatever you can tell me about him. He seems to be increasing his protests around the area."

Sam leaned back and studied the ceiling for a moment. "When I first met the damned fool, we were in the Enlisted Men's Club in Kuwait. He was at one end of the bar. Me another, nursing a beer, when a Butterbar Louie and another Butterbar strolled in. You might say we both were too unkindly to officers being in the EM Club—they had an O Club of their own they could go to." She leaned back and smiled as she recalled the incident. "I started putting the run on them and a fight started. Jonah tried to get into the thick of things, but I don't recall him doing much more than getting tangled up in the melee. Since then, he thought we had some kind of solidarity or something. Some connection between us, which is bullshit." She stood and stretched, and Arn had to look away. "This is about a couple veterans dying in an odd way, isn't it?'

"Where'd you hear that?"

She smiled. "Men come in here and tell me things. All sorts of

88

things like I'm some psychologist. But I ain't, even though I'm a pretty good listener when someone has something interesting to say. Or maybe they just want to get on my good side. So is this about those guys having their heart attacks at the VAs?"

Arn nodded. "But getting back to Jonah—did he ever try to recruit you?"

"For that silly group he is supposed to command?" she laughed. "He tried. I had just gotten discharged and landed a VA Service Officer gig and was in Sheridan—that's one of my stops—when I ran into those RSL fools protesting. I was there meeting with some orthopedic surgeon who had denied a veteran's claim and I ran into Quentin… Jonah now. We had a few friendly words and he asked me to dinner. Him! There's no lifeguard in the man's gene pool. If you stand close enough to Jonah, you can hear the ocean. The man is an idiot, for sure I wouldn't date him." She smiled. "But you… you seem a little sharper than him."

"Thanks for the compliment. I think."

"At least you'd know if I gave you the brush-off."

"And Jonah didn't?"

She shook her head and pulled a lock of hair behind an ear as she spoke. "I give riding classes in Rapid City on Saturdays during the summer. Jonah just *happened* to be there one day and hit on me again. Man couldn't understand *no*. But I'm certain you're not interested in my romantic relationship with that fool."

"I'm interested in the times you may have seen his group protesting during your travels. The VA website says you do travel a bit."

"A bit! I go all over hell with this job. Which is why I don't mind being single."

Arn thought she emphasized the word *single*. But it might just be his wishful thinking.

"I travel to VA facilities and outreach centers in South Dakota and Wyoming. Most veterans genuinely wish to see me to learn about benefits they're entitled to, and I advise them. Advocate for them. But some, like Jonah," she leaned forward, and a smile crept over her face. "Has he done something illegal you can connect him to, 'cause that would plumb make my day. Especially if he is involved in all those veterans' murders."

Arn sighed, wondering just where she had heard it. Wondering who had leaked the information about the vets' suspicious deaths. "I can't say for certain right now that they *were* murdered."

"Then why investigate deaths that were not homicides?"

Arn closed his notebook and took off his hat. He ran his fingers through his hair before putting his Stetson back on. "Sam, I've been a lawman all my adult life. Through dealing with criminals all that time, I've developed a sense of... what, I don't know exactly, but it's something that makes my gut churn when something just isn't what it seems. And whenever I think of the coincidences of those deaths to the presence of the RSL, it makes my gut growl more than a butter churn."

"Maybe it's not that," she said. "Maybe you're just hungry."

"I am a little gaunt. Missed my lunch today."

"I did, too," she said as she tapped his business card with her fingernail. "I am hungry, and curious what kind of Oldsmobile you mention on the card." She stood and stuck her head out the doorway. "Tell those other fellers waiting I'm closing up shop early today," she told the receptionist. She turned back to Arn. "You don't mind going for a bite to eat—my treat?"

A dinner date with a woman everyone else has been trying to land? He never looked a gift horse in the mouth. Even if she was a looker like Samantha Holder. "I have a few loose ends I need to sew up here. If you meet me at the Police Office downstairs in fifteen minutes, I'll take you up on that offer."

———

Arn took the down-elevator and caught Sgt. Wagner just as he was locking up for the day. "Did you get a chance to pull up Captain Sims' service file?"

"I did," Wagner answered. He looked both ways along the hallway before handing Arn a manila folder held tightly closed with a rubber band. "Remember, you did not get this from me. It's not Sims' whole file, but it covers his duty stations and what he did while in Vietnam."

Arn thanked him and slid the file into his briefcase.

"If I'm caught giving a civilian military records, I'll stand by my initial answer—if there's anything to your theory that veterans were murdered around the area rather than dying natural, then I'll do whatever it takes to find the SOB."

Arn turned to leave when Wagner stopped him. "I noticed the side of your face isn't red like I thought it might be."

"Red from what?"

Wagner grinned. "Getting slapped by Miss Ice Lady Samantha Holder when you put the moves on her."

Now it was Arn's turn to grin as he caught sight of Sam walking toward the Police Office. "Matter of fact, sergeant, I projected my Norwegian charm and landed a dinner date." He exaggerated a look down the hallway, "where is *your* dinner date?"

"What?"

"Winger?"

Wagner waved the air. "He just stopped by to show me his new boots he'd bought with all the overtime he made. Can you imagine paying a cool grand for a pair?"

"Not this cowboy," Arn answered.

"Back to Sam—where's that date you thought you'd line up?"

"We're going to eat in a moment."

"Sure you did," Wagner said with a grin. "You stick with that story."

"I will," Arn said as Sam stopped beside him and threaded her arm through his. "Ready for dinner?"

Wagner's mouth dropped and Arn winked at him. "I'd offer to take you along, but I don't think you'd fit in the back seat of my car. Maybe tomorrow, sergeant."

As they started out the door of the VA, Arn glanced over his shoulder at Wagner still staring at them. Mouth agape.

19

ARN FOLLOWED CHIEF OBLANSKI INTO the sound-proof room and closed the door after them. He turned the sound up on a speaker in the wall as Quentin Barb—aka Colonel Jonah Barb—sat upright and stoic in the chair on the other side of the one-way glass. "Only reason I'm letting you set in on this interrogation," the chief said, "is because you've done enough nosing around about Jonah that something he says might click."

"It might if you tell me a little more than you did when you woke me up."

"Fair enough," Oblanski said. "A homeless man found Brian Gibbs' body in back of the American Legion about sunup. He had been dead for four to five hours according to the coroner."

"You said Gibbs was bludgeoned to death."

"To put it mildly. There was so little left of the man's face that he was almost unrecognizable from his driver's license photo. If he didn't have his DL in his wallet, we might have taken a lot longer to identify who he was."

"Any money left in his wallet?"

"Four-hundred dollars and a few cents," Oblanski answered.

Arn's eyebrows arched. "Rules out robbery. Who's doing the interrogation?"

"Mike the Mauler," Oblanski said. Mike Sommers had acquired his nickname because he had an uncanny way of coaxing confessions out of people—even sometimes when they *didn't* commit the crime. And he did so without any threats. Without any intimidation they could later claim in court. "Here he is now."

Mike the Mauler entered the interrogation room carrying a single, thin file under one arm. At barely five foot, the investigator had been interrogating criminals longer than most officers on the department had been alive. He had developed that same gut-instinct Arn had developed over the years of listening to other men's lies. He sat on a chair across a tiny table from Jonah and laid the file on top.

"There must be some compelling reason why I'm here," Jonah said.

Mike smiled but remained silent as he scooted his chair closer to Jonah. He cleared his throat nervously like this was his first rodeo before asking, "Yu have been read your Miranda rights it appears."

"At the motel when your officers dragged me out of bed. But I was just a little bit groggy so I'm not sure what they said as The Mauler fished his rights card out of his shirt pocket and began reading it to Jonah.

Oblanski turned the sound down. "The patrol officers who found Jonah's motel room said it *appeared* as if he had been sleeping when they rousted him out of bed. Means he had either been sleeping *all* night like he claimed—."

"Or he killed Brian Gibbs e*arlier* in the night and really was sleeping."

"He's good for it," Oblanski said and turned up the speaker volume.

"Jonah Bard," The Mauler said, pausing as if not knowing. "*Is* that your given name?"

"I go by Jonah now. Like the biblical feller who got hisself swallowed by the whale and later escaped."

"So, you *do* equate yourself with Jonah in the Old Testament?"

Oblanski turned the volume down again. "Won't be much to hear for a while. Ol' Mike's just speaking small talk, loosening Jonah up, getting him comfortable talking before he drills the main point home."

Arn took off the lid of the Starbucks cup and blew on it to cool the Americano. "Why do you think Jonah is good for Gibbs' murder?"

"Some drunk—Harlan something-or-other, his name's in the report—claimed Jonah was in the Legion and had some words with Gibbs. He remembered you coming in and talking with Gibbs.

"But Jonah left after a few minutes, according to Gibbs. About an hour before I came in," Arn said. "Came back a few hours later. Drunker 'n Harlan if you can believe him. Jonah picked a fight with Gibbs which lasted all of twenty seconds before Gibbs gave him the bum's rush."

"What was the fight about?"

Oblanski nodded to the one-way glass. "Jonah thought it was his right to waltz into the Legion and recruit for his RSL. Gibbs thought otherwise. I'm leaning towards Jonah hanging around until Gibbs locked up for the night and ambushing him."

"What was the murder weapon?" Arn asked.

Oblanski wiped coffee dripping from Arn's cup onto his shirt front. "We don't now yet. Officers combed the alley in back of the Legion for six blocks either way. Nothing discarded. Nothing tossed in the dumpsters."

"And nothing in his motel room by the sounds of it?"

Oblanski stared at the glass and nodded. "If Jonah killed Gibbs shortly after he locked the Legion up for the night, he'd have more than enough time to dispose of any weapon."

"What kind of weapon you think it was?"

"Something big and round," Oblanski answered. "Pipe of some kind perhaps. Something that made deep, rounded marks in Gibbs' head and face." He turned up the volume to the interrogation room.

"We have two witnesses who will testify that you threatened to kill Brian Gibbs," The Mauler said.

Jonah waved the air. "That was just the booze talking. I'd never hurt him." He tilted his head back and laughed hard. "As big as that man is—was—do you think *I* could have hurt him any? Look at me compared to that big bastard."

"Any man can kill with the right tools," The Mauler said.

Jonah tapped his chest. "But not this man."

"Then how do you explain this? The Mauler opened a small envelope and shook out a small, silver colonel wing and laid it on the table. "Whoever killed the victim must have lost it in the struggle."

Jonah picked up the shiny wing that reflected the light as if they were just buffed.

The Mauler scooted his chair closer, his knee touching Jonah's knee.

"Looks like the wings that you wear when your group is protesting."

Jonah hung his head. "You can get DNA from those wings, can't you?"

"We can. And our crime scene tech is processing your motel room now."

Jonah shook his head, and Arn thought the man was going to confess when he said, "Then there's only one thing to say." He looked up and laughed. "Kiss my behind. I got nothing to say to you. Those wings," he flicked it with his finger, and it skidded across the table, "can be bought off the internet, or at any military surplus store. Just like I bought mine." He stood. "You got nothing on me. Process my room all you want, and when you're finished, prepare yourself and your department for a lawsuit. In case you didn't know, we have two attorneys living and organizing with us down in Winsdor." He straightened his shirt. "Now unless you're going to arrest me, I'm walking out the door."

The Mauler looked at the one-way glass and Oblanski keyed his portable radio twice, his signal to allow Jonah to walk.

He knocked the chair over as he turned and stormed out the interrogation room.

The Mauler walked into the viewing room and tossed his file folder on the counter. "I was certain he was going to break down. Sorry, boss."

"You did your best. Any read on him?"

The Mauler plopped himself in a chair, a disgusted look on his thin face. "Jonah is one cool customer. For the life of me, I couldn't get *any* read on him. I could not tell if the man was lying or not."

"Meaning he's a habitual liar and used to it," Oblanski said. "Or a sociopath who doesn't even know right from wrong."

"Or that he's innocent," Arn added.

20

"**WORD IS THAT YOU HAVE** a new squeeze," Ana Maria said. "Who's spouting that rumor?" Arn asked.

"Oblanski. He saw you having dinner at Poor Richards with an absolute knockout. Some young babe—."

"She's only twelve years younger than me."

"The chief says she could be your daughter."

"She just looks naturally... youthful. Good genes, she says."

"You could have brought her home for dinner," Danny said as he handed Arn and Ana Maria a plate with apple pie hanging over the sides.

Arn licked the side of the plate and sawed off a piece of pie with his fork. "I'd be afraid you two yahoos would scare her off with all the questions you'd have of her."

"We gotta look out for you," Danny said.

"And speaking of Chief Oblanski," Ana Maria said, "he'd give only the barest of facts at the press briefing this morning."

"Like he doesn't trust the media?" Arn said. "Hell, *I* don't trust the media."

"But you trust me?" Ana Maria said.

"Only if it's off the record."

Ana Maria nodded. "Ok, let's have it. Off the record."

Arn began by telling her the murder weapon was probably a pipe, or a wrench or some other heavy, rounded object, which Oblanski had kept from the press. He also said the department had located no weapon used in the homicide. Oblanski also didn't say police had brought in Jonah for interrogation. "Small, silver wings were found

96

beside the body like they were dropped by the attacker. Maybe Gibbs fought and ripped one off. Maybe not."

"But you said Jonah's a little fart," Danny said, "not much bigger than me."

"Not much."

"That means there must not have been much of a struggle. He had to have taken him quick. As big as Gibbs was, *anyone* would have had to take him quick."

"You knew him?" Arn asked.

Danny's face flushed. "Just from my drinking days. The Legion always treated us vets good." Danny finished his pie and washed it down with a sip of coffee. "And Jonah's right—you can buy those wings at most surplus stores."

Arn nodded. It *had* seemed too pat to Arn that colonel wings were found at the murder scene. As much as he wanted Jonah to be the killer, there was nothing to connect him to Brian Gibbs than an occasional fight and a tour in Iraq together.

"Anyways," Ana Maria said, "Chief Oblanski gave me nothing that I could air and I came home with nothing to show for bugging the chief. I thought maybe Captain Sims' file would have held something I could use so I could say I didn't waste the whole day."

Arn stopped his pie mid-mouth. "Tell me you didn't look at his file."

Ana Maria took another small bite of pie and *cooed*. "Great pie, Danny."

"Don't avoid the question," Arn said. "If you looked in the file you weren't supposed to—."

"Then don't leave it lying around where other people can peek at it." She stood and set her empty plate on the counter. "Did you read it yet?"

"I glanced over it," Arn said. The only reason he had even read Sims' military file Wagner gave him was that Arn was convinced Sims was *first* victim of the VA Slayer, as Ana Maria had labeled him. Or her. Even if the way in which Sims was murdered didn't fit the MO. Or supposed MO. Without more evidence, all Arn had was that Steve and Frank had overdosed on cocaine.

"I read it pretty thoroughly," Ana Maria said. "Apart from the man living a quiet life on his family farm after Vietnam, Robert Sims was one competent criminal investigator over there."

"You talking about Robbie Sims?" Danny asked.

"Ring a bell?"

"Like Quasimodo," Danny said. "Captain Robbie Sims was hell on wheels as a criminal investigator in 'Nam. He was CID—Criminal Investigative Division. And he was absolutely relentless. There was so much black marketing of cigarettes and booze, arms and ammunition before he was assigned to Saigon, half the American supplies probably walked north."

"But after he was transferred there?"

Danny ran his finger across his throat. "After he came into Saigon, he put the fear into all of us."

Arn nudged Danny. "You mean you dealt in the black market when you were over there?"

Danny shrugged. "Just a carton of Marlboros now and again to get some drinking money. Sold two bottles of Johnny Walker Black once and went on a week-bender." He held up his hands. "But ol' Danny never sold any arms or ammunition. Not so much as even one fragmentation grenade. The piddly stuff I black marketed wasn't enough to interest a hot shot like Robbie Sims."

"Ever meet him?" Ana Maria asked.

"Never," Danny said. "But he was written up quite a bit in the *Stars and Stripes*. Sims even got a general's commendation once for catching some Spec Sergeant named Bo Randall for stealing LAWs."

"What's— ."

"Light Anti-Armor weapon," Danny said. "Portable rockets. Bad-ass little numbers. We used the hell out of them, and Charlie always loved getting his hands on them, too. But when Robbie Sims busted up Randall's theft ring, I was long rotated back to the world."

"I'm still not convinced Captain Sims was our killer's first victim," Ana Maria said.

But Arn was sure, not so much because any evidence pointed to it, but because that old gut feeling that overcame him. He *sensed* that Sims was the first victim, and that the killer got better at his hunting and killing techniques in the next couple years. The next victims. Which did nothing to explain who had murdered Brian Gibbs.

Either way, Arn had other things to worry about… like who was killing the veterans. And why Ana Maria was leaving the house alone. "Where are you going?" Arn asked her as she put her shoes on.

"I do have a nightly broadcast I am responsible for."

Arn stood and stretched. "I think I'm getting cabin fever. Mind if I tag along?"

"Don't you *even* start with that," Ana Maria said. "I know what you're doing, and I won't stand for it. I have to function even with Doc Henry in town."

"It wouldn't hurt for Arn to tag along with you," Danny said.

Ana Maria shook her finger at Danny. "You either. Get off it. Besides, I have that little gun Arn gave me for protection." Her tone softened. "Thank both of you for being concerned. But I really do need to do things by my lonesome without having one of you looking over my shoulder."

"Understood," Arn said. "You won't don't hesitate to use it if Doc puts the sneak on you?"

Ana Maria nodded. "Believe me, after the last time, I won't."

Arn waited until Ana Maria had left for her nightly broadcast before he grabbed Sims' file. "Grab us fresh coffee," he said to Danny. "We're going to look at a military record."

"And you need someone who can decipher shit from 'Nam?"

"You a mind reader?"

———

As Danny was reading Sims' service file, Agent Kane from the South Dakota DCI called. "We have another body in the Hot Springs facility. Heart attack. He's slabbed-up and gone now, but you're welcome to come on up tomorrow and I'll let you see what we found out."

The old Olds would be getting more miles put on than he wanted, and he asked Danny, "What do you think?" Arn asked when Danny had finished reading Captain Sims' file.

Danny sipped his coffee, smelling so good after the green tea he had made for Arn. "I think Bo Randall was a gnarly SOB. He's lucky someone didn't frag Sims." Danny explained how men—usually officers hated by their men—would go to the latrine only to have someone rig or lob a fragmentation grenade in to settle whatever perceived score was outstanding.

"Lucky he wasn't knifed in the brig." Arn said, "By statements made by chasers, Bo Randall had spent time in some brig in Vietnam."

"Lucky he wasn't killed in the riot," Danny said, then explained when Arn shook his head. "Bo Randall was probably sentenced to Long Binh jail—that was located about twenty kicks northeast of Saigon."

"Sims' background on Bo said he spent time for assaulting an Army major," Arn said. "Don't that usually earn you a Dishonorable Discharge?"

"Usually," Danny said as he flipped pages Sims had compiled on Bo Randall's background. "But it looks like he was knee-deep in the riot at the brig in August '68. Bo was one of the few white guys in there according to Sims' report, and he saved a guard and a Spec Sergeant from a group of blacks marauding through the brig kicking the hell out of honkies."

"Even with that, he should have been drummed out of the Army."

"Normally," Danny sand and motioned to Arn's cup. "More tea?"

"Not tonight," Arn said. "I had too much of your *wonderful* tea last night and was in the bathroom half the morning. Damn regularity."

"Suit yourself," Danny said and filled up his own cup from a coffee carafe. "It looks like Bo Randall was… invaluable to Army command. A genius in the area of supply. Sims noted that—if a CO needed to… acquire an armored vehicle—an M113 for example—and there were none to be had, Bo could find it. That went for anything else the command needed."

"I read where Bo had stolen eight cases of LAWs from the 3rd Marines and gave to the Army 1st Infantry. He barely got out with his hide. You'd have thought he would be back in Long Binh over that."

Danny laughed. "Three was more than a little interservice rivalry back then, and the Army brass looked the other way. Same as the Marine brass would do if the tables were turned."

"It looks like Bo's shenanigans finally caught up with him," Arn said. "He was caught again when Captain Sims nailed him for his black marketing of weapons and ammo."

Danny tucked his legs under him and Arn marveled at the old man's flexibility. "As far as a connection to the other deaths you're looking into, I don't see a one linking Sims to any of them."

"Let me ask you this," Arn said. "If someone had wronged you to the point where it all but ruined your future, would you seek revenge?"

"I would. I'd make it slow. Painful."

"Then it is safe to assume that Bo Randall would have a grudge of the most intense kind towards Captain Sims."

Danny nodded. "I would say so. Why is that relevant to your victims?"

"Because," Arn handed Danny the background information on Bo Randall, "when he enlisted in the Army, he gave Custer in the Black Hills as his home."

"So?"

Arn leaned over and flipped to the next page. "He might have given his home as Custer, but he enlisted in Sheridan in 1966."

Danny grabbed Arn's glasses and held the light under the reading lamp drooping over his shoulder. "Damned if you're not right."

"Even a stopped clock is right twice a day," Arn said.

Danny handed the report back. "I'm not sure how it helps knowing Bo enlisted in Sheridan… there is no information about any friends or relatives of his living there. No one who might tell you where he might be living. I'm assuming you intend finding him?"

Arn stuffed the file back into the folder. "That'll be the only way to scratch him from the suspect list. Or elevate Bo to the top. Only other thing I have to go on is that Bo's home was in Custer before he enlisted."

"It might just be worth it for you to drive up to Custer and talk with that old sheriff about Bo."

"The ex-sheriff's not available for a couple more days. And I doubt if that croaker at the VA will wait a couple days for me. I'm going to ask Ana Maria if she wants an all-expense paid trip to Custer tomorrow."

"Good idea," Danny said. "The more she's away from town the less likely she'll run into Doc Henry."

"Or the less likely that he'll run into her," Arn said.

21

"**D**EANGELO SENT ME ALONG," ANA Maria said, "only because there might be something newsworthy at the end of your rainbow of suspicions."

"Just keep an open mind." Arn slowed to allow a small herd of whitetail deer to cross the road.

Agent Kane of the South Dakota DCI had called last night. "You need to get up here," he said. "We have an odd death that you might be interested in." Arn hung up the phone and began laying out his clothes to wear for his trip to Hot Springs so Ana Maria could approve. Something about she didn't trust his combining stripes with checks. Arn figured it must be a woman thing. He'd do his job even if he looked like he just fell off a clown car. "You're welcome to come see for yourself," Kane told him over the phone, "but this old feller died as peaceable and natural as you please."

They drove past the Mammoth Site, cars in the parking lot of the archeological dig showed no shortage of people wanting to uncover the bones of the animals, and crossed a bridge over a slow running creek, until the Hot Springs VA Center loomed off to their left. Once called Battle Mountain Sanitarium, it had been the first short-term medical facility for war veterans in the country. Last year the Veterans Administration had threatened to close the facility, but public outcry kept it open.

Arn recalled one weekend in the summer of his youth when he and his father—in a rare moment of actually being a parent—made the drive to Hot Springs. They soaked in the healing waters of the mineral springs, though it did nothing to heal his father's battle with the bottle, and he had reverted to being the mean drunk as soon as the weekend ended.

Arn parked his car in front of the enormous sandstone structure and led Ana Maria inside. The receptionist directed them to the campus police, and they walked a short hallway to where a man older than Danny sat under the "Police" sign." With his hat tilted over his eyes, and his head bouncing now and again on his chest, Arn *suspected* he was still alive. They stopped in front of the VA policeman and coughed. When Arn got no response, he coughed louder. The man's elbow fell away from the arm of the chair, jolting him rudely awake, and he rubbed the sleepers out of his eyes as he focused on Arn. "Don't look at me like that." the old man said. "I'm just catching a few ZZs is all. Not like anything ever happens here to need the police."

"Except that patient who died here yesterday?"

"Oh, that." He stood and stretched his back while he fished a pack of cigarettes from his uniform pocket. He put one in his mouth but didn't light it as he stood under the NO SMOKING sign. "Down the hall and to your left. Those DCI agents took over for us, and they're interviewing folks," he guffawed. "As if we couldn't do the job ourselves."

"Indeed," Ana Maria said.

The old policeman didn't wait for Arn and Ana Maria to leave to resume his duties. He sat back in his chair, pulled his hat down low, and started sawing logs, while his unlit cigarette still dangling from the corner of his mouth.

Ana Maria glanced back at the old man as they walked towards where the interviews were being conducted. "Good thing something bad *doesn't* happen in here."

"Like someone dying alone in the restroom," Arn answered and stopped outside a room with a DO NOT DISTURB—POLICE INTERVIEW IN PROGRESS sign duct taped to the door. Chairs had been placed along the wall outside the room, but no one occupied any. "Must be something more than just some old veteran keeling over," Ana Maria said and sat in a chair. "What did Agent Kane tell you exactly?"

"Just what I said—that there had been a death, unattended, like the others I was looking into. Asked if I wanted a firsthand look at the scene."

"Appears we'll know the skinny soon enough," Ana Maria said as the door opened and a woman wearing dirt-scuffed pants and the top of a janitor left the room. A stocky man—squat was Arn's first impression—followed her out of the room. "You must be Arn Anderson?" he said as the janitor disappeared down the hallway. "Please come in."

When Ana Maria stood to follow, Kane stopped her.

"She's with me," Arn said, leaving out the fact that she was reporter. "She's my secretary."

Ana Maria's face flushed and Arn smiled. "She does all the transcribing. Pencil sharpening. Small stuff around my office."

Kane hesitated for a moment before motioning her to follow. He pointed to chairs lined up at a long table, notes strewn across the tabletop, manila folders marked and waiting for reports to be stuffed inside. A laptop stood open beside the folders. Kane tapped keys and turned the computer so Arn could see it. "Scroll through the photos and tell me what you see."

With Ana Maria looking over his shoulder, Arn began scrolling through pictures of a man lying face down on the floor, his head partially inside a urinal. "This guy looks a lot younger than the others," Ana Maria said.

"Looks a lot like Steve Urchek and Frank Mosby's crime scenes to me," Arn added.

"Funny you use that term," Kane said, "because I think it is a *crime scene*."

"So you think my theory holds water—that there have been deaths at the VA facilities made to look natural."

Kane popped the top on a can of Red Bull and took a long pull. "The VA Police call us or the local law on every unattended death—more out of curiosity than policy. As many old vets die in these centers—just worn out or from complications of their service—we usually waiver the call. Tell the locals and the VA Police to handle it. After all, there hasn't been a suspicious death here since it opened in 1907. But," he took a longer drink of the Red Bull this time and tossed the empty can into a recycling bin by the table, "I remembered your... theory. I told them not to contaminate the scene until I got here, and to lock the facility down. No one in or out."

"Doesn't explain why you *think* this death is anything more than natural," Arn said.

Kane eyed another Red Bull but didn't assault it. Yet. "After I called you, I got to thinking maybe this veteran didn't die peaceable like I told you. So me and another agent searched the restroom where the victim was found. Nothing odd. Until we expanded the search to include adjacent rooms." He reached over and turned the laptop so he could read it before turning it back to Arn and Ana Maria. "That's when we found *that* stuffed inside a trash receptacle by the entrance to the center."

Arn donned his reading glasses, and stifled a smirk when Ana Maria had to do put on her own Walmart readers. A bent hypodermic needle stuck out of a plastic syringe partially covered with a crumpled Burger King bag. "Xylazine." He took off is glasses and examined the drug name pasted on the side of the syringe. "Not sure what that is. Did you look it up in a PDR?"

Kane turned the laptop around again. "Wouldn't be in any PDR. Xylazine is a horse tranquilizer. The syringe in on the way to the lab now, though I'm certain we won't find DNA or prints on the tube."

"What is horse tranquilizer doing in a medical facility?" Ana Maria asked.

Kane looked at her with an odd expression, and Ana Marisa quickly wrote in a long, reporter's notebook. As if she were taking notes for her boss—Arn. "That's the question we need answered. It might have absolutely no connection to the man's death. But— ."

"I bet you don't believe in coincidences," Arn said.

"I do not," Kane answered. "The closeness of this trash receptacle to the restroom—not thirty feet away—is just too handy. But we'll see what the lab comes up with."

"Did you find an injection site?" Arn asked, knowing that—if the victim was killed by horse tranquilizer—it could have been administered IM through the clothing. In the muscle.

"We found no injection site, though it means little at this point. If there is one, we'll find it at autopsy."

Arn turned the laptop again but could not see the victim's neck clearly. "Did he have bruising on his neck like the other victims I faxed you a couple days ago?"

"No," Kane said. "But the coroner said there might not be since the man was about thirty years younger than all the others you showed me. Skin too pliable. Resilient, she said. Not so prone to bruising."

"So, the victim's an Iraq War vet, maybe from the Syrian conflict if I figure his age right."

Kane gathered his notes and stuffed them into a briefcase. "You're not looking at *any* veteran. Our victim—Charles Boding—wasn't a vet at all. He was merely here giving his father a ride to Hot Springs for his annual checkup."

"But the hat," Ana Maria said. "The photo shows Boding wearing a Vietnam hat with gold embroidery of some kind on the bill."

Scrambled eggs," Arn said. "They call them scrambled eggs. Officers wear them."

Kent unplugged his laptop and slid it into a pocket in his briefcase. "Boding's father was wearing an identical hat when he visited his primary care doctor right before his death. Must have given his son a cap like his with *Vietnam* pasted across the front and those gaudy scrambled eggs on the bill."

"Then the victim could have been killed because he was mistaken for a Vietnam vet?" Arn asked.

"Very well could have." Kane snapped the clasp on his briefcase. "Still, at this point I have no proof that this *was* a homicide. We'll have to wait for the lab results and the autopsy." He snapped his fingers. "If you're staying in the Hills for the night you could come up and catch the autopsy in Rapid City," he winked at Ana Maria. "It'd be cheap entertainment for you and sweet cheeks there," he told Arn. "I'll bet secretaries don't get a chance to leave the office very often. I'll buy popcorn."

"We'll pass," Arn said. "We're staying over here in Hot Springs for the night to catch the hot springs in the morning. It's just late enough I hate to drive back at night with all the deer on the road. Besides, I wanted to visit with Ethan Ames if he happens to be here. Wanted to get his insight into the killer with this fresh victim."

Kane slung his briefcase over his shoulder "I wanted to talk with him myself, but he left for Cheyenne earlier. I'll catch up with him day after tomorrow as his secretary says he's in Rapid that day." He started for the door and called over his shoulder, "I'll let you know what we find in the autopsy and the lab results when we get them."

"What about the surveillance cameras?" Ana Maria called after Kane just before he left the room.

"What about them?" he asked without turning around.

"Did you look at them?"

Kane turned slowly. "Even us rubes get our jobs right now and then." He laid his briefcase on the table and talked slowly. "There was no one—except veterans and employees—roaming the halls."

"There must have been *someone* besides them. *Someone* wanting to kill Boding."

"Anderson, I'm still struggling with your notion that all those deaths are connected. And until I took a closer look at Boding, there just is *nothing* to prove homicide."

Arn nodded to Ana Maria. "She had a good point—did you see anything unusual at all on the cameras?"

"We talked before about those RSL fools," Kane said. "Two of them came into the facility and tried recruiting but they were tossed out on their keisters before they got a chance to spread their hatred."

"And they couldn't have slipped back in and killed Boding?"

"You mean sneaking by Earl?"

"That old man guarding the front door?" Arn said. "You could drive a dump truck past him and he wouldn't wake up."

22

*H*ow the hell could I *have screwed up that bad? If I had a gun, I'd cap myself right now. Right here as veterans walk past me in the courtyard paying me no mind.*

How? The man—I learned was a Charles Boding living right outside Rapid City—looked way too young to have served in Vietnam. Yet I was so careless thinking he just wore his age well. Good Genes, *as Dr. Oz would say.*

I got careless.

That's the one thing I said I would never do after I almost botched Captain Sims' killing. But I screwed this up simply because I assumed *a man wearing an officer's Vietnam hat was a Vietnam vet.*

On a positive note, luck was on my side today. As big a man as Boding was, he didn't go down like the others, but merely staggered. If I hadn't had the vial of Xylazine to… sedate him, he might have fought like Sims did. But unlike Sims, I had cocaine ready in the other syringe. I might just keep a syringe of Xlazine with me from now on. For such occasions. Except this time, I'll hang on to it and not drop it in the trash, though I doubt the inept cops will even think to look in the garbage.

The courtyard will help me think about what to do next. What I did was not right—Boding didn't need to die like the others. Not like the retired officers who probably trumped up charges against any number of enlisted men for things they did not do.

Even though killing Boding was a blunder of mammoth proportions, I owe it to myself to think straight. As I look around, I feel people staring a hole in the back of my head. But I know I'm just imagining it. I know no one suspects the man in the courtyard catching a few rays as the one

109

the police will be looking for. If they ever figure it out.

I need to move. To think deeper, and the presence of people surrounding me somehow focuses my attention and I move to the waiting room. Like a familiar part of the forest that is a cougar's territory, I have come to think of waiting rooms as my safe space. Where no one knows me. No one pays me the slightest bit of attention to me, like the mailman or the paperboy on their routes that no one notices—plain. Unobtrusive.

It surprised me that the police—I don't mean that old duffer snoozing by the front entrance—but the regular police, and now the state investigators, have been called. All the other times, they would take it for what it appeared—an old veteran who had just worn himself out and died as he was taking his last dump. Except Boding wasn't old. He wasn't helpless.

I think back to Aristotle when he said it is during our darkest moments that we must focus to see the light. *Focus. Think. I know the police will find nothing. The commotion will soon die down and I'll simply slip out one of the side exits.*

And I make a solemn promise to myself not to make the same mistake twice—never will I confront an innocent *veteran again.*

What kind of man would I be—after all—if I didn't recognize my mistakes and learn from them?

Hunting the VA Slayer

23

A RN AND ANA MARIA HAD left Hot Springs early after an early morning soak in the mineral pools. By the time they arrived in Cheyenne, Ana Maria was nagging him to grab a bite somewhere when Sam left a voice mail offering to buy him lunch.

"Might as well drop me off at home," Ana Maria said.

"Thought you wanted to get something to eat?"

She tapped Arn's phone. "With an invitation from the Ice Lady, you better go. And go alone if you ever expect to make anything of this relationship."

He had hesitated to accept her lunch invite. Their last dinner date had gone remarkably well, with Sam hanging on Arn's every word, complimenting subtly more times than she should have. In fact, it had gone so well, red flags waved in front of Arn's face as he tried analyzing her. A woman many years Arn's junior who could have her pick of suitors. Even with the single professional men who drooled around her office, she had come on to him. At first, Arn had been flattered as he felt his old mojo returning. Until he remembered he didn't recall ever having mojo enough to attract a beauty like Samantha Holder.

He had sat and thought about her last night as he soaked in the hot springs, without Danny or Ana Maria telling him just to enjoy her company and see where it goes. Which is just what Sam said when she called him this morning. "It'll just be at the cafeteria here at the VA," she told him. "Nothing fancy. Just to get together and visit. See where this is going."

Was she after something more than a relationship, like information

111

about his investigation? *Get a damn handle on your paranoia. Meet with the lady but keep an open door to your gut feelings.*

"I can bring you something from the cafeteria."

Ana Maria smiled. "Not to worry. Drop me off at home and Danny will throw *something* fabulous together for lunch."

——

When he passed the Police Office, the door stood open and he stepped inside. "Returning the file," Arn called out.

"Back room," Wagner answered.

When Arn stepped into the small, back office with Sims' military file tucked under his arm, Wagner sat at his desk, one sockless foot propped up on the desktop while her cleaned his toenails with his Buck knife. "Did you find anything in there?"

"Nothing that'll lead me to his killer."

"I told you there wasn't a whole hell of a lot in that file," Wagner said, "except Sims must have been some kind of investigator the way he went after those black marketers. I was hoping there'd be more in the after-action report I received from the Army archives this morning. If you think there was anything substantial in *that*, don't hold your breath."

Which is just what Arn did, holding his breath as he moved upwind from Wagner's stinky feet. "Care to let me look at the after action report?"

"Can't," Wagner answered, admiring his toes like a model admiring her figure in a full-length mirror prior to runway time. "But I can give you the quick and dirty of what I found."

"I see the quick and dirty," Arn pointed to Wagner's feet, "but tell me what you found out." He took out his notebook and a pen. "Shoot."

Wagner started slipping his sock back on when his big toe stuck through a hole in the fabric. "Funny you should use that term," Wagner said as he extricated hos toe from the hole in the fabric, "because that just what Bo Randall threatened to do to Sims at his court martial— that he was going to drill Captain Sims center-chest as soon as he got released from Leavenworth."

"I take it he's no longer in prison?"

"You got it. He got another year tacked on for that little courtroom outburst, but he served his time and was released in 1972. His trail goes cold from there."

"Did the Army keep track of him?"

Wagner tossed his holey sock in the trash can and put his boot on without one. "Bo served his time. Wasn't any reason for the Army to keep him on their radar. My guess is he went back to Custer."

"I have another favor to ask—."

"Not today," Wagner said. "And not the day after. Or the day after that. I have enough of my own work to do around here as it is."

"You wouldn't want to help solve these crimes?"

"Anderson, there *are* no regional crimes, at least as far as old vets go. It's just some old farts keeling over from heart issues."

"Suit yourself," Arn said as he closed his notebook. "I'll get hold of the South Dakota VA officers and ask them for help."

Wagner laughed. "And just why should they help a pain-in-the-behind civilian with his bogus theory?"

Arn shrugged. "Because when I put it all together—with their help—they'll be heroes."

"It'll take more than that."

"And they'll probably get nice promotion. Maybe even a transfer to someplace with more… opportunity for advancement for someone who takes a little initiative in their work." He started out of the office when Wagner stopped him. "How much work you talking about?"

"Not much," Arn lied. "But the reward could be well worth it. That is, unless you want to sit around bored out of your mind waiting to kick an occasional drunk out of the facility."

"All right. All right. What the hell you need me to do?"

After Arn explained that he needed Wagner to research each victim's record to see what doctors they were seeing at their respective VA centers, Arn needed to know if any of the victims served with Bo Randall in Vietnam. "That's all!" Wagner said. "Do you know how much time it'll take for me to do that?"

"What else do you have to do all day but sit around picking your toenails?"

———

Arn patted dry wall dust off his bib overalls before taking them off. "Where do you want them?"

"Just drop them by the washer," Danny said as he swiped at a spot of wet dry wall mud that had dropped onto his shirt front from his dry wall knife. He put one hand on his thin hip. "I swear you make more work for me than a dozen people trying to hang drywall. And you better run a brush through what little hair you have—there's enough drywall dust and mud there to hang another sheet."

"I just feel guilty about leaving you with the rest of the room to finish—."

"Believe me, you'll be doing me a favor," Danny said. "If you're not helping, I'll go twice as fast with half the mistakes. Now clean up and give that DCI feller a call back."

Before Arn walked out of the mudroom, he stuck his head under the faucet. He dropped his shirt and bibs on the floor before parading through the house and upstairs to his room. He put on clean jeans and t-shirt before stopping in the kitchen long enough to make a cup of green tea. He hated to admit it, but it was helping his regularity. His blood work came back yesterday and—except for itching where the nurse had wrapped the Kerlix bandage too tight, he felt fine.

He took the cup of tea and a plate of cookies into the sewing room and opened his phone.

"I see you left me a voice mail," Arn told Agent Kane.

"I did. Figured you'd want to know… the autopsy on that feller in Hot Springs, Charles Boding, is finished, and the lab results are back. I *believe* he was murdered. Boding died from a cocaine overdose, but he was no user. I talked with his father and he is convinced me his son never used any drugs."

Arn thought of what Oblanski said before. A lot of cocaine addicts lived a normal life—unlike meth heads—and often the last to know were the person's family. "Why you figure he was murdered?"

"That syringe we found in the trash," Kane said. "I fast-tracked the lab tests and the techs found traces of Xlazine. Faint traces."

Arn let out a breath. Although it gave him no peace to be right about the veterans' deaths, at least he felt some vindication. And a place to start looking for the killer. "Did you find the injection site?"

"Finally," Kane answered. "In the event the victim *was* a user, we looked at the usual places where people shoot themselves up—the veins in the arms and the back of the hands. We even looked between the toes. Nada. But," rustling of paper on the other end, "the ME saw a tiny red mark under the tongue. Bingo! That was where he was injected with the coke."

"Just to be absolutely certain," Arn said, "You are positive he did not inject himself?"

"I am," Kane said. "I have never run into a user who injects himself under the tongue."

"And the horse tranquilizer?" Arn asked. "Was that injected under the tongue as well?"

Arn waited so long he thought Kane had hung up.

"It's the oddest damn thing I ever ran into. At autopsy, there was a pinpoint discoloration on the victim's thigh—another injection site."

"He was hit with cocaine twice."

"He wasn't," Kane said. "Testing at the site and blood work showed Boding was injected with Xlazine high on his thigh. We'll know more after I run the samples to the state lab."

Arn closed his eyes, processing what Kane told him, and combining it in his mind with the crime scene photographs of Boding's death, reconstructing the crime in his mind's eye. The killer would have hit Boding with the horse tranquilizer to get him sedated before the needle was injected under the victim's tongue. That might work very efficiently with the older veterans who had died.

But Boding wasn't an old vet. He was a younger, stout man that the killer had to inject with the Xylazine to subdue before injecting with the cocaine

But how did the killer get the upper hand on a young man like Charles Boding?

24

ARN ENJOYED THE RIDE SOUTH on 85 as much as he had enjoyed it when he was a youngster growing up in Cheyenne. He and his friends now and again would sneak on down to Pierce, Colorado and east on an oiled road to climb the rolling hills of the grasslands. They would climb to the top of Pawnee Buttes with their warm beer in a backpack and watch the antelope chase one another through the buffalo and grama grass. And when the boys had a snootful, they would slide down, stopped only by the limber pine and chokecherry bushes and hang out until they were sober enough to drive back home.

As Arn headed east on the secondary road he passed a pump jack moving slowly up and down, like a giant pecking bird, pumping oil into one of five large holding tanks on the well site. Black White-Faced cows grazed beside the oil site, and a coyote scurried across the road in front of the Oldsmobile as Arn turned onto a drive. He started along the hard mud-rutted road for a quarter mile, the 442 bottoming out every so often, and Arn cursed himself for not getting his old International truck roadworthy.

When he reached the top of a slight rise in the road, it dropped off sharply and ended a hundred yards farther, passing a sign that read RIGHTEOUS SWORD OF THE LORD: TRESPASSERS WILL BE SHOT.

He pulled up slowly to a small guard shack positioned on one side of a gate made from well pipe heavy enough to stop a truck, and repositioned his revolver beside his leg. Just in case the two guards emerging from the building considered him a trespasser needing to be shot.

The two men—dressed in black uniforms punctuated by silver-colored embroidered *RSL* patches on each shoulder—kept their rifles slung as they walked toward the car. Before they reached the Olds, one man peeled off and headed to one side of the car. Arn's blind side. *Military.*

"You lost, bud?" the man approaching him asked while he discreetly switched the safety off his AR-15.

Arn stepped out of the car and stretched, keeping the man to his side in his peripheral vision. "No. I know just where I am."

"Then you know you don't belong here. Hop in that old beater of yours—."

"I'm here to see Jonah Barb."

"Got an appointment?"

"Didn't know I needed one," Arn said.

"You do," the man said, and Arn detected an imperceptible nod to the other guard.

"Even if I want to… join your merry band of men?"

"Scat!" the man said. "Colonel Barb is busy."

Arn motioned to the phone hanging on the side of the guard shack. "Maybe I'll just call him. Tell him a convert is here to enlist," and started for the phone when the man off to Arn side rushed in. He grabbed Arn by the arm, but years of custody control classes—and wrestling matches in high school—kicked in. He slipped from the man's grip right before he kneed him in the thigh.

He howled in pain and dropped to the ground when Arn caught movement from the first man. He had taken his rifle from his shoulder and cocked it behind his head to deliver a butt strike when Arn stepped into him. He slapped the guard *hard* across the face and—as his eyes rolled back in his head—kneed him in the thigh as well. As the man fell to the ground, Arn caught his rifle and stepped back. "You ladies are *some* guards," Arn said as he cradled the man's rifle under his armpit.

"I ought to kick their sorry asses down the road," another man said. Arn spun around when he heard the racing of a shotgun slide. He turned to the sound and towards the two men pointing pump guns in his direction.

Another man—unarmed—stepped from in back of the biggest man and stopped in front of Arn. "Just give the rifle back to that boob."

Arn dropped the magazine before handing it to the guard writhing on the ground holding his leg.

"There a reason you're beating up on my men?"

"*Your* men." Arn slipped his hand inside his trouser pocket and rested it on the butt of his revolver. Thinking back to Brian Gibbs' murder, Oblanski made it a point to tell Arn that Jonah had argued with the big bartender only hours before the man's death. "You must be Jonah Barb?"

"*Colonel* Jonah. And you still haven't answered my question—why are you beating up on my men?"

Arn stifled a grin as he motioned to the guards on the ground. "Let's say I take offense to men pointing guns at me."

Jonah stood on his tiptoes. He whispered to the men with the shotguns and they lowered them. "My men there," he chin-pointed to the two guards struggling to stand, "are new to the movement."

"Fresh out of the military, no doubt."

Jonah nodded. "They are. Joined our movement when they... saw the light. Realized the military treated them badly, and that we," he waved his hand over the prairie and their compound in the distance, "are doing all we can to change that."

"If they're going to man a guard post, they need to handle themselves a whole lot better."

"Oh, they can handle themselves," Jonah said as a white gelding pranced up to the fence. It hung its head over the top wire until Jonah walked to the horse and handed it a carrot sticking out of his back pocket. "You just ... surprised them. Now what is it you want? And who the hell are you..." he snapped his fingers. "I've seen you before... Ft. Meade little more than a week ago." He pointed to Arn's car. "I'd know that car anywhere."

Arn exaggerated reaching inside his shirt pocket and handed Jonah his business card. He turned it over in his hand before saying, "Okay Mister Mystery Man—what is a private investigator snooping around our compound?"

Arn motioned to the two guards still cradling their shotgun under their arms. "I'd feel more open to answering questions if men didn't wait to shoot me."

Jonah jerked his thumb at the two guards, and they retreated to the guard shack, still within range if they needed to assist their leader. "And you two—get back to the compound," he told the two just now regaining their footing. They glared at Arn as they walked, each holding the other like in a slow three-legged race They crow-hopped into a Jeep and disappeared over the hill. "Ok, Mister PI. Make it quick. Why are you here?"

Arn reached into his notebook and handed Jonah a sheet with dates when the VA victims were murdered. "Were you and your group protesting these places on these dates?"

Jonah glanced at the list and handed it back. "Without looking it up, I would imagine we were conducting operations then. Why?"

Arn turned so that he could look closer at Jonah, study his face to see if he lied as he said, "men were killed at VA centers in this region on those dates. All under suspicious circumstances."

Jonah glanced at the shotgun guards leaning against the shack. "Are you implying somebody in my organization might be responsible?" Arn detected nothing, no involuntary tic, nothing to reveal Jonah was lying as he asked.

"We are a peaceable movement. Our operations do not advocate violence."

"Folks have been hurt at your protests."

Jonah waved it away. "I *do* tell our people to defend themselves if attacked."

"Why would they need to," Arn asked, "if your protests are peaceable?"

Jonah half-turned and motioned to the tip of a chimney popped up just over the hill. Thin tendrils of smoke wafted straight upward on this airless day. "Most of our flock are prior military. They have seen the fallacy of pushing American values on unsuspecting people worldwide. Of the misery that war brings."

"And this justifies your group bringing misery to veterans who have sacrificed so much in defense of this country... to ensure your right to protest?"

Jonah smiled. "We bring our message to where it is most needed—veterans centers. Let vets know they are not alone in decrying anguish that our military has wrought. And to encourage them to join us."

"I'd like to talk with Nehemiah," Arn said suddenly.

"What?"

"Your *General* Nehemiah. I'd like to talk with him."

Jonah started pacing in front of Arn's car, his hand wringing, knuckles white before he blurted out, "The General is a very busy man. He cannot meet with anyone."

"Then what's his number?" Arn asked as he grabbed his phone from his pocket and flipped it open, finger poised above the numbers. "It'll only take a moment."

Jonah stopped pacing and motioned to the shotgun guards. They came off the guard shack and walked toward Arn while they unslung their long guns. "This isn't going to be another Jonestown thing where inquiring people are gunned down?" Arn asked, taunting Jonah, until Arn realized it *could* well end up bad for him and his hand went back into his pocket.

"Leave, Mr. Anderson, before I can no longer control my temper."

Arn backed up to the door of his Olds while he kept his hand on his gun butt. It might not stand him well against shotguns, but at least with his last breath he'd nail Jonah with his .38 if it came to gunplay. "By the way, did your temper flare a couple nights ago when Brian Gibbs put the run on you from the Legion? The night before he was found bludgeoned to death?"

"Leave."

"I will but hear me—don't ever slip by the television station and threaten Ana Maria Villarreal again."

"Leave, Anderson!"

25

A RN HUNG UP THE PHONE and stared it like it was a thing possessed.

"Well, what did Agent Kane say?" Ana Maria asked as she followed Arn into the sewing room. "No, wait. Tell me as soon I taste this great peach cobbler."

"Great?" Danny said. "More like *memorable* once you taste it."

When they had all seated with forks poised over the dessert, Arn said," Kane drove the syringe and tissue samples to the state lab in Pierre himself. They found small amounts of Xlazine in the victim's blood. But massive amounts of cocaine. Twice the fatal dose."

"Why do you suppose the killer used horse tranquilizer?" Danny asked. "And not even enough to do any damage?"

"The only thing I could think of," Arn said, "is the killer injected Boding with just enough to get him loopy before injecting the coke."

"So he is learning?" Ana Maria said.

Arn nodded. "Our killer's learning."

"And so am I," Ana Maia said. "I found Bo Randall."

Arn set his cobbler on the TV tray. "Are we going to have to guess where? He might be the key to all the VA deaths. We need to talk to him—."

"Bo and his wife were living on ten acres outside Custer, but she left him some years ago. Took their daughter and lit out, but she had to leave the boy—Bo threatened to kill her if she took him, too."

"So where is Bo?" Danny said. "You guys need to talk to him—."

"Not in this lifetime," Ana Maria said. A beat. "He's resting comfortably in a pauper's grave. The sheriff of Custer County at the

121

time Bo and his wife were living there said he'd show me just where Bo was buried if I came up there. Seems like he committed suicide six years ago."

"Because of the divorce?" Arn asked.

Ana Maria dabbed at her peach cobbler, stringing Arn along. "The divorce happened long before Bo shot himself. The sheriff wasn't sure why, and he thought at first Pudgy might have come back home and killed his own father."

"Pudgy?"

"The boy that Bo kept in the divorce." She downed a piece of dessert with coffee, the wonderful odor mingling with the acrid odor of Arn's tea.

"Does the sheriff know where Pudgy is now?"

"Nada," she said as she gathered plates. "He hasn't seen the kid in years. Didn't even come back for the old man's funeral. Sheriff says Pudgy ran away from Bo when he was sixteen, though never reported him gone. Sheriff heard rumors the kid enlisted in the Army when he was old enough and just stayed away from home. 'Good for him' the sheriff told me. 'Best thing the kid could do was get away from the old man, even if Pudgy was odd."

"Odd how?"

"He didn't say. He'll tell me more if I drove up to Custer to meet him."

"I hear a *but* in there somewhere," Arn said.

Ana Maria nodded. "The *but* is DeAngelo. He says I need to go on-air live with what I've found about the RSL. I can't go up there with you."

"If that old sheriff can give us any information, it'd be worth a drive back up there. Be another excuse to drive through the Black Hills."

Ana Maria winked at Danny and asked Arn, "and seeing Samantha isn't an incentive to drive up there?"

"I didn't say that," Arn answered.

26

"WATCH OUT FOR THAT DAMNED buffalo!" Danny shouted.
Arn laid on the brakes and the Olds slid to a stop mere feet from where the big bull was ambling across the road, not even looking their direction. If a two-thousand-pound beast can amble. "Crap," Arn said, breathing deeply to calm himself. "Guess I was a little distracted."

"With thought of that babe from the VA you've been seeing, no doubt."

When the buffalo had crossed the road, Arn motored slowly past him. "Hard not to be distracted by her."

"And you are disappointed that she is not going to be in the Black Hills area on her VA rounds?"

"Wish the hell you didn't know me so well."

Danny smiled. "Just trying to steer the hero in the right direction.

Danny had a good point, Arn thought as they meandered through twisting hills northbound, through Black Hills forests dotted with ponderosa and lodgepole pine, buffalo berry and chokecherry bushes. Arn's thoughts went seamlessly from Sam to Ana Maria. He worried about her being alone at the house with Doc Henry in town. Even though Doc hadn't contacted her, and Oblanski said his daily patrols never spotted Doc anywhere near the house, he worried. Oblanski even stopped at Mimi's only to learn that Doc worked late into the night and it appeared as if he had no time to stalk Ana Maria.

"You're concerned about her, aren't you?" Danny asked.

"Samantha?"

"Ana Maria."

"Can't help it. Even though the prisons tout the great rehabilitation programs, inmate recidivism is still terribly high. There're just some people that are unredeemable. Like Doc Henry."

Arn *was* worried about Ana Maria, especially since he climbed into his car this morning. He had said nothing to Danny, but Arn just *knew* someone had been in the Olds since last night. The seat had been pulled ahead; the rear-view mirror cranked down. But nothing else has been tinkered with, and he blew it off as some kid walking the neighborhood looking for something to jack from parked cars. Yet, that old gut feeling was that someone besides a kid had been in his car.

Doc Henry? The psychopath was the first who popped into Arn's head, yet he had nothing but that *gut* feeing that had served him so well for so any years to go on.

"I'm like you." Danny took off his ball cap and his stringy, gray ponytail fell onto his frail chest. "The more I think about this Pudgy character, the stranger it seems that he wouldn't even come back for his own father's funeral. It'd take a special kind of man of walk away from the death of a parent like that."

"It would take some cold bastard, that's for certain." Even though Arn's father had been an abusive drunk despite being a city cop, Arn had attended the funeral. He had even shed a tear, though it was more window dressing for the sake of his mother than genuine sorrow. Perhaps he would ask Ethan Ames the next time he saw him how certain people—like Pudgy—could turn away from a dead parent like that.

"I'm worried about her too," Danny blurted out. "Dammit, I still don't see how Doc Henry can be walking the streets."

"It's our system," Arn said, slowing and weaving the car through a herd of six deer walking across the road from one grove of trees to an inviting meadow on the other side. Arn explained again how Doc had earned several sentence reductions until he was paroled.

"Well, it's just not right, him killing all those women—."

"Which we could only tie Doc to the one."

"Just say the word," Danny said, "and some of my old AIM buddies will drive down to Pine Ridge and… show Doc the door, so to speak."

"Don't tempt me," Arn said.

They completed the four-hour drive to Custer talking about things that got their mind off Ana Maria and Doc Henry: how hot the weather was, and how the traffic seemed more congested with tourists the closer to the southern hills they drove. But despite Danny's ramblings about how he used to practically live in the Black Hills in his youth, Arn's mind kept returning to Ana Maria and her safety. She had been more on edge since that first night seeing Doc Henry, but she had recovered quickly, always keeping the small revolver handy. No matter how Arn scolded her about going out alone at night during her broadcasts, she marched to her own drummer. It was almost as if she went out of her way to defy Arn. Just like a rebel child would do to her parent.

"Where's this retired sheriff supposed to meet you?"

"The old courthouse," Arn answered. "The one your American Indian Movement buds trashed in that '73 riot."

"Was no riot to it," Danny said. "It was a demonstration against white abuses."

"You were there, I suppose," Arn said as he pulled in front of the Victorian-looking brick courthouse.

Danny unlatched his seat belt. "I was. I marched with the two-hundred other poor bastards freezing our *cojones* off. Marching on the courthouse in peaceable protest."

"We studied that in high school when that went on," Arn said. "As I recall, AIM torched the courthouse and burned some police cars. Beat up some locals."

"So we got a little... rambunctious. At least we drew attention to ourselves."

Arn laughed, recalling Danny's *rambunctious* side. A year after the Custer riot, Danny and two other AIM activists had planted bombs in a building in Minneapolis meant to shine attention to the plight of Indians. Fortunately for Danny and his cohorts, the building had been condemned, empty and awaiting to be torn down, and the explosion had actually done the city a favor. After many years—like so many arrest warrants—Danny's had sat idle long enough to be expunged.

They walked up and through the steps past the colonnades on either side of the entrance where an elderly man sat behind a reception desk reading a copy of the *Custer County Chronicle*. He looked over the top of his half-glasses before returning to his newspaper. "Self-guided tour," he said without looking up as he pointed to an empty gallon pickle jar on the counter. "Tips appreciated."

"We're not here to tour the courthouse—."

"You got something against our local history?" the old man asked as he turned a page of the newspaper.

"No," Arn said. "We're just here to speak with Sheriff Mick Ridley."

The man put his newspaper down and stood to his full height of five feet and some change. "Ain't been called sheriff in a long time. You must be Arn Anderson."

"I am. And this is Danny Spotted Elk."

The old sheriff's eyes narrowed. "Spotted Elk... I ever arrest you?"

"Some policeman did during the '73 protest," Danny said. "But the charges were dropped."

Sheriff Ridley dug into the pocket of his bib overalls and retrieved a pipe. He filled it from a pouch on the counter and lit it. Waving smoke out of his eyes, he stood face-to-face with Danny and said, "guess we both learnt something during those awful times." He held out his hand and Danny shook it before facing Arn. "Now what was this about Bo Randall that caused you to drive up thisaway?"

Arn explained the suspicious deaths at the VA centers in the region, and the possibility that Bo Randall was somehow connected. Even though he was long dead.

"If Bo was alive, I could see him doing that. He was a little feller— not much taller than me—but wiry. With an evil glint in his eyes. Took out his frustrations on his wife, and that's when we got involved with him—breaking up their damned family fights." The sheriff spit in disgust. "Son-of-a-bitch had an attitude since he was released from Leavenworth."

"Attitude about what?" Danny asked.

"About getting drummed out of the Army like he was I guess. Or born with a nasty-ass attitude. Hell, I don't know. Some men are just plumb nuts. Every now and again Bo'd come into town and raise hell. Start cleaning out bars, especially if he thought there was some retired officers in there drinking. And that's when he'd go home and tune up his wife."

Sheriff Ridley knocked burnt ashes into the trash can beside the counter and pocketed the pipe. "Like I said, Bo would be good for it. But I personally cut him down from the rafters in that old horse barn of his after he hung there for a week, so I know he's dead. "He spit. "And I'm here to tell you I'm not sorry."

Arn took off his hat and laid it crown-down on the counter beside the tip jar. "Tell me about the missus and the kids."

"Not much to tell about Beth—that was Mrs. Randall. She lit out with the girl to parts unknown. Never heard from either since. A shame too, as that girl was a cute little pot licker."

"But the boy wasn't so cute, if the description you gave to Ana Maria is right."

The ashes in the trash can started smoldering and Sheriff Ridley looked at it for a moment before calmly tossing his coffee onto the ashes. "That boy Pudgy—that's what everyone called the fat, crazy little bastard—was a lot like his old man. Always a chip on his shoulder. Once when I responded to their place for a family fight, I came out of the house to find one of my tires slashed and Pudgy sitting on the stoop whittling with an old Barlow knife of his. 'You outta' take better care of your car, sheriff,' he says and grinned. I'm telling you, just the way he looked at me with that knife in his hand sent shivers down my spine. If I could have proved he done it, I would have hauled him in that night." He spit in the trash can. "And a week later when all my tires were slashed sitting smack in front of the courthouse I figured it was Pudgy, but no one would come forward and say they saw him."

"Sounds like he was trouble?"

"That's an understatement. If I got a nickel for every time he ran from us law dogs I could have retired early."

"Driver was he?" Danny asked.

Ridley nodded. "Ever since he could see over the wheel, Pudgy would take Bo's car and hop it up. Come to town with that cute little sister of his beside him. He'd boil tires right in front of the courthouse and police station until one of us took the bait and chased him."

"Might there be a booking photo somewhere of Pudgy?"

Ridley shook his head. "He was sneaky enough—and damned cunning enough—that he never got himself arrested."

"Whatever happened to him?" Danny asked.

"Army if rumors are right." Sheriff Ridley said, "Thank God. Pudgy got into the Rangers from what I heard, but I can't verify it. Some folks said he came back now and again to visit Bo before he hung hisself but I can't prove it." He chuckled. "As much as Bo and Pudgy fought, he might have come back and done the old man in himself during one of his visits, he was just that cold hearted."

27

ARN DRIED HIMSELF ON THE towel Evans Plunge had rented him and snapped Danny's bony butt. It *twanged* and Danny howled. "That hurt."

"Figured I'd urge you along. I'm late for my appointment with Ethan Ames at the VA," Arn said and tucked his shirt into his jeans. "I'll be waiting outside."

Arn walked to the car parked in front of the mineral hot springs, the breeze finishing what the terry cloth towel missed. He put his Stetson on while he walked towards the Olds, a group of kids gawking at it.

"That's some ride you got there," pone boy of about sixteen said. His arm encircled a girl's waist as they peered inside. "But what's that *thing* sticking out of the floor?"

"In my day," Arn said, "we called it a *gear shift lever*."

"Cool, dude," he said and backed away to allow another boy to look inside. "I'll bet pink slips I could beat you in the quarter with my car," he said and pointed to some foreign outfit—Honda, maybe Toyota or Nissan, Arn never could tell the Japanese cars apart—parked at the far end of the lot. "No thanks," Arn said as he tapped his chest. "Not sure this old ticker could stand one more race." But Arn knew that most tuners the kids fine-synched today could beat any of the old muscle machines. And that's with half the motor size.

Danny emerged from Evans Plunge, his stringy, wet ponytail blowing across his face. The kids looked oddly at him as he climbed into the passenger side of the car. "Fans?"

"Kid wanted to race me in that tuner car of his."

"You'd have lost."

"I know," Arn said, and drove out of the parking lot.

By the time they drove the few blocks to the VA facility, Danny's hair was dry, and he tucked it under his ball cap. "Been here many times to pick up meds and for my yearly checkup."

"Your want this to be your last time here?" Arn asked.

"How's that?"

Arn tapped the brim of Danny's hat, the outline of Vietnam on the front, scrambled eggs on the brim. "No reason to advertise you're a retired officer—."

"I wasn't an officer," Danny said. "I just bought this 'cause it looks cool." He set it on the seat. "But I see your point. I'll go down to the cafeteria and grab us coffee. Unless you want tea."

"I'll pass."

They entered the enormous sandstone building, Danny peeling off toward the cafeteria, Arn standing staring at the legend hanging on the wall. Dr. Ames' office was situated at the far end of the hallway, and Arn stepped around a Korean War vet slowly making his way down the hall with the aid of a walker as a younger man wearing an *Occupation Iraqi Freedom* t-shirt walked beside him, ready to help if necessary.

When Arn entered the outer room of the mental health wing, a PATIENT CONSULTATION IN PROGRESS sign hung on the door by a suction cup. "Doctor Ames will be finished shortly," a woman said from somewhere under the counter. She stood holding file folders, her glasses hanging by a chain from around her neck. *Navy* under a ship's anchor had been tattooed on one forearm. "Please be seated," she said after she took her pen from her mouth and glanced at her desk pad, "Mr. Anderson."

Arn sat and sifted through the magazines splayed across a coffee table beside the chairs. Unlike most doctor's offices with their *Good Housekeeping* and *Pregnancy Today* and old copies of *Reader's Digest*, the reading material here consisted of *Guns and Ammo* and *Western Horseman* and *American Legion* magazines. He picked up a copy of last summer's *American Legion* and was half-way through an article on the Marines at Belleau Wood when Dr. Ames' door opened. He led a man wearing an *Operation Enduring Freedom* hat out of the office. "Get with Michelle and make an appointment for next week. I think that's when I'm here again."

The veteran merely nodded as he plodded towards the secretary's desk, his gaze never leaving the floor.

Ethan stood in his doorway. "Mr. Anderson—we seem to pass one another in our travels. Michelle said you wanted to see me, but I'm scheduled to be in Cheyenne again later this week."

"I was in the area and thought I'd drop by while I was here."

"And you hit the mineral springs I'd wager?"

"Did me wonders," Arn said.

Ethan motioned for Arn to enter and he pointed to a chair. "If I got a nickel for every veteran I've seen lately with PTSD I could retire and live on some fancy ranch somewhere."

"I've heard it's become more common with this new crop of combat vets leaving the military."

Ethan sat behind his desk and unwrapped a piece of gum. He popped it into his mouth, folding the silver wrapper neatly into a tiny square. "It *is* more common. I've even treated women who had support roles in Iraq and Afghanistan suffering from Post Traumatic Stress Syndrome." He lobbed the piece of wrapper into a trash can beside his desk. "We know how to better diagnose and treat the affliction now."

"Would someone suffering from PTSD be able to function for any length of time?"

"Of course!" he snapped, then held up his hand. "Sorry, Mr. Anderson. I just get a little emotional when people begin thinking that veterans can't handle society."

"Understood," Arn said.

Ethan propped a scuffed boot on an open desk drawer and looked up at the slowly rotating ceiling fan. "Veterans have suffered from what we psychiatrists called shell shock in World War One and, later in World War Two, CSR, or Combat Stress Reaction. The medical community has been treating diseases like dissociation disorder and psychogenic fatigue for years until we *really* got a handle on it. We can even screen for predisposition of PTSD by testing for low levels of cortisol."

"But you treat it with therapy?"

A smile crossed Ethan's face as if reliving his fight against the disorder. "Cognitive Behavioral Therapy is now the drug of choice. But to answer your question, most veterans can function in society without anyone knowing they have PTSD. With proper treatment." He dropped his boot on the floor and leaned his elbows on his desk. "But you didn't come here for a lesson in Post Traumatic Stress Disorder. You came here to ask about my insight into these deaths you believe were murders."

Arn set his hat on the chair beside him and ran his fingers through his hair that was still damp from the mineral springs. "Frank Mosby's body and Steve Urchek's were both exhumed. Both had injection sites under their tongues. Both toxicology tests came back as overdoses of cocaine. Remember that list I gave you with the names of the victims?"

"How could I forget?"

"I got word this morning that you treated one of the men—Johnny McGomerary—a few years ago for substance abuse." Wagner had researched all the names on the victims' list and called Arn this morning. Lieutenant McGomerary, living and unemployed in Cheyenne, was Dr. Ames' only patient on the list.

Ethan stood and looked out into the parking lot. "How did you get this information?"

"Does it matter?" Arn said. "All I need to know is some background on McGomerary."

"I cannot help you," Ethan said. "Patient confidentiality."

"The man's dead, for God's sake!" Arn blurted out. "I'm sure he'll give you no grief if you tell me about him. Might help other veterans from being murdered."

When he faced Arn again, his mouth had downturned in sadness. "You are absolutely right, and I apologize." He sat back into his chair and leaned on his elbows once again. "Lieutenant—Johnny—McGomerary was a troubled soul. Homeless." He held up his hand. "Before you ask, he didn't want help. He didn't want to go into a shelter. He came to me with a cocaine addiction two years ago. He'd lost his job. Lost his family. He was at his bottom. But with therapy, he was on the right track to full recovery. Or so I thought."

"What changed it?"

"Denver," Ethan said. "Johnny had an early appointment at the Denver VA, but he had no way to get there."

"I thought there is a DAV shuttle that goes down there daily."

"There is," Ethan said, "but it *leaves* from Cheyenne at eight o'clock—the time Johnny's cardiology appointment was. I took the day off to drive him there." He looked away to the photo of a young Ethan Ames in a color guard in Casper hanging on one wall. He seemed to be gathering his thoughts as he straightened the photo. "After Johnny's appointment, he wanted to buy cigarettes. I don't abide by smoking, but that was the least of his worries. He said he knew a tiny smoke shop along E. Colfax that sold cheap cigarettes and I stopped there. Bad idea."

Ethan started pacing, gesturing with his hands. "Johnny walked out back of the smoke shop after he bought his cigarettes. I figured he needed to take a leak, but after ten minutes, I went to check on him. His drug dealer was just pocketing the money Johnny paid for an eight ball." Ethan dabbed at his eyes.

"That's not cheap."

Ethan shrugged. "He had gotten a job at Albertson's bagging groceries, and I figured he saved up a couple paychecks to buy his dope. I figured he was planning to go off the wagon for some time." Ethan sat on the edge of his desk. "Johnny went downhill after that. Skipping therapy sessions. Hanging with some other druggies in town. So it doesn't surprise me that he died of a cocaine overdose." He stopped and looked down at Arn. "So you see, I doubt Johnny was murdered. My guess is he just OD'd on his own. Like so many other poor souls have."

"I disagree, "Arn said. "I've developed a certain *sense* of when something isn't right. And these deaths stink. Including Lieutenant McGomerary's."

Ethan spit his gum out and popped in a fresh piece. "Let us say— for the sake of argument—that you are correct. Let us say that there is some malevolent man—or woman—stalking and killing vets. Who would you put at the top of a suspect list?"

"Like you said before, Ethan, someone like you. Someone who

travels to VA hospitals where deaths have occurred."

Ethan smiled. "And what motive would I have?"

"Don't know that you would."

"Then I would run one suspect by you. Or I should say, a bunch of suspects—that Righteous Sword of the Lord fanatics. I've been following Ana Maria Villarreal's coverage of that bunch of fools, and they are even scarier than she depicts them."

"You've had run-ins with them?"

"They have been protesting at several facilities the day I had appointments. And every time, I literally had to fight my way past them." He smiled again. "But they're nothing that I can't handle,"

"Then tell me, have you treated their leader, Jonah Barb?"

"Why would he be a patient of mine?"

"Anger issues," Arn said. "Seems he kicked the hell out of an officer in Iraq and earned himself an Undesirable Discharge."

"I cannot treat anyone with an Undesirable or a Dishonorable. Doesn't mean I would rule out him as a suspect." Ethan stood and grabbed his briefcase. "But I have to run, Mr. Anderson. I have a date with destiny."

"How's that?"

"I have been ordered to attend a class with Winger... Steven Hays."

"Never heard of a doctor needing to go to a custody control class."

"Well, it's heavy on control," Ethan said as he led Arn out his office. "VA regs say anyone dealing with violent patients needs to attend. Believe me, if there was some way I could beg out of it I would. But Winger is here just for this makeup class that I conveniently missed the last time."

Arn rubbed his neck as if still feeling the impact of the brachial stun Holder whipped on him. "Go to the restroom first."

Ethan stopped rigid. "Why should I do that?"

"Because if it's anything like the class I went to with Holder, you're likely to pee your pants after he's done."

28

*A*nderson and some anorexic old *Indian pull away from the VA center. He wasn't inside long—just enough to make his stop and grab a bite at the lunchroom. But then, I figured he wouldn't be. I thought he might have learned something significant from Sheriff Ridley before coming here, but what could he learn? I haven 't been back home since... well, since pappy hung himself. I attended the funeral, though I had changed enough no one recognized me anyway. Except old bucktoothed Mary Ann whom I ignored when she called my name on the street.*

What could Anderson hope to learn here? There were no witnesses to my latest... victim as Anderson and Ana Maria calls them, and I kick myself in the butt again for killing an innocent man. But not hard enough to waltz into the police station and confess my dastardly deeds.

Ana Maria's last nightly Cheyenne broadcast about the RSL was followed by little more than a teaser about a special to come covering the veteran's deaths. She had no idea who is behind the suspicious death or if they even were murdered, though it's more dramatic for her to purport she knows. Teasing!

But what if the law, and Anderson and the reporter do *have more information? I began to lose sleep, wracking my brain, thinking where I made a mistake. Until I realize I made none.*

I confounded and will continue to confound the law, dumb as they are.

Still, I have read everything about Anderson I could get online: former homicide detective who solved every case assigned to him. And he solved a case of serial killings in Cheyenne two years ago when the local law could not. For a brief moment, I wish Anderson were an officer, but I checked that, too. He's not prior military. He's not one of us. It would make it so

135

easy if he were. I could—in good conscience—rid myself of that bastard before he found out more.

But he won't find out about me. He won't find out how bitter I was when pappy hung himself, and he won't find out that Pap's intense hatred for the elite was passed down to me. All those years living with a man incensed with the officer class of life rubbed off onto me. Or perhaps I welcomed it, I don't know. Perhaps I ought to seek therapy somewhere.

When I attended his funeral—keeping well away from Sheriff Ridley and another deputy, the only ones attending—I couldn't fault Pap for hanging himself. As he was lowered into his grave inside a rough-hewn pine box, I thought how I wish I would have had the chance to talk him out of it. I know *I could have talked him down, once he saw me in uniform. Once he saw what I had become.*

Pap, why did you do it? Did the hate you felt all those years finally catch up with you? I know why you felt as you did—Lord knows I had enough run-ins with officers myself that didn't turn out well. Your inveterate hatred for officers was always at the periphery of my thoughts.

Mama.

How many times have I searched online for her, for where she and Sis lit out to when she and Pap broke up? Surely, she would have some insight into how I should deal with my feelings passed down over so many years by the man she once loved. She would know what I should do.

But try as I might, she and Sis' whereabouts are unknown to me.

I suspect I will have this hatred and fury inside me until someone like Ana Maria Villarreal or Anderson catches me.

But that's something I cannot allow.

29

"HAS OBLANSKI FOUND JONAH YET?" Ana Maria asked as she placed the dozen roses in a vase and set them above the fireplace mantle. Arn wondered who her benefactor was, but figured she'd tell him in her own time.

"Not yet." Arn answered. "I talked with Chief Oblanski and he put out a region-wide BOLO for Jonah Barb, and Kane did the same from the South Dakota end."

"I thought you'd given up on Jonah as a prime suspect?" Ana Maria said.

Danny entered the room with a piece of key lime pie for he and Ana Maria and set them on TV trays.

"What's that?" Arn bent and looked closer to whatever Danny set before him.

"Diet pudding."

"Jonah as a suspect," Ana Maria pressed Arn for an explanation.

"It was me that changed his mind," Danny said proudly.

"That right?" She asked as she sniffed a rose.

"In a manner," Arn said, keeping his cell phone close. "Danny and I talked at lunch in Hot Springs and we kicked around what Ethan told me how he had to take a class in controlling violent patients. On a hunch, I called Sgt. Wagner—he served in Iraq about the time Jonah did. Wagner said violent patients where the norm in field hospitals. Just where Jonah worked as a medic assisting doctors."

"But it was me who figured it'd only make sense that medics would be taught controlling techniques," Danny seemed to beam. "Including that stun thing that knocked Arn on his keister."

"I'm still not sure about your theory," Ana Maria said. "If you think someone can be stunned long enough for someone to hurriedly inject cocaine under your tongue—."

"Believe me," Arn rubbed his neck as if still feeling Holder's slap, "a person would *not* be aware of it." Arn stabbed a piece of pie. "Oblanski said Jonah was nowhere to be found when Colorado deputies went to his compound. Right after your broadcast, it would seem. So, you watch your backside."

"Don't even start with suspending my special again," Ana Maria said. "If Jonah comes anywhere near my broadcast, Oblanski has plain clothes officers ready to snatch him up."

"I checked their website and the RSL doesn't have any protests scheduled," Danny said. "If they did, you could bet Jonah would be among them."

"Unless he's on the run," Ana Maria said, putting a tiny piece of pie on the end of her tongue. "Perfect," she winked at Danny. "Sorry Arn," she motioned to his pudding with her fork, "but we're getting you in shape."

"I'm liking the shape I'm in the more diet food and green tea I put down me."

"Apparently Samantha Holder does, too," Danny said.

Arn chuckled. "You mean the Ice Lady? That's what Wagner calls her. Seems it's easier to suck-start a Harley than wrangle a date with her."

"But you did," Danny said. "And that's what's odd. No offense, but did it ever occur to you how strange it was that she came on to you that first day? And a few more times since?

"You don't think it's my undying charm?" Arn said.

"Arn," Danny said, "you *have* no charm. She's after something else, and it's not your wit or your Oldsmobile."

Arn took a small spoonful of his *diet* pudding and laid it down without eating any more. "Don't you think that's been gnawing on me? She travels to VA facilities in the region where veterans are murdered and comes on to me just when I'm looking for answers?"

"That's enough!"

Arn and Danny stopped arguing and stared at Ana Maria. "There's nothing linking her to any of the deaths any more than there is linking Winger Hayes to them just because his job takes him to various VA centers."

"What *did* Wagner find about Hays, now that Ana Maria brought him up?" Danny asked.

Arn took out his pocket notebook right after he forced himself to scoop another spoonful of runny pudding into his maw. "Winger swerved in Iraq. Never went to the field but was assigned Headquarters Company. Self-defense instructor for security police. When the drawdown happened, he was transferred to Ft. Sill, Oklahoma. He got into a row with his CO when Winger got a little too… physical with the recruits in defense class and Winger saw the writing on the wall. Got an early out and nailed a position with the Veteran's Administration little more than three years ago. This traveling classes is his first duty station with the VA."e gotH

"That's it?" Ana Maria said. She stood and went to the roses and once again sniffed deeply. "That's what you're hanging your suspicions on with Hayes?"

Arn thought about what she said. When he was an investigator at Metro Denver Homicide, he would never have tried building a case based on something as flimsy as what he had learned about Winger. Or Samantha for that matter. He hated to admit it, but his thoughts were getting tangled up. He would have to run the gauntlet of Gorilla Legs and talk with Chief Oblanski once again. "I'll get a fresh start tomorrow." He motioned to Danny. "You're closest to the television—turn it on so we can watch Ana Maria's taped broadcast."

"Not before you explain why," Ana Maria said.

"Why what?"

She sniffed a rose. "Why *these*? It's not my birthday, so I figured you had them delivered just to cheer me up."

"I didn't send them," Arn said, "as much as I'd like to take credit for being a hero. What did the card say?"

"There was no card."

"I didn't send them, either," Danny said. "I'm broke."

"Come in, guys—admit it. You two were in Hot Springs this morning when they were delivered. I know they have FTD there."

"I was with Arn most of the time," Danny said, "and can vouch he was too cheap to send them."

Arn stood and walked to the bouquet of eleven red roses. And one white one. "Who always left a single white rose atop his victims for law enforcement to find?"

The color left Ana Maria's face an ashen pallor as she staggered back and dropped into her chair before her trembling legs gave out. "Doc Henry," she breathed.

30

A RN CONNED OFFICER SMITH INTO letting him through the door that led to Oblanski's hallway. "If Gorilla Legs interrogates you," Smith said, "tell her it was my twin brother that let you in. And give me a heads-up if she heads this way so I can beat feet from that witch."

Arn thought he had successfully sneaked by her when that witch stepped from a side room in front of him. "Step aside," he commanded. "I got no time for your horseshit this morning."

Gorilla Legs balled her fists up for a mere moment before she read something in Arn's demeanor this morning that gave her pause, and she stepped out of his way.

When he busted into Oblanski's office, the Chief jotted on a piece of paper as he held a telephone receiver in the crook of his neck. "I'll call you back," he said and hung up when Arn stopped in front of his desk. "I got this feeling that you're about to kick someone's ass."

"Not kick," Arn said. "Kill. Doc Henry."

Oblanski walked around his desk and motioned to a chair. "You better sit down before you have a heart attack."

Arn dropped into a chair while Oblanski sat on the edge of his desk. "Now tell me what's going on with Doc Henry."

Arn breathed deeply as he settled back. "Doc Henry sent Ana Maria flowers."

"She see him?"

"No," Arn answered, the throbbing of his veins in his head telling him Oblanski could be right—he'd better calm down before he had the big MI. Since he figured it out that it was Doc who sent the flowers, the only thing controlling his rage—and controlling his impulse to drive to Mimi's Restaurant and throttle him—was a sliver of common sense remaining. And Ana Maria and Danny's urging him not to. "Underwood Florist delivered them while I was in Hot Springs, but she wasn't home either. They were instructed to leave them on the stoop. No card."

"Did they have Doc's name on file as paying for them?"

"No. When I checked this morning, they said the man who ordered them paid cash. Some little guy with a gray handlebar mustache."

"Lots of fellers have handlebars around here," Oblanski said. He grabbed a pencil and began gnawing at the eraser. "Ana Maria has a lot of fans. Could have been anyone."

"Not some old man sporting a full head of wavy gray hair and a battleship tattooed on his forearm." Arn recalled Doc arguing for leniency at his sentencing hearing in Colorado twelve years ago. As he pulled up his shirt sleeve to show his tat, Doc claimed he had served with distinction two stints with the U. S. Navy. But the only stints Doc served were two long ones for cutting Marines on two different bar fights.

Oblanski grabbed the pencil from his mouth and tore off a fresh piece of notepaper. "I'm going to talk to Judge Michaels. Get a restraining order on Doc fast-tracked—."

"Ana Maria refuses to apply for one."

"Refuses? Doesn't she realize what Doc is capable of? I did some research on that asshole, and he is one sick puppy. I hate to hell to have him in my community and something like this might get him revoked."

"She remembers too well what Doc can do."

Oblanski put his pencil down. "Without a restraining order, there's not much my department can do. You know that. But what reason does she give for *not* filing one?"

"Pride. Ego. I don't know," Arn said, "except she says she doesn't want to give the son-of-a-bitch the satisfaction of knowing she's afraid of him."

"At least I can double the house checks at your place," Oblanski wrote down. "And I'll tell my guys to swing by the television station more often, too." Oblanski tossed the chewed-up pencil in the round file. "Just what I need right now with the RSL in town."

"In town as in protesting?"

"Affirmative," Oblanski answered. "Sgt. Wagner called an hour ago. A bus load of them showed up and are amassing just outside the east gate to the VA, with another bus load on the way from Colorado."

"You sending troops that way?"

"Got no choice," Oblanski said. "The VA police don't have enough men to handle it. Just had an emergency staff meeting with my lieutenants twenty minutes ago." He grabbed his hat. "Show yourself out."

"You headed there now?"

"As fast as I can. Why?"

"Sgt. Wagner called me this morning. He's been researching the deaths like I asked and put the word out on Jonah. Surveillance cameras caught the wily Colonel at VA centers five of the nine dates that vets have been found dead of apparent heart attacks. If the RSL is protesting, he's probably close. I might blend in a little more without all that riot gear your officers will be wearing?"

"All right," Oblanski said. "But stay out of the way."

"I'll just be another set of eyeballs looking for Jonah Barb among the protestors."

———

By the time Arn and Oblanski had pulled into the VA compound, the other bus of protestors from Colorado had arrived and were off-loading RSL people and signs denouncing the American military. Six police cruisers were already on-scene blocking the road into the VA, while officers—Cheyenne PD and VA Police—in riot gear had formed a skirmish line across where the protestors would march.

Sgt. Wagner saw Arn standing by Oblanski and left safety behind his sawhorse barricade. He walked hurriedly over while keeping an eye over his shoulder at the developments at the main entrance. "They got bad intentions this time," Wagner said. "If you can spare a couple officers to cover the rear doors, Chief, I'd appreciate it. If they get inside, there'll be no containing them." He looked back nervously. "We just don't have the manpower. I've corralled everyone—my custody control officer before he left for South Dakota, and a janitor who spent eight years as an Air Force AP. I even ordered Samantha Holder to suit up once her secretary locates her."

"Samantha's in riot gear?" Arn asked.

Wagner winked. "She will be and looking hot. Her primary MOS was military police so she ought to be familiar with riot formations. Bad thing is, if these fools get inside the facility, they'll overwhelm us in no time."

Oblanski whistled to a large Sergeant looking even larger in his riot gear as he padded over to them. "When the sheriff's deputies and state troopers arrive, send them out back. We don't want any of these shitheads getting inside."

"What do you want me to do?" Arn asked.

"Nothing," Oblanski said. "I can't risk a civilian getting hurt. Just stay back and out of the way when feces hits the wind rotating device."

"Then I'm going inside. See if I spot Jonah."

"If you are, take this and show it around." Oblanski handed Arn a copy of Jonah's Colorado driver's license photo before turning to his sergeant. They walked toward the other officers on the skirmish line awaiting the shit to hit the fan, paying Arn no attention.

He looked around at the scene at the officers stationed around the perimeter and at the entrances. Soon, the back doors would secure, and no one could get in that. But what if the commander of all this mess was *already* inside? When if Jonah Barb had entered the building and blended with the veterans hours before his troops arrived to begin their protest?

Arn started for the front door when he spotted the TV van pull up and Ana Maria jump out just ahead of her cameraman. She pulled her hair back and straightened her top while she waited for her cameraman to set the beast on his shoulders. Arn walked close to the van and motioned her aside. "You going to be all right here?"

"What do you mean?" she asked.

"Roll in twenty!" her producer shouted at her.

"I mean, Oblanski's got no one to shadow you. If Doc Henry should come near you now— ."

"Arn, there are a hundred people around here. Doc's smart enough not to risk doing anything to put him back behind bars until he's worm food."

"Ten! Come on Ana Maria."

"Gotta run." She turned to join her producer and cameraman when she asked, "just what are *you* doing here?"

"Jonah's got to be directing things. He wouldn't put off being in the limelight for this. I'm going to find him."

"And if he you don't, there's bound to be some protestors wanting to get their mug on camera in exchange for a little information. Like where their commander is. Gotta run."

Arn watched as Ana Maria and her crew approached the protestors chanting and holding their signs. Through the bulge of clothing, Arn saw that some wore shin and knee pads. Others had stuck weapons down their trousers—a pipe here, a homemade blackjack there. Things designed to make the police glad they wore riot equipment.

He turned and entered the facility, pausing just long enough for is eyes to adjust to the dim hallway. *Where the hell are you, Jonah?* "You'd have to be somewhere where you could direct operations without being spotted." Unless... some type of disguise? A janitor's garb. Kitchen help perhaps?

Arn walked into the primary care waiting room packed with vets waiting to see their doctors. Normally. To a man and several women they stood staring out the window at the festivities about to begin. One vet handed some folding money to another, and Arn wondered if he was betting on the police or the protestors.

He dug Jonah's driver's license photo out of his pocket and began walking the room, showing veterans the picture, asking if anyone had seen anyone even remotely looking like Jonah. Arn came up empty, but then he figured Jonah would have radically changed his appearance. He surely knew the law was looking for him now and he'd be hard to spot.

He began walking the halls, trying doors, looking into those empty yet unlocked. As he arrived at the end of the hallway, he found himself outside the Service Officer's room and he entered. "Is Samantha in?" Arn asked.

The secretary, the same one he'd spoken with before, grinned. "You're that old feller she's been seeing?"

"That's me," Arn said. "The *old feller.*

"Sam took an early lunch and she hasn't returned yet," she checked the wall clock. "And she's overdue."

"I think Sgt. Wagner was looking for her to man a position outside."

"Damn protesting bastards," the woman said. "If they're not cleared out by the time I get off I might just have to run one or two over getting home. You think for a minute I'm going to miss Jeopardy for them, you got another thing coming."

"Tell Samantha I'm wandering the halls whenever she gets back."

He continued down another hallway towards the cafeteria and poked his head in. Jonah wasn't filling his belly, but Ethan Ames stood in line waiting to order. He motioned for Arn to join him. "You keep me company and I'll buy you lunch."

"I'm looking for... somebody."

"Found him yet?"

Arn shook his head.

"Then maybe he's not here."

"Maybe not," Arn said. *And maybe he never was.* "I'm cutting down, but I'll let you buy me coffee."

"Deal." Ethan slid his tray down the line to the cashier and paid for his burger and fries. "Pick out a booth while I fill my soda cup."

Arn filled his cup and sat in a booth away from two nurses and a doctor studying some kind of lab results laid out across his table. "You following those protestors outside?" Ethan said.

"Hard not to. They're getting worked up to do some real damage unless they're contained."

"And all they want is for the U. S. military to disband," he took a bite of his burger. "Or so they claim. I think they're just a bunch of drunks and dopers and losers who have no problem with the military. I'd wager they're here just to act up and get crazy."

"You don't sound very tolerant for a... shrink."

"Not of idiots like them," Ethan said. "Pushing their weight around like they're somebody, and all the while all they want to do is disrupt people's lives."

"You think all the elaborate games are a cover?"

Ethan wiped ketchup from the corner of his mouth and speared another French fry. "I do. They follow some charismatic leader who has convinced them that they can belong to a group. At any expense. They will storm the line of police, getting their heads busted, earning a night in jail just to belong. That's why they are dangerous—crowd mentality."

Arn dug Jonah's photo out of his pocket and slid it across the table. "That's their charismatic leader you mentioned. He's nowhere to be found, but I'm thinking he must be close to his followers outside. Seen him in the facility today?"

Ethan held the photo to the light before handing it back. "I passed him in the hallway… a few hours ago. And last week I spoke with him briefly under the veranda at the VA in Hot Springs."

Arn did the math. If Jonah was in Hot Springs this past week… "Can you be more specific as to what day in Hot Springs?"

"I'll look at my planner when I return to the office," Ethan said. "Are you thinking this man might by the one you *suspect* is killing veterans?"

"He just floated to the top of the suspect bowl," Arn said, finishing his coffee, "and I'd like nothing better than to pull the handle and watch him swirl down the crapper."

31

The perfect storm—what a cliché. But that just what this is. Righteous Sword of the Lord troops protesting outside the facility. VA security and the local police tied up. Everyone inside distracted with what is happening right outside their windows. Like drivers motoring slowly past a gruesome traffic accident—they have to watch. They have to know. But when they actually see the spectacle that nightmares are made of, they turn away in disgust, vowing never to look at another accident like that again.

Until the next time.

That's what I told myself after killing Captain Sims three years ago— never again will I look at another accident. Never again will I kill another. But like drivers slowing to gawk in passing, I only slowed down until I could no longer look. And I killed again. And again. Until now I am unable to stop. But do I really want to stop? I keep telling myself what I do is necessary. That I am selective. I tell myself it is only officers who have wronged others beneath them. And all have been guilty of pushing their weight upon lower ranks. Except that one veteran's son in Hot Springs. But at least I moved on—it was an honest mistake that I'll never repeat.

But I know better.

I would kill to protect my mission that is so pure. So genuine. Unlike those RSL fools outside the facility, making noise and doing damage for what? Some perceived notion that has no chance of succeeding?

I would even kill Anderson if I had to.

I wondered if I would be forced to a moment ago. When he entered the waiting room where all the old veterans sat, watching the events unfold outside, he almost saw me. I had just returned from checking the restroom.

148

Making certain no one was inside. Making certain nothing had changed. Taking nothing for granted anymore.

I would have run right into Anderson. He would have asked questions, like what the hell was I doing in this waiting room? If I hadn't seen the cowboy hat perched on his big, gomby head I might have been spotted. But I backed out of the room with him none the wiser.

Just another vet wandering the hallways.

I hope I never have to confront him. I hope I never have to dispatch Anderson. All I really want to do is saddle my sorrel and take leisurely rides to clear my head. Or hit the blackjack table at Deadwood and wager my ass off. Anything to get my mind off off him. From what I'm afraid I'll have to do eventually.

On the other hand, it would *be exciting to see him writhing on a tile floor as I slip the needle under his tongue.*

Or slice through a jugular with this old Barlow knife of mine.

32

SAMANTHA SLID INTO THE BOOTH beside Arn. She took off her ball cap and pink knitted scarf and dropped them beside her while she waved for the waitress. "I'm a little more than worried. Arn, what should I do?"

"Do?"

She waited until the waitress dropped off her iced tea and left with their order before lowering her voice. "Yes. I was at the VA yesterday when the police locked it down. Right *there*. *At* the facility when that janitor discovered that poor man's body in the restroom. I'm no prude. I have two tours in Iraq under my garter belt and some time in Kuwait and have seen enough not to be squeamish. But I just *know* that man didn't die of a heart attack like Wagner speculates. What should I do?"

"Again, what do you mean, do?"

"What if I had walked in on the killer in the restroom as he was murdering that old man?"

"First thing I'd do is turn around and walk out if I were you."

"What?"

"If you were in the men's restroom, you went in the wrong door."

She elbowed him in the ribs. "You know what I mean. A man killed right under the noses of all those vets watching the riot."

Samantha had returned to her office too late—the protest had already begun, and she was spared the duty of suiting up in riot gear. When Arn left the VA center as the riot got under control—and still no sign of Jonah—he had caught a ride in a police cruiser following a police van full of angry, arrested protestors being transported to

150

the county jail. One ambulance had already departed for the hospital Emergency Room with a protestor sporting a busted head, the other EMS unit treating an officer and a protestor by the VA entrance.

He had only learned about the latest victim when the policeman dropped him off at the Public Safety Building.

"What did the police chief tell you?"

"The bare minimum after he found out I saw nothing unusual while walking the halls."

Arn told her he had scoured the VA all during the riot but failed to locate Jonah. If he were *ever* there.

"Got another body here at the VA," Oblanski had stammered out of breath just as Arn pulled to the curb in front of his house. "Some Vietnam vet dead in the shitter by the waiting room. Looks like a heart attack." Shouting in the background drowned out Oblanski's voice until he apparently shielded his phone with his hand. "DCI evidence van is in route, and I'm up to my ass in alligators with these rioters. Talk later," and hung up.

"You might have seen the killer and didn't know it," Sam said. She wrapped her hand around her mug of hot chocolate. "God, what if he saw *you* and suspects you'll eventually realize it—."

"Nothing to recognize. I still don't know that he—or she—looks like."

"And you don't think this Colonel Jonah was there, somehow directing his troops and," she shuddered, "staging the murder in the restroom?"

The waitress brought their lunch: Sam a double-stacked burger with onion rings spilling out of the bun, Arn a chicken salad. *Hold any dressing that might make the salad palatable.* "All Jonah Barb is right now is a person of interest," Arn said, his mind drifting to the real person of interest sitting next to him. "The only reason the police need to re-interview him might be more coincidences than anything else. Jonah was in VA facilities or on the grounds at VA centers during the dates of five of the nine suspicious deaths." He stabbed a piece of chicken. "Wandering the halls by the looks of the surveillance cameras."

"But you don't buy it?"

"I don't buy it," Arn said. "I think Jonah was at those VA centers scouting ahead of time. Looking for where the surveillance cameras were placed. Noting exits and entrances. Things he'd need to know if he were organizing a protest."

"When will you know more?"

Arn checked his watch. "Chief Oblanski told me to stop by after five o-clock—hopefully after Gorilla Legs leaves for the day—and he'll fill me in."

"Who's Gorilla Legs?" Sam asked.

"Some bohunk woman who wants a piece of my ass 'cause I yelled at her earlier. I'll call you when I know more."

"Let's just talk about it over dinner," Sam said. "Danny said he's making something special."

"Danny?"

"Yes. Your... *house man*. Ana Maria invited me over. Seems like she's got a problem with an old truck she's working on."

"That old International I bought off some Hutterites right outside Ethan in South Dakota? But what's that got to do with supper?"

"The old binder's got a diesel motor, and Ana Maria said she's light on diesels. But she knows I worked on them in the Army. She said if I stopped by and took a look at it, Danny would fix something special."

"Everything Danny makes is special," Arn said. "See you later."

————

Arn dreaded confronting Gorilla Legs. He had to be certain when he was buzzed through the door and walked past her that he stayed away from her powerful arms. But as Arn walked through the door on the way to Oblanski's office, she stepped closer, and Arn was sure she wanted a rematch. She stepped from around what Oblanski called "her throne," smoothing her skirt that stopped just below her thick knees. Her hair had been pulled back in a neat chignon and held together by a bright red, bone holder. She smiled at Arn—something he thought her incapable of.

"Chief Oblanski said you'd be stopping by," her voice soft, yet a slight *hiss* as she talked through ill-fitting dentures. "Just go into the conference room. He's expecting you."

Arn cautiously walked past her as he caught a *whiff* of some cologne, strong enough he imagined her falling into a fifty-five-gallon barrel of Channel No. 1.

He kept her in the corner of his eye, expecting some ambush that would leave him bruised and bleeding, but her smiled remained pasted on her face until he walked into the conference room "I ought to have you come by more often," Oblanski said. "Gorilla Legs has been… well, you saw her."

"I did," Arn said, "but I wasn't sure it was some variation of *Invasion of the Body Snatchers* or something. She's actually pleasant—bite my tongue."

'She was nice to me, too. Ever since I came in this morning, all she could talk about is the great retired Denver Metro detective Arn Anderson."

"She detests me."

"Seems like she finally found a *strong* man that's not afraid to put her in her place when necessary," Oblanski said. "Your show of strength yesterday when you bulled past her made an impression." He winked. "Want her number?"

"What?"

"Her phone number," Oblanski said, smiling, obviously enjoying this. "She's not spoken for. She's single. Just like you."

"Now you can bite *your* tongue. All I want to do is find out about the body the VA found yesterday."

Oblanski motioned to photos spread out on the long table. "Here's what they found—same thing as Frank Mosby. And the others if your theory is correct. Slight bruising on the side of the neck consistent with a blow of some sorts. He just retired from a civilian position at F. E. Warren Air Base last month. Major Leonard Mills. At least he was a Marine Major in Vietnam when he was there. Still had his officer bumper sticker on his BMW that we found parked in the lot."

Arn studied the photos. The victim lay slumped on the floor, his head resting against the door of the stall. His double-breasted western shirt was half-out of his Wranglers and one polished boot had been trapped under the sink when he fell.

"Killer must have spotted the victim's "O" sticker on Mills' car as he parked, if your theory is right."

"Or our killer has learned to spot officers."

Oblanski chuckled. "Now you're getting a little far afield, thinking this is some kind of Superman who can tell an officer when he sees one."

Arn picked up a photo and donned his readers. "Some years ago when I worked in Denver I had a case involving an Air Force Academy student who had been knifed to death. I went to the academy in Colorado Springs and spent nearly a week talking with other students and instructors, trying to get a handle on who might have killed the airman. By the end of the week, I got so I could ID officers even when they were in civilian clothes. Their swagger. The way they stopped at doors so others could open them for them. Subtle things." He tapped the picture. "Our killer is a predator. Our killer has developed a sense where he—or she—can pick out officers in a crowd."

Oblanski nodded in agreement. "I don't doubt that. And you'll notice I mentioned the Major was a *victim*. I'm leaning toward your theory that these deaths are connected—at least the ones here in Cheyenne. This victim, though," he ran his finger over another crime scene photo, "had no injection."

"None?"

"Nothing except from the blood draw he must have had earlier."

Arn put on his readers and held the photo against the glare from the window. A bandage covered a small part over the vein in the major's arm, and Arn thought back to his own blood draw a few days ago, to the itching from the Kerlix wrapped applied too tightly. "Did he actually have a blood draw today?"

"What?"

"A blood draw. Check to see if he actually had his blood taken."

"Of course he did." Oblanski circled the major's arm with his pencil. "The bandage proves it. They put one over the site where they tab you with the needle so it doesn't get infected. Or have you never had a blood sample taken before?"

"I have. A few days ago. And then—as every other time I had a blood draw at the hospital—the nurse taking the sample secured the Band-Aide with a couple wraps of Kerlix gauze. The major's Band-Aid doesn't come off." Arn handed the photo back. "Do you see any Kerlix on his arm?"

"Shit," Oblanski said. "You're right. There is none. And now that you bring it up, I've always had the Band-Aid secured with a wrap as well. Shit. Frank *didn't* have Kerlix."

"And neither did the other victims if their photos are correct," Arn said. "Ned, that's how the killer got away with injecting his victims without us realizing it—he put a Band-Aid on after injecting their vein with the coke to make it appear as if they'd just had a blood draw. Simple."

"And we would never have e caught it without asking for a specific test for cocaine," Oblanski breathed and slumped in his chair. "We'll know more at autopsy, and the DCI is expediting Major Mills' tox report."

Arn took off his hat and dropped into a chair. "I bet no one saw a thing?"

Oblanski looked around until he found a pencil in a cup holder and started nibbling nervously. "We showed Jonah Barb's photo around—."

"As did I. Got no takers."

"And neither did we. And neither did the surveillance cameras. Jonah might have been scouting other centers other times, but not this time. All the cameras captured were vets that folks could identify and employees working for the VA. If Jonah's our man, he's disguising himself pretty good."

"The back doors," Arn said at last. "As I recall, there are two that have no surveillance camera coverage. There was a lapse of time from when your officers arrived, and you sent deputies around back to cover them."

Oblanski chewed the pencil eraser off and looked around for a fresh victim. "I have no argument for that. He—or *anyone*—could have slipped in those back doors before officers arrived to cover them." He snapped the pencil in two. "But dammit, Jonah Barb is still MIA."

"And none of the protestors would say where he is."

Oblanski sat beside Arn, an exhausted look on his tanned face. "We arrested eleven—nine men and two women, including the two who had to make a trip to the hospital to get patched up before we dumped them in the pokey. To a person, they claim they hadn't seen their commander in over a week."

"Then who organized the protest?"

"Jonah," Oblanski said. "Through a secret email account that our forensic computer gurus discovered. So we're back to square-one suspect wise."

33

A RN WALKED INTO THE HOUSE to voices coming from the kitchen. He took off his boots before Danny-the-Cleanliness-Nazi reprimanded him for wearing them inside, and headed toward the noise. Ana Maria sat at the kitchen table across from Samantha, the sleeves of their plaid work shirts rolled up. Grime and grease had collected under their perfectly-manicured nails, and they both hugged mugs of steaming coffee. They looked up for a moment before continuing their conversation. "Hope I'm not interrupting anything," he said.

"You are excused," Sam said and flashed a wide smile. "See, Ana Maria, even a famous Metro Denver detective can blush."

Arn felt pretty good about himself, having a beautiful woman flirt with him. Until he remembered Gorilla Legs doing the same thing and his ego instantly deflated. "I take it you got the old truck running?"

"Like a new one," Ana Maria said. "Thanks to Sam."

"And thanks to Ana Maria, I've managed to calm down over that body at the VA. Have they found out anything?"

Arn grabbed a cup from the cup tree. "Let me grab some coffee first."

"We're outta coffee," Ana Maria said. "But green tea is brewing in the pot."

Arn figured this was no time to discuss his irregularity and poured tea before sitting at the table. "Correct me if I'm wrong, but I didn't see the truck sitting outside."

"That's because Danny took it," Ana Maria said.

"Danny hasn't had a driver's license since 1979, and I haven't bought current plates for it. Or insurance. What's he driving it for?"

"For an emergency," Samantha answered.

"That's right," Ana Maria said as she stood and walked to the tea pot. "A major emergency—he drove to Safeway to buys some fresh lobster. We all—collectively—figured with the killings so close to home and us working our tails off, we needed some comfort food."

Arn groaned. Even if Danny didn't get arrested for driving without a license and the truck impounded, several pounds of fresh lobster would set Arn back more than if he'd taken them all out for supper. "Did Danny take my Visa card?"

Ana Maria nodded. "Relax. Even with the cost of that, Sam didn't charge for getting the truck running. In the long run, you saved a ton of lucky bucks. So quite being a cheap skate."

"Did you find out anything?" he asked Sam.

"I did some heavy duty asking around the VA this morning. A couple people *thought* they saw someone matching Jonah's description walking the hallways during the protest."

"Good." Arn took his notebook out of his pocket. "I'll want to talk with them."

"Crap," Sam said. "I didn't get their names, and I don't know who they were. I only get here once a week. I'll ask around tomorrow again before I go to the outreach clinic in Gillette. If I get names, I'll call you."

"Just watch yourself." Arn said, "Snooping around, asking about Jonah might not be safe."

"I doubt I have anything to worry about," Sam said. "I was neither an officer and—if you hadn't noticed—I'm not a man either."

Arn blushed, rescued when Danny entered the kitchen. He plopped down two Safeway bags and handed Arn his Visa card. "How much, I'm afraid to ask?"

"You can't put a price on comfort food," Danny said and patted Arn on the back. "Don't think for a moment that we don't appreciate it."

———

After Arn saw Samantha out to her car with the promise that they would get together the next week when she was in Cheyenne, she pecked him lightly on the cheek and sped off. By the time he came back in the house, Danny had finished the dishes, and he motioned to the coffee pot. "After springing for that lobster, you deserve a cup of fresh *coffee*. Picked a bag up at Starbucks."

"About time. Where's Ana Maria?"

"In the sewing room. She got some new information."

Danny trailed Arn into the sewing room as Ana Maria's taped broadcast was ending. "We here at KGWN intend staying on this development until the killer is corralled and brought to justice. We are but a half-step away from unmasking the killer of innocent veterans," and she signed off.

"Rewind that a few seconds," Arn said.

Ana Maria tickled the buttons and her night cast rewound in double time.

"Stop! Hit play."

Ana Maria started the DVR again while Arn bent close to the TV screen and squinted. "Stop!"

"What are you seeing?" Ana Maria asked.

"There," Arn jabbed the screen with his finger. "Look at the crowd behind you wanting to get into the frame."

Ana Maria's hand began trembling, and Danny took the remote before she dropped it. "What is it?" Danny asked.

"Behind me," she said. "It's… him."

Doc Henry stood among the crowd that had gathered in back of Ana Maria listening to her broadcast. Watching her.

Within grabbing distance of her.

———

Arn drank a beer now and again. Danny, never since he stopped altogether and joined A.A. ten years ago. Ana Maria—on the other hand—could, belt down all sorts of libations with the best of them when she felt the urge. And tonight, she felt the *urge*. "How could I be so stupid," she asked, but it came out *schtupid*, her words slurring badly this last hour, "to allow Doc Henry to get that close?"

"Couple reasons," Arn said. "You let your guard down. And, you refused to file a restraining order against Doc."

"The court wouldn't issue one on something as flimsy as Doc standing close to me. Not doing anything— oh shit, I forgot how you cops put it—."

"Overt," Danny said, "is what I think you mean." He nodded to her empty glass. "I'll grab refills," and left the room.

"Overt." She tried snapping her fingers, but coordination eluded her. "That's it. They wouldn't issue an order unless he did something *overt* towards me."

Arn knew Ana Maria was right. She'd covered the police beat enough to know Doc had to do *something*—threaten her. Show up at her work place repeatedly. "It would have still gotten the police involved. Got something on record."

Arn hit the TV tray. "I guess I need to have a private talk with Doc."

"And get yourself tossed in the hoosegow?" she said.

Arn, and Ana Maria, had few options. She was right—Doc hadn't done anything to her. He could argue that he happened to be outside the capitol building when she aired, merely watching the broadcast like the other thirty people who had gathered in the hopes of getting their mug on television.

Danny returned to the room and placed a bottle Jack Daniels on the TV stand in front of her. Arn snatched the bottle before Ana Maria could and poured two fingers, not the four she'd been belting down the last hour before emptying the last bottle. "You need to slow down or Danny will have a big mess to clean up in here. You dropped your guard, but you're all right."

She watched through bleary, red-rimmed eyes as Danny left the room once again. "I'm not all right," she said, sounding as if she talked through a hollow barrel. "Doc's here and there's nothing I can do about it."

This wasn't the first time Arn had run into a false bravado by someone, only to reveal how frightened they were once the booze started flowing. Ana Maria had put up a strong front about Doc

Henry when she was sober. Drunk, her fears surfaced. As they should have. "Maybe you ought to stop your live updates," Arn said. "At least for a while."

Danny came back balancing three saucers of double-chocolate cake. He set one in front of Ana Maria and handed Arn a much smaller piece. "Tell me you didn't frost this with Ex-lax, 'cause I don't need anything to help my regularity after Ana Maria's broadcast." He leaned closer to her. "I about shit when you claimed the authorities were close to finding the killer. We're not. What *were* you thinking?"

She shrugged and her fork slid from her fingers. Danny picked it up and handed her one of the slices of cake. "I thought I'd prod the killer into thinking we have more than we do. Worked before, didn't it?"

Arn agreed. Except now, with Doc Henry in town, she had other things to worry about beside the killer thinking she had more information than she did. She had to worry about Doc.

"Give me the word and I'll put in a call to some of my old AIM buddies," Danny said, running his finger across his throat. "Ana Maria'd never have to worry about Doc Henry again."

"If it were only that simple," Arn said.

"While you've been looking for Jonah Barb," Ana Maria squinted through one eye and managed to cut off a corner of cake, "I've been talking to suspects."

Arn stopped his fork mid-mouth, a bad feeling coming over him. "What suspects?"

"That beautiful woman we just had as a dinner guest. While you were gallivanting around, wasting your time today, she and I... bonded over that old truck of yours."

"I don't follow you."

"Do you really think I invited her here to help fix your old pickup?" Ana Maria said. "Hell, all it needed was new glow plugs. I've replaced a bunch of those when I worked my dad's shop. I didn't need her to do that for me. But while we were both turning wrenches, I asked her about the dead veterans. In my own way."

"I thought you said you were talking to suspects?"

Ana Maria set her fork down and grabbed for the bottle of whisky, but not before Arn snatched it our of her reach. "All right already. She told me the dates that she at the VA centers for her benefits job. In all but three, she *was* at the VAs where the men were found dead."

Arn landed closer to her. "Sam is no suspect, but I appreciate you looking out for me."

Ana Maria seemed to clear her head for a moment and looked at Arn, her voice—though slurred—taking on a serious tone. "Remember us talking about a beauty like her chasing after you?"

"How can I forget," Arn said. "You brought up something about it being unnatural for a looker like her—her age—to come on to an older man like me." He looked at the bottle in his hand, now tempted to take four fingers himself and he handed it to Danny for safe keeping. "In some circles a mature man—even fifteen years older— would be considered a catch. Did it ever occur to you that she sees me as a stable part of her life?" But Arn knew just where Ana Maria was coming from. He'd had his doubts all the while Sam and he had been seeing one another.

At some point, he admitted to himself, he'd have to stop thinking of her as a romantic part of his life and more as a suspect.

Especially after what Ana Maria had just told him about Samantha.

34

ARN SPENT THE MORNING TALKING with investigators in South Dakota, but none were any more interested than Wyoming authorities about exhuming the bodies of the other victims. "A drug overdose," Agent Kane said, "is not uncommon with veterans. It would take a whole lot more influence than I have to go through that expense."

"But you agree there could be a connection, given Frank and Steve's deaths—and Charles Boding's in Hot Springs?"

"I'm just telling you what's reality," Kane said. "The state's not going to shell out the bucks to exhume four bodies on a theory."

Finally, Arn gave up and did something to take his mind off his failures—*helping* Danny rewire a room. "Stick your finger in that light socket," Danny told Arn when they had finished running Romex three-strand through the guest room. "Go on—just for a second to see if it's hot."

"Are you serious?" Arn asked.

Danny kept his straight face for as long as possible before busting out in laughter. "Of course, I'm not. Besides, I haven't tripped the circuit breaker yet so it would have been all right."

"Thank goodness," Arn said and checked his watch. "'Bout lunch time anyway."

After watching Ana Maria's noon broadcast consisting of a road closure towards Denver on Interstate 25, and how there was a high-

163

wind warning on the pass outside Laramie, Danny shut the television off. "You barely touched your club sandwich I made," Danny said, "plus your coffee is getting cold. I *know* you like your coffee, hot and strong. Better than that tea you've been drinking."

Arn stared into his cup, silent.

"These deaths are bugging the hell outta you."

"I can't help it," Arn said at last. "I might not be so angry at myself for not figuring things out by now, except it's personal. One of the victims was Frank Mosby, and you know how many times I talked about him."

Danny chin-pointed to one wall opposite the television. "There might be a reason you didn't want to finish this room just yet."

"How's that?"

"The white wall. It's still just drywall. We haven't painted it yet. Just perfect for notes."

"It is," Arn said, looking at the wall that had faint traces of marker bleeding though the coat of primer from the last time he had scribbled notes on a case.

Danny handed Arn a marker. "I think you're gonna need this."

Arn shook his head, amazed at the old, skinny Indian who he'd rescued from homelessness two years ago had grown to read him so well.

He stood and uncapped the marker. *Suspects* he wrote first and underlined it. Just the writing on the white wall started him thinking and he wrote *Jonah* beneath it and stood back.

"That's it?" Danny said. "If it is, you don't have to look any farther. Just ask Oblanski to draw up an arrest warrant and you can tell your friend Helen you've solved the case."

"You think there are others who might be good for the murders?" Arn asked, not turning around, staring at the wall, knowing he had to write *Winger* underneath Jonah.

"And why do you think either man killed those veterans?" Danny asked.

Arn faced Danny, grateful that he had someone to bounce thoughts off of. Grateful for someone to ask the questions that he ought to be asking—if this case hadn't gotten him in the dumps so badly. "Winger travels this area. It's his territory. He would have opportunity, and ability to put someone down quick before injecting them with coke."

"Have you asked Wagner to pull up Winger's service record?"

"I was reluctant to ask. Winger and Sergeant Wagner have known one another professionally. I didn't want to cast dispersions on Winger—."

"I'd better write that down for you," Danny said as he dug a pen and notepad from a pocket hanging from his TV tray. After he wrote down that Arn needed to look at Winger's service record, Danny said, "as much as I hate to bring it up, you're missing another name—Samantha Holder."

Arn stepped away from the white wall, as if stepping away from the thought that the woman he had feelings for was involved in the murders. After long moments, he wrote her name to one side and started listing the reasons he should consider her. "Like Winger, she travels the VA system."

"And her primary MOS in the Middle East was military police—."

"For which she never worked in," Arn said.

"But for which she knows police techniques. Such as stunning blows," Danny said, and Arn jotted that on the wall as well.

"She could certainly blend in," Danny said. "Maybe that's why the surveillance tapes showed only veterans and employees. Maybe no one thought twice if they looked at the tapes and saw her walking the hallway."

Familiar with the VA he added under Sam's name. Arn had thought of that before and dismissed it. Danny saying it aloud gave credence to the notion. "She *was* gone for several hours the day of the protest."

"Even factoring in an hour for her lunch break or workout," Danny said, "that would give her an hour where she could have wandered into the men's restroom and killed the major."

"But why?" Arn said and waved the air. "I know—ask Wagner to look at her service record."

"I notice you didn't write Pudgy's name on the white wall." Ana Maria had entered the house without Arn or Danny knowing about it.

"What the hell?" Arn turned to her. "The alarm didn't go off."

"I was wondering why it wasn't armed," Ana Maria said, "when I tried punching the code in."

"Danny?"

The old man seemed to slink farther down into his chair. "I guess I forgot to re-arm it after I took out the garbage this morning." He held up his hand. "I ought to know better with Doc and Jonah roaming the town."

"No damage done," Arn said. "But don't forget——."

"I won't," Danny said. "But Ana Maria was right: you didn't write Pudgy's name under suspects. With what you found out about him, he'd be right at the top of the list."

He would be, Arn thought, and wrote *father hated officers. Crazy and appears to have socio-pathological leanings.*

"Based on...?" Danny asked.

"Based on his dealings with Sheriff Ridley. Even some kid right out of puberty knows it's not right to slash tires of a sheriff's car. But all he did was merely grin at Ridley. I'm thinking if the sheriff would have come after the kid to arrest, that old Barlow knife would have been sticking in the lawman's gullet."

Ana Maria set her purse on her TV tray. "But he hasn't been back since he enlisted in the Army."

"That we can prove," Arn said. "Kane did some checking with contacts in Custer. He found a girl—Mary Ann something-or-other—who swears she saw Pudgy the day of his father's funeral."

"If my math is correct," Ana Maria said, "Pudgy would have to be in his late thirties, early forties, assuming he did enlist at eighteen. A man can change a lot in that time."

"Kane gave me her phone number. I'll know more after I call her when she gets off work at the diner."

"I almost hope he did return," Danny said.

Arn and Ana Maria looked at him. "As much as I detest Jonah Barb, he is providing entertainment. And I could get used to having Samantha around, too. Winger does nothing for me, except he spent a tour in the Middle East. To his credit. If Pudgy were the killer, it would make it easy to prove motive."

Arn sat in his chair and leaned closer to Danny. "All right, mister investigator, let's hear it?"

"Officers." Danny said with a wide smile. "Pudgy's old man hated officers, apparently since Sims nailed Bo for black marketing guns and ammunition. It wouldn't be too much of a stretch to believe Pudgy started avenging his father's reputation and suicide years later." He stood and gathered the empty coffee cups. "Fruit not falling far from the tress, and all that Perry Mason shit. So that's my analogy."

"You should have been a detective," Arn said under his breath as Danny left the room.

He stopped in the doorway and said over his shoulder, "don't even suggest that, big guy," and grabbed his toolbelt on the way out.

———

"What did Mary Ann say?" Ana Maria curled up in her chair with her legs tucked beneath her. She unfolded broadcast notes on her lap. "Did she actually remember Pudgy?"

Arn jotted in his notebook before answering. "Mary Ann was walking Main Street in Custer the day after Bo's funeral, when she passed a man in his early thirties perhaps. It was Pudgy. Or so she thought. 'Pudgy,' she called out and the man stopped for the briefest amount of time before ignoring her and walking on."

"That's it? That's her recollection of someone who *may* have been Pudgy?"

"According to Mary Ann, Pudgy wasn't pudgy anymore. She said he was fit and trimmed up. If it wasn't for a small scar on the back of his head where a bull gored him when he was a youngster, she might not have known him."

"Possibility," Ana Maria said. "People can change dramatically in twenty years."

"Mary Ann dated Pudgy when they were in high school until Bo pulled him out to homeschool him. She told me she's know Pudgy anywhere."

"Was she helpful with anything else that might help you find him?"

167

"No," Arn answered. "But she did tell me a story that'll help us once we *do* locate him. She said Pudgy was a wrestler in school before Bo pulled him out, and he was at a meet in Davenport when the other kid was about to pin him. Seems like Pudgy took offense to it and gouged the other wrestler's eye. Damn near put it out. Mary Ann said when the team returned to Custer the principal pulled him into his office and suspended him.

"A week later, the principal promptly resigned and left for parts unknown."

"At the prodding of Bo Randall I would imagine?" Ana Maria said.

"That's what Mary Ann figured."

"What did she tell you about Beth Randall? I heard you ask about her."

Arn stared at the white wall like it was a television set. "'If damn Pudgy would have stopped,' Mary Ann told me, 'I would have told him where his Ma and sister moved to.'"

"She knows?"

"She knows," Arn said. "Beth came back for a day a couple years after she fled Custer to settle her mother's estate. Mary Ann ran into her and they had coffee."

"Tell me she knows where Beth is?"

"Sort of," Arn said. "She said Beth and the girl Jenifer—who'd grown into a real cutie—just wanted to say away from that crazy-ass Bo Randal. She wrote her new address for Mary Ann on a napkin but told her never to tell anyone. To keep it strictly secret."

"Mary Ann has Beth's address," Ana Maria sighed. "At least we have a starting point to line up an interview—."

"Mary Ann ate the address."

"She what?"

Arn shrugged. "My impression is that Mary Ann's kind of a dingbat, and she thought the only safe way for no one to learn where Beth loved was to eat it. Figured she'd remember the address."

"I have the sinking feeling she doesn't."

"Bingo!" Arn said. "She was lucky to recall the city—Seattle. She did recall that Beth took her grandfather's name of Schwartz, knowing Bo would try to find her." He nodded to Ana Maria's notebook. "What do you have going?"

"Doc Henry," she said. "I've had about enough of that SOB as I can take. He placed a white rose in the front seat of my VW while I was inside the TV station." She held up her hand. "And before you ask, I am not going to give him the satisfaction of filing a restraining order on him. I am, however, going to do my best to get his parole revoked."

"How do you intend doing that?"

She tapped her notebook. "You looked into Doc's parole and found he is not to have contact with his victim—that'd be me."

"That's what Sheila down at the Parole Office in Denver said. And she also said she got word to his PO here in Cheyenne who gave him one warning about being even close to you."

Ana Maria waited until Danny's pounding upstairs stopped. "That's my point. Doc is fascinated by these killings and by the RSL it would seem. Twice, he's been spotted in the periphery of my broadcasts. Mostly concealed by the crowds, but he was there. The next time he'll be nailed and sent back to Florence."

"Still doesn't explain how that's going to come about?"

"I talked at length with DeAngelo and gave him my two-week notice. 'I'll take it back,' I told him, 'if you give me free reign to run with these VA deaths *and* the Righteous Sword of the Lord fanatics.'"

"He was just looking out for you."

"I can look out for myself. My decision."

"You're leaving and going back to turning a wrench?"

"Not today," she answered. "DeAngelo agreed to let me go ahead. After all," she grinned, I am his star."

"Just make sure that star doesn't wink out before it's time," Arn said, absently looking over the white wall again. "It sounds dangerous. Doc might not be a rational man like we think of rationality, but he *is* a genius. Thinks things through before he acts."

"Don't you think I know that. But by going live every night, it just might draw Jonah out, too. He must be worried, with the emails he sent me—."

"What emails?"

"Just garbage," Ana Maria said. "Says to drop my coverage of *his* RSL or he'll kill me."

"You never mentioned that before?" Arn said, facing her. "This is serious. You need to report it."

"I did this morning," she said. "Oblanski is going to have his computer forensics geek try running down the ISP Jonah used to send the emails," she gagged. "Better than the dead cat he sent me."

Arn threw up his hands. "Why the hell don't you tell me these things?"

"Nothing to tell. He must have found out I loved cats—."

"Now don't give me hell again, just because I'm allergic to them."

"I won't," Ana Maria said. "But he sent it from a post office in Central City—."

"By Denver."

She nodded. "Oblanski got hold of the postal inspector and he's running down Jonah from that end as well."

"Well excuse the hell out of me, but these are things that you need to tell me."

"Didn't want to alarm you for no reason—."

"No reason!"

"Not much reason, anyway. Call it women's intuition that you're so dependent on now and again, but I'm not worried." She held up her notes. "But what I think will happen after tonight's special airs is that one or both of those bastards will be lurking around my broadcast."

Arn snatched his cell phone. "I gotta call Chief Oblanski. Get some security—."

"Already taken care of. The chief says he will have a couple men in plain clothes among the crowd. So let's cross our fingers Doc or Jonah shows."

"As long as you stay safe," Arn said, facing the white board. *Something is wrong* he thought to himself and snatched his notes from his TV tray. He thumbed through them hurriedly, until he dropped them and turned back to the notes scratched on the wall. He grabbed the marker and wrote *Two Killers* on the wall. And underlined it.

Ana Maria joined Arn in front of the wall. "What's that all about?"

"We have been going on the assumption that whoever killed Captain Sims killed the others as well. Probably out of hatred of officers. But what if," Arn grabbed his notes again and showed her, "there were two killers. Sims was murdered in a gruesome way, while the other vets were killed surgically. Neatly. Without a drop of blood shed."

"Two killers," Ana Maria breathed out deeply. "If that were the case, would they be working separately? Or together."

"You mean as a team?"

"It's not uncommon," Ana Maria said. "There have even been men-women killer teams in the past."

"If that's the case, I'd put my money on Pudgy. Sims' overkill—from what little we know of Pudgy right now—seems more like his style."

"And he'd be working with... who?"

"Someone who might have hated officers because of Bo's suicide."

"The sister?"

"It's a stretch," Arn said. "But one that complicates things for us even more."

And Maria agreed. "The sooner we get a photo of the sister—and of Pudgy later in his life—the sooner we might know to exclude him from the suspect list or not."

Arn groaned. "Oblanski *and* Wagner are going to love me for this."

35

ARN WAS ON THE PHONE most of the morning with Lieutenant Waddie asking more about the RSL protests on the day Steve Urchek was killed. He had asked her if she could connect the RSL in any way to Steve, but—as of this morning—she could not.

Agent Kane was even less pleased to hear from Arn. He asked him to check with veterinarians in the Black Hills Region to see if any had given Xylazine to anyone.

"Do you know how many veterinarians there must be in these parts?"

"I wouldn't ask if it wasn't important. I'm going to do some checking here in the Cheyenne region. You might start with those vets specializing in large animals. Servicing ranchers."

———

Arn had only to wait for a few moments at the pet clinic for Dr. Church to invite him back to an examination room. "I hear you're asking if we give out Xylazine. We do to ranchers. Occasionally."

"What do they use it for?"

"It's horse tranquilizer," Church said. "Ranchers use it for all sorts of things—when their mare is about to foal it helps ease the discomfort. Now and again ranchers use it when they have to treat an animal that is pain-sensitive. Puts the critter at ease."

"Have you given any out recently?"

"Not recently," Church said. "We're mainly a small animal clinic. But I can give you a list of veterinarians who deal mostly to ranchers.

Traveling vets, you might say."

He left the room and returned within moments with a computer readout. "Most of those folks work out of the backs of their service trucks. Good luck," he smiled, "and run if they have a set of nut nippers in their hand."

———

It was mid-afternoon by the time Arn got to the last two veterinarians on the list. He had met with three others working at local ranches, but none had given out Xylazine recently. He was about to give up when the fourth one on the list—Seth Barnes—answered. "Sure you can come down and jaw," he told Arn. "I'm at the Nadier Ranch a mile east of the Terry Bison place tending to a mare that's having some difficulty."

Arn drove the eight miles to the Nadier place, a hobby farm of forty acres. A newly-planted shelter belt lined one side of the long driveway, the budding pines having been beaten and bruised by the latest hail storm. The barn was a pole barn costing more than Arn made in a year in retirement, and two shiny Cadillacs sat on a concrete pad in front of a new, mid-century house, their license plates bearing DR1 and DR2.

"Dr. Barnes!" Arn called out.

"Back here," he called out and Arn followed the sound of his voice.

Seth Barnes was bent over a mare in labor, her panting telling Arn she was not yet ready. Dr. Barnes glanced up at Arn and looked around, but no one was with him. "Lady here isn't close to her time. Her nipples aren't even waxy yet." he said. "Damned fools running hobby farms know just enough about livestock to be dangerous." He used the side of the stall to stand and stretch. "She'll be all right. Now what is it you wanted you talk about?"

"Xylazine. Have you given any out recently?"

Seth looked away just as Arn saw that faint micro-tic at the corner of his eye. *He's lying.* "I haven't given any out for ages."

"It's important—."

"I said I haven't given any Xylazine out!"

Arn summed him up. He stood as tall as Arn, and his *Enduring Freedom* t-shirt rippled beneath muscular arms. He would be a handful if he chose to…

"Just what the hell do you want from me?"

Arn backed up a step and set himself. In case Seth became more worked up. "Do you keep records of medications you issue?"

"Of course. We all do."

"But if a vial or two of horse tranquilizer slipped by… well, that might be understandable, as busy as you are," he motioned to the mare lying in the stall.

"I said I didn't—."

"Of course you did!" Arn snapped. He had dealt with enough professional liars in his law enforcement career, he couldn't take much more of this amateur. "Now you can tell me what I want to know, or I can place a call to the State Veterinary Board."

Seth dropped his head and grabbed a can of Skoal. He stuffed his cheek and snapped his fingers to rid them of the excess before pocketing the can. "I gave a dose to a… friend a couple weeks ago that I've known since Iraq."

"And…?"

"All right. I gave another dose a couple days ago."

"Who was this friend of yours?"

Seth paused. "I am *not* going to tell you. I'd hate for them to get in trouble just 'cause they needed to doctor their horse. They helped me out when I came back from the war."

"Helped how?"

"Listened." Seth turned back to the mare and squatted down, running his hand gently over her protruding abdomen. "All the Army did when I returned from theater was change my MOS—made me a cannon cocker. Bad idea. My mood just got worse after my enlistment was up. I was a mess. Drunk all the time. Couldn't hold down a job. *Listened.* That's all. Understood where I was coming from because we spit out some of the same sand over in Iraq for a time, so they knew what I was going through. Convinced me I was worth something and steered me toward this," he motioned to the horse. "So I'm damn sure not going to give them up."

"But if I run names by you, you'll tell me if I'm on the right track?"

Seth spit tobacco juice and it *splat* against the side of the stall. "Not even if you waterboard me."

———

Arn sat across from Chief Oblanski and Sgt. Wagner. He glared at Arn when he walked through the door. "This better be good, Anderson. I'm about beat to a draw."

"I don't understand."

Wagner jerked his thumb at the closed door towards the chief's secretary's desk. "That woman out there—that WWE wrestler or whatever the hell she is—grilled me for fifteen minutes. I thought once she was going to leap over the counter and throttle me before Ned here came to my rescue." He turned to Oblanski. "Why the hell *do* you keep her around?"

The police chief slapped a ream of paper sitting on the corner of his desk. "Because of this. If I didn't have her threatening me every day, I might screw off and miss my deadline. Which reminds me, Arn, Sgt. Wagner's right—this better be good."

Arn opened his briefcase and handed both men sheets of paper that he'd printed out last night. "I'd like you to locate Beth Randall. She's going by Schwartz now and apparently moved to Seattle. I've asked Agent Kane out of the Rapid City DCI office to do some checking, but he's had no luck yet."

Oblanski leaned across his pile of paperwork. "I know just where you're coming from, Arn, and it's not going to work."

Arn exaggerated batting his eyes and remained silent.

"You're thinking that, because I worked at the Seattle PD before landing this job, that I have contacts there."

"You *are* the astute one," Arn said. "I wouldn't ask it if it wasn't important. Veterans are in danger the longer it takes to catch this killer."

"All right. All right," Oblanski said. "I'll make some calls this afternoon."

"Thanks," Arn said. "And thanks for sending a couple officers to look after Ana Maria at her broadcast last night."

Oblanski shrugged. "They didn't spot Doc Henry or Jonah Barb in the crowd, but that doesn't mean either won't show up tonight."

"By the way, any luck locating Jonah?"

Oblanski shook his head and hunted around for a victim-pencil to chew on. "He's some kind of shrewd bastard. Our computer forensics people traced the ISP—it's a routing network out of India. they put in a call to the FBI and hope they can run it down."

Wagner chuckled. "Looks like you got your work cut out for you with that Seattle thing."

"Ned has it easy," Arm said, "As you'll notice if you turn to the next page."

Wagner scanned the entries and handed Arn the paper.

"Keep it. You'll need it to locate all those."

"You want me to pull the service records of Winger and Samantha? And who's this Seth Barnes?"

"He gave Xylazine to a friend. But he won't give up the friend."

"Want me to have Mike the Mauler talk to him?" Oblanski asked.

"Won't do any good. Seth is too grateful to his… friend that he won't give him—or her—up. He was that vague."

"What's that got to do with Winger and Samantha?"

"Seth alluded to having served with the person he gave the Xylazine to. Both Winger and Sam served in Iraq during that time. And both have horses. And that was the time Jonah served as a medic there as well."

"If I do manage to get their service records," Wagner said, "what do I do with it?"

"Cross-reference Seth Barnes' name with the three of them. See who among the group he was stationed with."

Wagner sat back in his chair as he shook his head. "It might take a while, but I can do that."

"Hope it doesn't take too long," Arn said. "Or we'll have another crime scene to look at."

36

"IS THIS GOING TO BE a date or an interrogation?" Ana Maria
asked. She stepped back and examined the knot she'd tied for
Arn, reaching out and making a slight adjustment before she patted
him on the shoulder. "You look like you're ready for the town."

"I don't know," Arn said. "I've never put up some front like this
with a woman. It's... dishonest."

"Didn't you ever tell at least one little fib to a lady?" Danny asked,
seeming to enjoy Arn in a tie and sport coat. "Just one?"

"No."

"Even when you'd get on-line to one of those sites you...
experimented with?'"

"Maybe just a tiny fib," Arn said. "But this?"

Sam had called Arn to tell him that she was free tonight. No, it was
more a suggestion from a strong-willed woman, but Arn didn't know
if he should. She was—after all—one of the people she suspected in
the killing of innocent vets.

It was Ana Maria who had talked him into it. "She dropped her
guard a few days ago when we were working on your old truck. If you
loosen her up with your... what's the word, Danny?"

"It's certainly not charm," Danny said. "Maybe old cop bullshit."

"Whatever it is, you might hit pay dirt," Ana Maria said. "She
might just slip up."

"Let's hope so," Arn said. "Outback Restaurant's not cheap. Hope
to get something out of this evening."

"Romance?" Danny asked, and Arn blushed. "Loverboy."

―――

Outback's parking lot was packed tonight as it usually was, and Arn parked the Olds at the far end of the lot next to Home Depot. Ana Maria had called in a reservation for seven o'clock, and it looked like that was the same time everyone else had reserved.

He climbed out and loosened his tie the tiniest bit. He wasn't used to wearing them, or a sport coat, but Ana Maria assured him that dressing up would impress Sam enough that she might slip. If she *were* involved in the VA deaths.

He shut the door and the dome light went out, plunging this part of the lot into darkness. *Is this a date or an interrogation?* Ana Maria had asked, and Arn still had no answer. He liked to think that she invited him out—in a roundabout way—for a dinner date. As for the interrogation—would this be he interrogating her in his own way, or would it be Sam subtly interrogating *him* to learn how his investigation is coming along?

He patted the fender of the car as if saying goodbye to an old friend before taking a last, deep, calming breath. He started for the door when…

…his periphery. Coming fast. Coming hard. Something shiny…

…he turned into the object crashing onto his head, absorbing the blow. Dropping to his knees. A mask in the darkness.

Lashing out, his hand jutting beneath the mask. Grabbing hair. Falling.

Something shiny reflecting the light over the door of Outback. His attacker cocking the object for another blow as…

"Hey!" a voice boomed out. "Bobby, you run thataway and I'll cut the bastard off this other way."

Feet running across the lot. A woman kneeling beside him. Calling 911 moments before the night went even darker.

―――

"He's coming around," Sam said and Arn's eyes flickered.

"Don't try sitting up just yet," a woman in blue nurse's scrubs said, and handed him a glass with a bent straw sticking out of it. "Just relax for a while and your friends can take you home."

"She's right," Sam said. "You need to take it easy. That's a nasty bump on the side of your head."

"Lucky it only took six stitches," Ana Maria added.

"Funny, I don't feel lucky. What the hell happened?"

Sam forced a smile. "What happened is you missed our dinner date. Somebody waylaid you in Outback's parking lot."

"Then you saw what happened?"

Sam shook her head. "I was a little late for dinner changing a flat tire, and I turned off Lincolnway just as the ambulance was pulling out. All I know is what Ana Maria knows," Sam said as she stroked his forehead, voice soothing even as his head throbbed.

"I got the call from my cameraman to roll to Outback Steak House," Ana Maria said. "I interviewed the two guys and their dates who saw your attacker."

"Oh hell," Arn said, "just leave me in the dark about what the *hell* happened."

"I'm getting to it," Ana Maria said. "Two ranchers from outside Wheatland were in town with their wives shopping, and thought they'd grab a steak at Outback. When they came out the door and saw you lying there clawing up at whoever attacked you, they chased him."

"At least you put up a fight going down." Oblanski stepped into Arn's hospital room and grabbed a chair. He sat backwards and draped his arms over the side.

"Who was it?"

"Haven't the foggiest," Oblanski said. "Those ranch boys might have been heavy in the bull dogging but they sure lack in the running department. By the time they hit the end of the parking lot, your attacker was nowhere to be found. Kicked the afterburners in and was just *gone* they said."

Oblanski's phone rang and he stepped out into the hallway to answer it.

"Didn't you see anything?" Arn asked Sam.

"I told you I was tied up changing my tire." She continued stroking his head, the pain easing even as she spoke soothingly. "I feel so guilty. If I had been on time, I might have been able to run the person to ground—."

"Samantha," Oblanski said when he stepped back into the room pocketing his cell phone. "I just got off the phone with my investigators. I need you to come down to the PD with me."

———

"Don't get up," Oblanski told Arn.

"Don't worry," he gingerly patted the bandage on his head. "I won't."

"Would you like a nice big slab of rhubarb pie, Chief?" Danny asked.

"Rhubarb's my favorite."

"I'll take one, too," Ana Maria said.

"Not tonight," Danny's voice trailing off on the way to the kitchen. "You're starting a diet along with Arn."

Arn sat up in his recliner and Ana Maria propped a pillow behind him. "Let's have the bad news."

"There is *no* news, good or bad. Sam wouldn't come off anything except she was late changing a tire on her truck."

"That ought to be easy enough to verify."

"One of my guys is checking with Big O Tires now to see if she dropped one off as she claimed."

"Apart from that," Ana Maria said and scooted her chair closer to Oblanski's, "why did you even suspect her?"

"Off the record?"

Ana Maria nodded. "Of course."

"Ok, here's the skinny—when those ranchers chased your attacker through the alley, we had a direction of travel. Brought the K-9 in and Harpo got right on the track. We found this." Oblanski punched a photo icon on his phone and handed it to Arn.

Arn pulled the reading light closer over his shoulder and expanded the image.

"That *Craftsman* crescent wrench was found a half-block from

Mimi's parking lot. See the etching on the side next to that smear of your blood?"

Arn could just make out the initials, s.h. "Samantha Holder," Arn breathed. "But that can't be."

"She knew you'd be there in the parking lot. I thought of that as I was wrapping up my broadcast on it," Ana Maria told Oblanski. "But that's not enough to hold her."

"It wasn't." He advanced a couple more images on his phone. "But here," he showed Ana Maria, "is a fresh injury on her knuckles consistent with Arn struggling with her."

"Mechanics get scuffed knuckles all the time," Ana Maria said.

"That's what Samantha claimed. Scuffed her knuckles when the four-way slipped off a lug nut. And when the officers checked her truck parked across from Outback, they found a pair of running shoes."

"There you have it!" Arn said, finding himself suddenly defending Samantha. "A pair of running shoes. I'm sure she'll get sent away to the Women's Prison in Lusk for that."

Danny entered the room with a tray containing four coffee cups and one piece of rhubarb pie. "*Bon appetite*," he told Oblanski and handed him the plate and a fork.

"Ned," Arn said, "a lot of people run nowadays. I'd be running myself if—."

"If you weren't a… bit overweight."

"I am not overweight," Arn said. "I'm just undertail for my weight."

Oblanski took the first bite of his pie, and Arn became jealous.

Until the chief's lips puckered up like he was going to bend over and kiss Arn and he grabbed for his coffee cup. "Danny, did you forget to put sugar into your recipe? Oblanski asked when he was able to speak again.

Danny wore a slight grin as he said, "I didn't put *any* sugar in. Like you said, Arn there needs to cut down on his sugar intake."

When Oblanski didn't take another bite, Danny prodded him. "If you finish it off, I can get you another to take home to the missus."

Arn understood. Danny'd had enough run-ins with the law that he was no fan of police. Even Oblanski, and it was Danny's subtle way of getting back. *Passive aggressive?* He'd ask Ethan next time he talked with him.

"Sam gave us a sample of her blood that the lab will compare to the dried blood on the handle of the crescent wrench, but I think it's yours," he told Arn. We'll know in a day or two if there's a match. But it'll take longer to get a DNA match on the hair."

"What hair?"

"You grabbed a clump of your attacker's hair and came away with enough for a test. Sorry," Ana Maria said, "didn't mean to steal your thunder."

"Steal away," Oblanski said and held up his empty coffee cup for a refill. When Danny left, he whispered to Ana Maria, "any place to… deposit this pie?"

"Here," she passed a small trash can to Oblanski and he dumped the pie right before Danny came back with more coffee.

"Another piece?" Danny asked as he handed the chief his cup.

Oblanski patted his stomach. "I need to cut down myself." He leaned into Arn. "There were four strands of hair stuck between your fingers that you pulled out in the scuffle. They could have belonged to half the population by the color. Certainly, could be Samantha's hair. Our evidence tech says there are two of the four strands that have been pulled. With roots. More than enough to test, and I've put a rush on the DNA test. Until then, I'd suggest stay away from her as we told her the same thing—stay away from you."

"Did she give you blood and hair samples?"

"She volunteered to give samples without us needing a search warrant."

"That should show she wasn't involved. Did she say anything profound?"

"She didn't she say *anything* about the attack when The Mauler questioned her, except 'you're nuts if you think I'd attack Arn Anderson with a Craftsman wrench. I've always been a *Snap-On Tool* girl.'"

37

What a pisser! And the *day was going so good up until tonight, too. I'd scored dope with my... supplier for future use, which, I'm certain, I will soon need. I knew Anderson would be arriving early to Outback. At Night. Pitch black. The perfect time to ambush him. Scare him off. Make him think twice about his crappy investigation. All I had to do was hit the big bastard a solid blow on his noggin with the wrench and that would be the end of Anderson for the night. By the time he recuperated, he would have the notion out of his head that the veterans' deaths are connected. Or at least that's what he'd tell everyone as he secretly worried about being the next victim.*

So unlike the others with their stark cleanliness. Anderson wouldn't have the luxury of just lying down as if he'd had a heart attack. His warning would be... bloody. But wasn't that my point—make it as dramatic as possible so he and—subsequently—that reporter roommate of his would drop it.

Everything was going so good tonight, hiding on one side of that horse trailer with Anderson dreaming of what the end of the evening might bring. Until those two peckerwoods straight out of Hee Haw came busting out the door and spotted me. They gave chase, in a manner of speaking. Even if they were runners, they would have little chance of catching me. I am, after all, former Army and used to physical exertions. Like running.

I look in the mirror at the hair that Anderson yanked out on his way down, and I see I can comb other strands over the missing clump. No one will be the wiser.

In the end, I am of the opinion that Anderson got the message. That was my goal tonight, wasn't it?

Then why am I so down in the dumps? I wonder that as I set here watching veterans stroll by at the VA Center here in Cheyenne... that's why I am so down on myself right now. As much as I wanted to send Anderson a warning, I wanted something more. If those ranchers hadn't come out of the Outback when they did, I would most assuredly hit him again. And again. And again, until his death would be the warming I wanted to convey.

But once again, I know it is not my fault. I cannot beat myself up over a twist of fate like those hayseeds walking in on the attack.

That which does not kill us makes us stronger. I just hope Anderson never read the writings of Friedrich Nietzsche. The last thing I want is a stronger Arn Anderson.

38

ARN WANTED TO GET OUT of the house before the walls closed in on him. Or before Danny's constant pounding with his dry wall hammer threatened to crush Arn's already-throbbing head. He started for his car when he thought it better to check if Sam was in Cheyenne today. He so wanted her not to be involved, but there were as many factors pointing to her as the killer as there was Jonah and Winger.

Sam's secretary ran offices for two other traveling VA people, and she told Arn that Sam took a personal day off. "She stormed in here this morning, and I thought she was going to kick somebody's butt. 'If that little bastard who interrogated me last night were right here—right in front of me—I'd put a boot in his rectum. Accusing me of attacking Arn Anderson. I'm going home.' And that's just what she did."

"To Rapid City."

"Uh, huh," the secretary answered. "Sam has a little bit of a temper, if you haven't noticed."

"I noticed."

"And when she blows her top, the only thing that calms her is to saddle her mare and take a ride through the hills."

That was all right with Arn. Though he had growing feelings for Sam, he also knew those feelings could cloud his judgement. Something he didn't need right now. His head was clouded enough already, and not just from the pain.

He pulled into the Cheyenne VA lot and stepped around a legless Vietnam veteran being pushed in a wheelchair by a woman the vet's age. *Thanks for all you've sacrificed* Arn thought as he passed the wounded man before he stopped. How many times had Arn *secretly* expressed his gratitude for veteran's sacrifices as if ashamed to say it aloud to the very men and women who gave so much so that Arn could walk here free?

He waited until the man's wheelchair came abreast of him before thrusting out his hand. "I want to thank you so much for all you've done for our country."

The man looked up at Arn through one good eye, the other camouflaged by a milky white and he took Arn's hand. Even wounded, the veteran displayed a vice-like grip as his calloused hand held Arn's for a long moment. "Wasn't always gratitude for us boys returning from 'Nam," he said. "Mostly, people spit on us. Mostly piss-ant little school kids who'd gotten a college deferment because their daddies had enough money to keep them in school." A tear ran down his one good eye and he chin-pointed to the woman pushing his wheelchair. "Like I told Emily, now and again someone thanks me. Now and again someone is genuine in their gratitude." A smile crept across his face and he snapped a three-fingered salute. All he could do with his blown-up hand. "Thanks, pard'ner."

Arn stepped aside, humbled by the old man's graciousness. How many more veterans were treated the exact same way as he described, with such abject disrespect, no one could know. But what Arn did know is that—if he dug deeper and found the VA Slayer—no one else need die.

He found Sgt. Wagner tapping keys as he squinted at his computer screen. "I'm getting goofy looking at all these records, but I finally got all them sent to me." He stood and grabbed file folders and tucked them under his arm. "Let's take a walk to the courtyard… there are no ears there."

They stepped outside just as a Korean War Marine made his way on a wobbly walker to the door and disappeared. "Tell me you've found something."

Wagner lit a cigarette and blew smoke rings upward. "Here's what I found—Winger got an article 15 twice for fighting, and he had nasty words with his CO, so you know he's got a hard-on for officers. Jonah we already knew about because he earned himself an undesirable discharge, compliments of his Executive Officer. Seth seems to have had a chip on his shoulder ever since joining the Army, but then there's a lot of Special Forces guys like Rangers have a chips on their shoulder. It what sets them apart and makes them such gnarly soldiers." He leaned closer. "Even women started joining Special Ops some years ago."

"And Sam? Was she ever written up?"

Wagner looked around, making sure no one else had slipped into the courtyard and turned to his file labeled *Samantha Holder*. "Except for getting in bar fights and receiving verbal reprimands, Samantha didn't seem to have a problem with officers. Except," Wagner turned to the back page, "she had to testify on the court martial of her CO. The major was charged with an article 134 in Iraq."

"English," Arn said. "Speak-a-English."

Wagner tapped the paper. "Samantha was called to testify against her Commanding Officer she had been dating while stationed in Kuwait. The military frowns on fraternization. An officer just *can't* have relations with enlisted personnel."

"I wouldn't think her commander getting prosecuted for it would cause her to hate officers."

"It might if the officer was seeing *two other women*," he closed the file, "at the *same time*. A woman scorned, and all that. At least that's how my third wife put it when she tossed my clothes out into the yard one night when I came home… late."

Arn stood from the picnic table and stretched the kinks out of his legs. "Essentially, we have all four of them potentially hating officers for various reasons enough to want to carry a grudge."

"But did that hatred escalate into homicide?" Wagner asked. "That's what I'd be asking."

"It could," Arn said. "I guess I need to talk with Ethan Ames again. Besides giving me some muted profile of our killer, Ethan knows more than he told me. He *knows* the killer, I'd bet."

A woman testing out a new prostatic leg stumbled into the courtyard while a boy—perhaps her son—remained close to her in case she fell. They sat at a table at the other end of the courtyard and paid Wagner and Arn no mind. "Did you find out if all four of them served together?"

Wagner lit another cigarette from the one burned down between his fingers and snubbed the butt out in the grass. "Winger and Samantha and Seth Barnes all have some things in common from their military careers. Two—Seth and Sam—were both in Iraq at the same time— Sam in the motor pool, Seth in the Rangers before he rotated back to the states. They sent him to Ft. Sill and was there when Winger was stationed there after his tour was completed in theater."

"Did you find that any knew each other before coming to this part of the country?"

Wagner shook his head. "They could have, there just was nothing to prove they ever did. Except Samantha and Jonah having served together, but we knew that.

"On a positive note, I learned that Frank Mosby had a rare allergy to cocaine. He underwent a nasal reconstruction down in the Denver VA fifteen years ago and was given cocaine for pain during the procedure."

"They use cocaine in the hospital?"

Wagner flipped through his notes. "Apparently. There is one company manufacturing pharmaceutical grade cocaine for medical purposes, but it is highly regulated by the DEA."

"But a doctor could have access to it?"

"A medical doctor. Anyway, seems like your friend went into cardiac arrest when he was given medical grade coke."

"So he wasn't a user," Arn said. "Helen will be glad to hear that, though she already knew it." Arn popped a piece of gun and moved upwind from Wagner's smoke, wondering how the ME could have missed something as obvious as Steve's allergy when it appeared as if he OD'd. "How about the other victims?"

Wagner shrugged. "Nothing to connect any of them except they were all officers. None served with each other in Vietnam, and none had the same jobs. They were as strangers to one another as ever can be."

He stood and closed his files. "So you see, all the work it took to get their files was a waste of time."

"I don't see it that way," Arn said. "You came up with a lot of excellent information."

39

A RN STOOD IN FRONT OF the white wall so long his legs went numb before he sat in his chair.

"Looks like you added some things," Danny said, and set a plate with pie on Arn's TV tray.

Danny plopped onto his stained and tattered La-Z-Boy that he had found beside a dumpster in the alley in back of the Salvation Army. "Pretty bad when the Salvation Army doesn't even want it for donations," Arn had said, not sure if he was angrier at having the ratty recliner in his house or the fact that Danny—without a license—had driven Arn's old truck that had no license plates and no insurance.

"Well, it's mine now," Danny said, even as he used half a bottle of *Febreeze* on the recliner.

Arn continued eying his notes, kicking them one way in his mind, then another.

"Let's hear it."

"Hear what?"

"Whatever's puzzling you," Danny said and daintily sipped his coffee.

"Ok, here's what's bugging hell out of me—*anyone* on that list up there could be the killer. And *no one* could be the killer. And," he picked up his plate, "any two of them could be working *together.*"

"I see you've lumped names together, but I'm not sure why."

"Look." Arn set his plate down and walked to the wall, He grabbed the marker and underlined Sam and Seth. "They were in Iraq at the same time, and briefly in Kuwait, though Wagner said they were in different units. And, Ana Maria saw them having dinner last night when she went to supper last night with DeAngelo."

"You sound a little... down with her seeing another man."

"Not hardly," Arn said. But he *was* down. When Ana Maria told him, and he kept telling himself he didn't blame her. *If* she and Seth dined together because of romance.

He pointed to the wall again. "Winger and Seth were artillery at Ft. Sill for several months, though again there's nothing to prove they ever had contact with one another. Samantha and Jonah served together for certain and they knew each other as recently as the night Samantha kicked hell out of him at the Legion." Seth also knew the... person he gave the Xylazine. He won't give the name up but was in Iraq when Brian Gibbs served two tours there."

"Now I am confused," Danny said. "What's all their associations with each other even matter if you're looking for that *one* killer."

Arn tapped the white wall with the marker. "I thought so at first, but been thinking: what if there *were* two killers? One sloppy and brutal as when Steve Urchek was murdered, the other meticulous. Organized. Bringing death in a painless, quick way with lethal doses of cocaine. A manner that would ensure instant death with a minimum of commotion. The perfect way to avoid being caught in the act."

Arn sat back and grabbed his fork and plate before he paused. "This is rhubarb pie."

"It is."

Arn set the plate down. "I saw the way Oblanski's face puckered up when you gave him a piece."

Danny waved the air. "I threw *that* pie out. This is fresh and it is a masterpiece."

Dany was right—the pie was *sooo* good. Arn let the sugary fruit and crust slide down his throat ever so slowly. "Did you mess up the recipe with the last pie?"

"Not hardly," Danny said as he grinned. "I knew he was coming by and I thought I'd make something special for him. I just bet Oblanski doesn't come around any time soon asking for pie."

"Passive aggressive is what you are," Arn said. "I'll ask Ethan Ames how to cure you the next time I see him."

Danny stared at the wall for a long moment before he said, "where does Pudgy fit in?"

Arn gestured toward the wall with his fork. "That's the biggest puzzle of all. As crazy as he was as a kid, I can't help but think it just escalated when he enlisted."

"I take it Wagner hasn't found out who he is?"

Arn shook his head. "Lord know, the good sergeant has tried, too. He cross-referenced men who had enlisted in Sheridan with their home being in the southern Black Hills. He came up with two that enlisted there with their homes listed as Rapid City and Hill City, but both those men are listed as KIA in Iraq. Wagner found out the data base to cross-reference servicemen wasn't developed until five years ago. But," he turned on the television, "if Pudgy was familiar enough with Sheridan, I can only assume that he knew his way around the VA there. And he night have run into Sims at the center some years later."

"Why do you think Pudgy enlisted in Sheridan and not his home?"

"One more thing I'll grill Ethan about."

"Turn it up a skooch," Danny said and Arn reached for the television.

"I attempted interviewing the leader of the group, Colonel Jonah Barb, as he calls himself," Ana Maria said as a crowd looked on from the steps of the state capitol," but the Righteous Sword of the Lord refused to allow me access to their compound."

"When did she drive down there?" Arn asked, a sinking feeling overcoming him. Ana Maria was safe now, but it would have been just as conceivable that some of the RSL zealots would have harmed her, especially given the bad attention Ana Maria had given them this last week. As Arn recalled from his visit to the compound, there was enough acreage to hide a body and never be found.

"All she told me couple days ago is that she had an interview with a person of interest in the case," Danny said.

A stiff wind whipped Ana Maria's hair across her face, and she pulled it back with one hand, the other holding a microphone as she said, "we need your help in solving these murders. The RSL is part religious fanatics, part activists that wish for all American military to cease to exist. We believe they—and especially their leader, Colonel Jonah—know something about the deaths of these innocent veterans. We believe they know the VA Slayer."

"I'm surprised DeAngelo allowed Ana Maria to continue her special after what Jonah's lawyers did."

"That old Greek is not someone to be pushed around," Arn said. "Even by a couple of fancy suits." Ana Maria said two RSL lawyers came to the TV station. They threatened to file a lawsuit against DeAngelo if Ana Maria didn't cease her on-air insinuations. 'DeAngelo went livid,' she said that night after work. 'He told security to toss both attorneys out on their ears. Not *usher* them out gently—*physically toss* them out.' She had laughed telling the story. 'It was a thing of beauty seeing those two rolling in the parking lot.'"

"We are not directly accusing the RSL of killing veterans," Ana Maria wrapped it up, "but members do know something that will help us connect all the killings."

"That," Arn motioned to the television, "was a disclaimer DeAngelo felt he needed to get out there to be legally safe with the broadcasts."

"Especially in light of the death threats she's been receiving."

Ana Maria has gotten four and five death threats a day from Jonah in her work email. In gruesome and graphic terms, Jonah outlined what he would do to her should she continue accusing him—and his RSL group—of committing the unsolved murders. Oblanski's computer forensics officers had no luck finding out where the man sent his email from. "Every email he sends was routed through another ISP. He never mails from the same place twice. He could be sending the threats from the house next door," Oblanski said.

"That's nuts," Arn said. "You must be able to track the server down."

"It's not that simple," Oblanski told him. "He's hiding himself very well. Hell, he doesn't even think we'll catch him the way he's ballsy enough to sign his name to the threats."

The camera stayed on Ana Maria as she fielded question, and Arn's attention stayed on the crowd. Oblanski had two men posted undercover somewhere in the crowd and Arn strained to spot them. He could not, and he sat back with a sigh of relief.

The crowd broke up, the broadcast ended. Arn knew Jonah was

a small man and suspected he could blend in most anywhere. If he were able to avoid surveillance cameras at the VA by altering his appearance the day of the protest, he might have been among the onlookers. Arn put on his reading glasses and focused on a lone figure that had broken away from the rest of the group heading towards their cars.

A familiar figure by his gait. The way his head was on a swivel as if expecting trouble. And when the man turned so the side of his face showed, Arn cursed to himself for not being in the crowd watching.

Doc Henry.

40

As I stare at the television set and listen to Ana Maria's nightly broadcast I DVR'd—I am riveted to anything she does—I wonder how can she be out there in the open? With people around? Anyone who could do her harm, especially since she's spouting off about those veterans' deaths. I tell myself I've done everything I could to warn her off: first the dead cat sent to the television station, then the threat through the email. A normal person would be more frightened, but not my Ana Maria. I guess that is one of the reasons I am so fascinated by her. So attracted to her, even if I feel it is taboo.

But some days you feel like the dog, and some days you feel like the hydrant. Today, I am the hydrant, for no warning I have given her has caused her to quit meddling in places she does not belong. Do specials on the county fair or traffic accidents in the abominable roundabout that are causing so many wrecks. Anything else. But not the veterans' deaths. If she finds nothing else about them, there will be no reason for me to fear detection.

Should I teach her a lesson as I did Anderson? I don't trust myself, for—as much as I admire her spunk—I might go off the deep end, as shrinks say, and fail to stop with that one blow of the wrench. Like I would have done if not interrupted the night I caught Anderson in the Outback parking lot unawares.

But I have to warn her off. But how… I have a way, I think. She is—after all—a gear head who loves her cars."

195

41

ARN SIDESTEPPED GORILLA LEGS AS she refused to budge. Their bellies brushed against one another and she flashed a wide grin. "The chief is expecting you," she seemed to *coo*.

"She's been asking about you," Oblanski said after he shut the door. "Comes in handy, too. Every time she gets a case of nasty, I mention you'll be stopping by and she mellows out. I'm telling you, she loves you big, strong men who can put her in her place."

"If I were to try putting her anywhere it would throw my back out of place."

"Would you rather have her on the verge of throttling you every time you need to come by?"

"Would you rather I bring a piece of Danny's pie for you every time I drop in?"

"I'm reeling from the last time. Take a seat. Gorilla Legs said you needed to talk."

Arn took off his hat and dropped into a chair. "Did you see Ana Maria's broadcast last night?"

Oblanski nodded. "She all but came out and accused the RSL of being directly involved in the veterans' deaths. And that horseshit disclaimer would mean nothing to the RSL attorneys. But why broadcast that if she has no proof? If we have no proof?"

"She thinks if she pushes hard enough in her broadcasts that it will force the killer to make a play and slip up."

"That's a dangerous line she walks," Oblanski said. "I don't have enough men in the department available to be her full-time bodyguards."

"Which is why I'm here. Doc was at Ana Maria's broadcast last night."

"You sure?"

"If you go to the TV station and review their tape, you'll see Doc right at the end walking away."

"Shit!" Oblanski punched a button on his phone and Gorilla Legs' raspy voice asked what the hell he wanted. "Get Sergeant Roth on the line. Tell him to ask his two officers on the Villarreal case last night why the hell they didn't spot Doc Henry."

"I should have been there myself," Arn said when Oblanski had disconnected. "I'd know Doc in a crowd no matter how he disguises himself."

"We talked about that before," Oblanski said, picking up a pencil and examining the eraser for a moment before gnawing on it. "Even if you spot him, I know you—you'll confront him and that'll lead to bad things for you. He's already filed a report with us concerning that first night you talked with him at Mimi's. Claims you threatened him by intimidation." He held up his hand. "I know it's bullshit, and I told him so. But it's his right to file a report for the record."

"I'm not going just sit around and wait for him to grab Ana Maria."

"As soon as I talk with Sergeant Roth I'll make sure the officers on her detail are especially observant for him." Oblanski turned in his chair and grabbed the coffee pot, the aroma strong.

"Not tea this time?" Arn asked. "What's the special occasion?"

"The celebration is my old FTO, Hank Rydell in Seattle, found Beth Randall Schwartz. She moved from there a few years ago down the road to Olympia."

"Are you going to give me her phone number?"

"It's not going to be so easy. Hank tells me Beth *might* talk with a woman. She was reluctant to even admit who she was when Hank found her. She's got a distrust of men; she won't talk with you. And certainly didn't to Hank."

"One of your female officers then?"

Oblanski laughed. "You get funnier every time I talk with you. Sure, I'll just tell the city council that I sent one of my women officers on an all-expense paid trip to Seattle to interview a woman who may or may not have absolutely *any* information about Frank Mosby's or Leonard Mills' deaths."

"Don't forget the others—.""

"As cold as it sounds, they are not within my jurisdiction. Sure, we'll share information with other agencies, but spending that kind of money for an officer to traipse to Seattle is out of the question. Now if you could positively link Pudgy to any of those two deaths…"

"You know I can't."

"Then you will have to line up another women to go there. I'd bet you could talk Gorilla Legs into going there and interviewing Beth." Oblanski winked. "As long as you're along to keep her company."

———

Arn pulled into the TV station lot and parked beside Ana Maria's Volkswagen. She leaned against it, arms crossed, a look of potential murder in her eyes.

He climbed out of his Olds and walked around the car. "You're right—someone did your VW a number."

"Son-of-a-bitch got all four tires. I'm waiting on the wrecker now."

Arn bent and ran his hand over one sidewall. It, like the other tires, had been slashed cleanly.

"Someone wants me off the air pretty bad," Ana Maria said. "I'd put my money on Colonel Jonah." She hit the side of the VW. "Dammit, I just put new skins on it last month. Has there been *any* sign of him?"

Arn shook his head. "Oblanski's guys have been working with the FBI to find out where he's emailing from. But just when they locate the ISP he's making from, he send another from a different ISP."

"He's got to surface sometime, right?" Arn had asked the chief in his office. "He can't go back to that RSL compound or he'll be caught."

"Colorado Bureau of Investigation agents and deputies executed a search warrant on the compound just this morning," Oblanski said. "Nada. Jonah was nowhere to be found. He has to surface sometime. When he does, someone will recognize him, especially with the coverage you're giving him." Every night for the past week, Ana

Maria began her coverage of the Righteous Sword of the Lord group with a photo of *Colonel* Jonah Bard as she danced around the group being connected to the VA Slayer.

"So this," she kicked a flat tire, "might not have been done by him? Could have been one of his followers."

"He's got enough zealots he could have ordered any one of them to slice your tires."

"You mentioned before his General... Nehemiah, could get him out of the country."

"That," Arn said, "is what worries me the most. There's little chance that Jonah could be whisked out in a commercial aircraft. Even less in a private flight. But that southern border... there's been so much emphasis on illegals crossing *into* the country that folks forget there's people who *leave* into Mexico every day. If Jonah flees south, General Nehemiah has enough contacts to keep his Colonel hidden for many years."

The tow truck started into the parking lot and Ana Maria ran over to the driver. She jumped onto the step and said something to him before he drove away.

"You change your mind about getting this towed to the tire shop?"

"No. I told the wrecker driver to come in the back way where he'll be less likely to be spotted by DeAngelo." Ana Maria glanced nervously at the back door of the TV station. "I didn't tell him that my tires have been slashed. If the old man knew, I'm just afraid he'd pull my special. There's only so many warnings I can get before DeAngelo cancels my special on the RSL."

"You are convinced one of Jonah's followers did this?"

"Who else?" Ana Maria asked.

"Think about it: your nightly broadcasts cover the RSL fools *and* the veterans' deaths. Tying them together. But what about one of the other suspects we talked about? What if one of them slashed your tires."

"Like Sam or Winger or Pudgy, if we ever find him?"

"Or, have you thought that maybe Doc Henry did this?"

"That was my first thought," Ana Maria said. "I know he hates me, but this isn't Doc's style. It's not big enough. Not... flamboyant

199

enough. Believe me, when he finally makes his move, it will be *memorable*."

"Which reminds me, how would you like an all expense paid trip to Seattle?" Arn asked.

"On whose dime?"

"On DeAngelo's, of course. That's if he doesn't find out about this tire incident."

42

"**GIVE ME THE BAD NEWS**," Arn said. He poured Ana Maria a cup of coffee before refilling his own and sat at the kitchen table. "Did Beth turn you down?"

"I haven't felt this exhausted since I rebuilt two motors in one weekend." She wrapped her hand around her coffee mug. "I thought I'd never get her to open up even a little. She finally agreed to talk with me *in person*. So you're right—I need to sweet talk DeAngelo into sending me up to Seattle."

"You can do it if you convince him Pudgy's whereabouts may be the key to solving these veteran deaths."

"I'm still not convinced myself Pudgy's involved, but I'm willing to talk with her. *If* DeAngelo springs for the plane ticket." She took a chocolate chip cookie Danny made that morning and broke off a piece. "What did Wagner say?"

Arn eyed the cookie and thought he'd better hold off. Until he reasoned he had burned his chance with Sam anyway, so it meant little what his shape is, and he grabbed one. "Sam had appointments scheduled all day in Sheridan. Wagner's going to verify she actually made them, and that Winger was in Scottsbluff for training."

"He could have easily slashed my tires and still make it to Scottsbluff. It's not that far away."

"I liked it better when you figured Jonah was your mad slasher."

Arn jumped when the alarm beeped, and Danny came in the house. The beeping continued and Arn imagined Danny fumbling to rearm the system. The noise finally stopped, and Danny walked into the kitchen, trailed by an Indian man who had to turn sideways to fit

201

through the doorway. Danny stopped and put his hand on his thin hips. "So condemn me because I don't do technology."

"It's not your problems with our new alarm system." Arn looked past Danny to the man towering over him. "Who's your... large friend?"

"Chauncy Big Eagle," Danny said. "But everyone always called him *Bulldog* 'cause once he got onto something he never let go until the job was done."

Arn looked at Bulldog's massive forearms covered with jailhouse tats inked by some prison artist with less than ideal skills. Colors ran together, as did the two teardrops tattooed on Bulldog's left cheek beside his eye. Spiderwebs adorned both elbows, and the wristwatch tattooed on his wrist had no hands.

"Don't just stand there," Danny said as he craned his neck up. "Shake hands with Arn."

"But you said he's a cop."

"Retired," Danny said. "But he's a good guy. Now shake."

Bulldog hesitated a moment before sticking out his hand missing the little finger. Arn shook it, noting *A. C. A. B.* tattooed on the fingers. "All Cops Are Bastards," Arn said. "Haven't seen one of those in a while."

Bulldog's grin showed only four teeth left in his uppers. "I like to think it stands for Always Carry A Bible."

"Do you have a bible on you?"

Bulldog's grin faded. "Why the hell would I carry one?"

"Let's talk out back," Danny said quickly and ushered Bulldog out the back door.

Ana Maria let out a long breath. "Now *that* man's scary."

"He ought to be if I read his prison tats right. The spider web shows he was in stir for a *long* time, and the two teardrops means he killed two men in prison."

"Then why's he out of jail?"

Arn shrugged. "Like Doc Henry, Bulldog probably gamed the system."

Danny came back into the kitchen and went to the freezer as if nothing happened.

"You're missing a friend," Arn said.

"Bulldog," Danny said as he kept his back to Arn, "don't like certain… company. No offense."

"Danny, turn around for a minute."

When Danny faced Arn, he asked, "Did Bulldog just get out of prison?"

"Naw," Danny answered. "He's been out of the state lockup in South Dakota for nearly a year. Been living on Rosebud Reservation doing odd jobs."

"Odd jobs? That include enforcing someone's will upon others?

Danny feigned hurt. "Why do you think that? Bulldog's just a big… pussycat."

"I say that because he had an American Indian Movement tat on one forearm."

"So, a few of my old A.I.M. buddies are still kicking."

"And they just drop in unexpectedly?"

Danny turned back to the sink and began unwrapping the frozen hamburger. "Bulldog dropped in for a visit. You know, reminiscence."

"Your reminiscences wouldn't include Doc Henry by any chance?"

"Of course not," Danny said.

Ana Maria stood and walked to the sink. "Don't tell me you sent for him to hurt Doc. As much as I despise the man, I don't want to see you get involved."

Danny smiled. "Who, me? "The only thing I did was recommend Mimi's Restaurant if Bulldog wanted a nice steak."

———

That night as Ana Maria's shower was running and Danny's snoring echoed from down the hallway from the sewing room, Arn looked through his wallet until he found Ethan Ames' business card. "Call any time you need to talk," he had told Arn that first day. "All my other clients do."

Ethan picked up on the third ring and breathed heavily into the phone. When Arn identified himself, Ethan said, "let me grab a towel and some water."

"Is this a bad time?" Arn asked.

"Not really. I just came back from a three-mile jog and a little out of breath. Not as young as I used to be and all that."

"Running at night?"

"Less traffic here in Rapid City," Ethan said and Arn heard water running on the other end. "Back," Ethan said. "What do you need, Mr. Anderson?"

Arn had thought long if he should even talk with Ethan about Pudgy. Arn had nothing at all to connect him to the VA deaths other than what Sheriff Ridley told him, and Pudgy's father who hated all things officer. And unlike the others on Arn's suspect list on the white wall, Pudgy wasn't an employee of the VA. Unless, Arn thought, Pudgy *was* an employee. Somewhere in the government system. But at this point, Arn didn't even have a name. Arn didn't even know if the man was still alive. "One of the people I want to talk about is a kid... he's a grown man now if he's alive, named Pudgy."

"Pudgy who?"

"I don't know yet," Arn said. "He lived in Custer with his father, Bo Randall, but he enlisted under another name apparently as there's no record of him being in the Army. But I found witnesses who saw him at the time of his father's funeral wearing an Army Ranger uniform."

"What do you want from me?" Ethan asked, his voice coming in muted gasps as he fought to catch his breath. "And before you ask, I can tell you I've never treated a soldier named Pudgy Randall. Or anyone named Pudgy. Or Randall for that matter."

"That's not what I wanted to talk about," Arn said. "One of the leads Ana Maria and I were working was Bo's divorced wife, Beth Randall, though she's going by another name now."

"Have you found her?"

"We have," Arn said. "Ana Maria's going to fly to... Washington state to interview her about her son."

"And you think this woman is Pudgy's mother?"

"Almost positive," Arn said. "What I need to know is what should Ana Maria be asking Beth about Pudgy that might help us identify him?"

There was a long pause on the other end of the line. "Sorry, had to grab another water. Tell me what you know about this Pudgy Randall."

Arn explained to Ethan that Pudgy's lacked respect for law enforcement or anyone else, including his teachers and principle. He told Ethan that Pudgy had been raised by a psychotic father after Beth fled the marriage with the sister, a father who undoubtedly brainwashed his son into hating most everyone. Especially military officers. "Ana Maria is going to have one shot at her, as Beth is highly suspicious."

"As she ought to be," Ethan said, "after the way Bo treated her."

Another pause. "Beth might not be able to be much help, given that the last time she saw her son was…"

"More than twenty-five years ago."

"Let me think," Ethan said. A long pause. "I would ask this Beth if there was anything to distinguish Pudgy physically. Maybe he was taller than most. Stockier as he might be with a name like Pudgy. Maybe the way he walked. His unique eye color. Anything that Pudgy couldn't change in that amount of time.

"Then I would ask her what she remembers about the way Pudgy dealt with his father as opposed to dealing with her when it came time for discipline. The way in which a boy interacts with both parents tells us a lot and helps paint a psychological profile."

Arn jotted that on his notepad and added, "Pudgy had few friends, according to his ex-girlfriend, Mary Ann Hester. She's still living in Custer and actually remembers Pudgy well."

Ethan dropped the phone and Arn heard the chink of a glass on a tabletop before he came back online. "If I understand you correctly, this girlfriend is still in South Dakota?"

"Living and working as a waitress," Arn said. "The way she tells it, Pudgy had even more trouble associating with people after the mom left."

"Abandonment," Ethan said. "Your Pudgy kid felt he had been abandoned. Betrayed when mom left. That would undoubtedly shape his world view. But I still don't quite grasp why you consider Pudgy a suspect."

"Remember me telling you about Captain Sims' murder in Sheridan?"

"How could I forget," Ethan said, "the way you described it so... graphically."

"And I recall you said it sounded like a crime of rage?"

"It did."

"Rage against military officers," Arn said. "Or, former military officers. And I thought back to when you told me serial killers are usually very intelligent. At least the ones that get away with their murders for any length of time. I believe it is a distinct possibility that Pudgy Randall killed Sims brutally and, later, evolved."

"And you think this because Pudgy's father was done wrong by officers? That is a bit of a stretch. But thinking back to other serial killers, they have gone on their killing sprees for less provocation than that. But you mentioned you think your suspect evolved?"

"If it is just *one* killer involved, I think he—or she—did evolve. Learned from their mistakes. Which is why I think it's so difficult to identify them now—their method of killing is so... surgical. Clean."

"Copy that," Ethan said. "But I'm afraid I haven't been much help. I'll be happy to sit down with Ana Maria when she returns to go over what Beth Randall said to her. Maybe I can help establish a profile."

"At least Beth may give her enough insight and information that Sgt. Wagner can run it through a database and we can finally ID Pudgy."

"Good luck with that," Ethan said. "And do me a major favor."

"Sure," Arn said, "I think I owe you after interrupting your cool-down time."

"Let me do a forensic interview with Pudgy when you do find him. He sounds like a deliciously fascinating guy even if he might be a serial killer."

43

"THE VICTIM WAS LAST SEEN** hanging around your house," Oblanski said.

Arn didn't have to pick up the photos, nor did he have to study them even though the face was crushed and showed little resemblance to a human being. The spider web tattoo on the big man's elbows and the wrist watched inked on his wrist told Arn all he needed to know whose time had run out. "Bulldog."

"The South Dakota parole board knows him better as Chauncy Big Eagle. He hasn't showed up at a meeting with his PO for over a year. Now why the hell was he at your house?"

Arn took off his hat and massaged a rising headache spreading across his forehead. "He was an… acquaintance of Danny's."

"There's more to it."

"There is," Arn said. "Danny had some romantic notion that Bulldog was going to… persuade Doc Henry from bothering Ana Maria."

Oblanski tossed his pencil into the round file. "What a dumb assed idea. Doesn't your man servant— ."

"Roommate."

"Whatever," Oblanski waved it away. "Doesn't he know better than to try pulling off some bonehead plan like that? Now we got us another dead body and no one to pin it on."

"Sure you do."

"And who might that be?"

"Doc Henry," Arn answered.

Oblanski picked up the photo. "It took four men to lift this… man

207

into the meat wagon, and you think some old guy like Doc Henry could do this," he tapped the photo showing Bulldog bloody and unrecognizable and left in a downtown alley.

Arn's headache only increased as Oblanski forced him into remembering what Doc was capable of. "Every one of Doc's victims—."

"I thought Doc was convicted of just *one* murder?"

"That's all that we could prove. Each victim had been strangled and bludgeoned worse than the previous one. It was as if Doc was learning the best way to ensure no one could identify them. As for besting some big bastard like Bulldog, Doc was found straddling a two-fifty-pound inmate while he was in Florence High. Only because guards pulled Doc off the guy did he manage to pull through. Doc had everyone in the block so scarred they all claimed he was acting in self-defense."

———

Ana Maria picked at her casserole while Danny hung his head, and Arn rubbed his headache. "Aren't we a sorry bunch," Arn said. "Danny's friend has been murdered, I have a headache bordering on a migraine from talking to Oblanski half the afternoon, and you're having some issues," he motioned to Ana Maria. "What's going on with you?"

"Just the old good news-bad news thing," she said and dropped her fork on the plate. "You want the bad news first?"

"If you're talking to me," Danny said, "I'd like the good news first. Maybe it'll cheer me up."

"Ok, here it is. Remember I told you I've been working my tail off to convince Ethan Ames to submit to an interview," Ana Maria said.

"Sure I remember," Arn said. "I recall his superiors wouldn't approve it. Something about patient confidentiality."

She nodded. "My argument was that there is no confidentiality issue if the patients are dead, but he said his hands were tied. Well, he called me this morning—he'd convinced his supervisor in Rapid

City that my argument held water, and that he could talk freely about the victims."

"What's there to talk about?" Danny said. "They're dead."

"A profile," Ana Maria answered. "Ethan will go on the record and talk about the victims and he will offer a psychological profile we can put out to the public. His supervisor agrees with me—any information out into the public domain might help us catch the killer."

"That's great news," Arn said. "I hate to spoil our festive mood, but what's the bad?"

"The bad news is I arranged to talk with Beth Randall Schwartz tomorrow afternoon. The same time my interview with Ethan's here in town. He's giving me an hour for an interview."

"Could you reschedule either one?" Arn asked.

"I don't see how. It took all my persuasion for her to agree to even talk. I am just afraid if I postpone it, she'll think something's up. I can't say for certain, but I got the impression that Beth is deathly afraid that Pudgy will find her. As for Ethan, he has to catch a red eye out of Denver for a conference in D. C. tomorrow night, so he won't be available for another week."

"*Someone* has to make that interview. If Pudgy is involved, Beth may have the one piece of information we need to find him," Arn said. "I'll go."

Ana Maria picked at her food with her fork. "Didn't you hear a word I said? Beth is so paranoid; I know she won't agree to talk with you. The minute you call her and tell her you're replacing me, the interview will be off. She might even skip town."

"I didn't plan on calling her."

"How's that?"

"I'm not going to call her. I'm just going to show up at the time you've arranged and hope to hell she agrees to talk."

"How are you going to get her to talk?"

Arn flashed a grin.

Danny groaned. "Not that old Anderson charm again."

44

ARN WAS ABLE TO SWAP his name for Ana Maria's on United at the last minute. DeAngelo had bulled-up when Arn dropped by the TV station and told him he wanted to fly to Washington state and interview Beth. "Why the hell should I pay a private investigator to fly all the way up there? If Ana Maria can't go, I'm getting a refund," the old man said.

"What if I go on my own dime and glean enough information from Beth that I can solve these deaths? And suppose that I give that information to an affiliate in Denver, perhaps the ABC affiliate?"

"I see your point," DeAngelo told him. "Doesn't mean you have to hold me hostage."

As it turned out—Arn thought as he looked at the seat assignment online—DeAngelo had held *Arn* hostage. Or at least got some vengeance when the old man cheaped-out on the ticket—he hadn't even paid for Business Class or Economy. The cheap skate had paid for Luggage Class—all the way in the back of the plane right next to the toilet.

Arn got through the security line at DIA and headed to his boarding gate when his phone rang. "You sound like you're in a stadium or something, "Agent Kane said.

"Hold on." Arn walked to the gate labeled *Pakistani Airlines*. There was no one sitting waiting, and Arn just figured there weren't many brave souls who wanted to fly there. "What cha got?"

"Nothing earth shaking," Kane said. "I put a man on Samantha Holder—not literally, though he would have loved to once he saw her—and followed her to those private stables west of Rapid. She

210

was giving private riding lessons to Duane Dagbe."

"I know that name from somewhere."

"You should. He's a Ghana national who is a *major* supplier of meth and coke who beat the rap in state court last year. Since then, he claims to have reformed."

"Don't they all," Arn said as he watched a woman push a double stroller while the little darlings screamed loudly as she got onto the escalator. "Is that what you wanted to tell me?"

"No," Kane said. "My agent trailed her to those stables, and—when she and Dagbe disappeared into the hills—my man... stumbled onto Samantha's toolbox in back of her truck. He might have been looking for something else—I won't be able to testify if it comes to that. She was telling the truth—every one of her tools is *Snap-On* brand and they all are engraved. with her initials. It looks like she wasn't the one who waylaid you outside the Outback after all. "He chuckled. "Unless she stole someone else's *Craftsman* crescent wrench."

"That is good news," Arn said, a sinking feeling overcoming him. He had considered her a suspect. Even brought her name up to Oblanski and thought that Mike the Mauler would tweak a confession from her.

But if she hadn't attacked him, who had?

———

Arn waited patiently to get onto his flight. They had just now started to board the Neat and Elite—the First-Class passengers, and he had enough time to call Oblanski. "The flight's going to about forty-five minutes late arriving in Seattle."

"I'll pass that along to Sven." Oblanski's old Field Training Officer in Seattle, Sven Olesen, had retired last year. Oblanski said he had contacts all over the state and had put out feelers until he found where in Olympia Beth Randall Schwartz had moved to. "He'll pick you up at the airport," Oblanski told had told him. "Man doesn't have much else to do now that he's retired. You and Sven ought to have a lot in common—you're both Norwegian."

The only thing Arn and Sven had in common was they were both Scandinavian. Arn had waited at the curb side pick-up area, looking frantically for Sven, walking the length, seeing no one until he heard the sound of a motorcycle idle up and stop in front of him. "You must be Arn Anderson."

A man nearly as big as Arn, but older—in his early seventies perhaps—shut the Harley off and swung his leg over the bike, his bare leg protected by leather chaps. "Ned said you'd be traveling light" he nodded to Arn's overnight bag. "Strap it on the sissy bars and hop on."

"On this?"

Sven took off his helmet and twirled his handlebar mustache as he frowned at Arn. "Sure, on this *Harley*. Don't tell me you're a BMW man. Or worse, someone who rides one of those Japanese bikes like a Gold Wing."

"I don't ride *any* bike," Arn said. "At least I haven't since I was in high school. And then just piddly little dirt bikes. Not like this... behemoth."

Sven tilted his head and laughed heartedly. "Then this will be a learning experience for you." He unsnapped another helmet from the back of the sissy bar and handed it to Arn. Buckle up tight... we're not going to let any grass grow under us on our way down there."

Arn had no choice. He had to get down to Olympia and try to convince Beth that he only wanted to find the killer of innocent vets. And convince her he would never reveal to Pudgy her whereabouts.

Arn strapped his bag onto the sissy bar using bungie cords that dangled from Sven's side saddles. He had instantly considered renting a car and following him down to Olympia when his phone saved him. For the moment. "Did Sven make it there?" Oblanski said.

Arn turned his back and said quietly, "You never said he'd be picking me up on a motorcycle."

"Did I forget to mention that?"

212

"You did."

"Oh well," Oblanski said. "Don't look a gift horse and all that. But I wanted to tell you that a Lt. Ordway in Denver called—."

"Did Matthew find Jimmy's dope dealer?" Arn had asked Matthew Ordway, a detective who had trained under Arn, to find Jimmy's dope dealer. "He located a pusher who operated behind a small cigarette shop on Colfax. The man knew Jimmy as a regular. But he did not know any of the people Jimmy conned for a ride to Denver. Seems like someone different brought him down every time, and the only thing the dealer knew was that Jimmy's rides were squares—dressed like they had a job. Or dressed like they were Jimmy's chauffeurs. That help any?"

"Not much," Arn said. "Could you send a man down to Denver with Jonah and Winger's photos. And for the hell of it, throw in Seth Barnes' picture. Maybe the dealer can ID one of them."

"You don't suspect Barnes, too?"

"Let's say he was a little too guarded as to who he gave the Xylazine to."

"I got just the man to send down," Oblanski said. "A single officer who just loves to hit Shotgun Willie's when he's down in Denver. He says it's for the free buffet, but who goes to a strip club wanting to eat… meat?"

Arn pocketed his phone and looked warily at the big motorcycle like it was an evil thing come alive. "Don't just stand there," Sven said. "Put your helmet on and flip down the visor. Wouldn't want you talking to the lady with bugs stuck all over your face."

———

Arn had seen footage of World War II Air Corps crew members drop down and kiss the ground when they landed in their shot-to-hell B-27 bomber. Although Sven didn't damage his motorcycle, Arn felt the same way as those air crew members must have felt. The sixty miles from Seattle had taken a little less than an hour. Through bumper-to-bumper traffic. Arn stretched his leg that had brushed against a florists' delivery van when Sven had cut it a little close and he was grateful for the face shield when the bike rode for miles in back of a smoke-spewing Mercedes diesel.

"We walk from here," Sven said. He locked it and Arn's helmets in his saddlebags and walked down the street. "Beth Schwartz' house sits back from the street a ways sheltered among some trees. I did some homework—she's a little goofy. Neighbors say she only comes out of the house to run to the grocery once a week. Hires her yard work done, so they rarely see her outside. One of the neighbors came up to her to visit and she jumped like a rabbit, her top flopping up and showed a small automatic in a belt holster."

"Hope she don't pull it on me," Arn said. "Only thing I got going for me is that Beth's expecting Ana Maria at seven o'clock sharp. That first instant when she opens the door and sees it is not Ana Maria will tell if I get an interview. Or get shot."

"Might as well wait here," Sven said, and leaned against a pine tree. He pointed through other trees to a beige ranch-style among other houses much bigger. "Thirty minutes until your interview time," Sven said. "Might as well take the opportunity to figure out what your game plan is going to be, 'cause I know it won't include me. She sees two burly bastards like us at her doorstep she's as likely to start shooting as slamming the door in our faces."

Arn had thought of what he would say to Beth that first moment when she realized Ana Maria hadn't come. After all, he had spent the two-hour flight gathering his thoughts between grunts from passengers visiting the restroom directly in back of seat, and countless flushes that threatened to interrupt his thoughts. *Too damn much green tea.*

"Time for me to head on up there," Arn said as he checked his watch. "If I'm not back in an hour, better call 911 because Beth decided to shoot me for deceiving her."

He walked slowly, accessing the front of the house leading to the entrance. Heavy curtains had been pulled across the windows, and faint light showed between cracks in the curtains. Arn kept his eyes on the windows as he mounted the four steps onto the porch. He kept to one side of the door before knocking.

Arn put his ear to the side of the house.

214

Footsteps approached slowly and paused for a long moment before opening the door. Beth Randall Schwartz was a small woman who came up to Arn's chest, but the bulge under her apron told him she was ready for whatever came along. She didn't see anyone through her screen door, and opened it, craning her neck out when…

…her eyes locked on Arn's.

Her hand snaked under her apron.

Arn held his hands flat in front of him as he sputtered, "Ana Maria Villarreal."

Beth stopped and blinked several times before asking, "What did you just yell?"

"Ana Maria Villarreal. She had an appointment to speak with you. It was important to her."

"Who are you?"

"I am her friend," Arn said, keepings his hands in front of him, even though she was close enough that he could disarm her if she drew on him. "And I dearly need to speak with you."

She looked both ways along her porch. "I keep to myself, so if you can kindly step off the porch—."

"More innocent veterans might die if you do not talk with me."

Beth took her hand away from her gun butt and her head drooped. "That is just what Ana Maria said when she talked me into visiting with her. Said my Pudgy is a suspect."

Arn nodded. "Please. Just a few moments of your time."

"You are not going to tell anyone here I live?"

"You're afraid of Pudgy, aren't you?"

Her eyes widened. "By now, he is as crazy as his father. Sure, I'm afraid. But he don't know where I live."

"If we can find you, so can he. Help me locate him so you are not in any danger anymore."

Beth looked a final time outside before opening the screen door wider and motioning Arn inside. "This way to the parlor," she said and started through the house, all the while keeping Arn in her peripheral vision. She motioned to an occasional chair across from a recliner with a knitting project sitting on the seat. An afghan. Perhaps a sweater, with the pink colored yarn intermixed with lavender.

Beth picked up her knitting and grabbed needles stuffed in the cushion. She resumed the *click, click, clicking* of them loudly in the quiet room until she said, "You want to know about Pudgy?"

"I do," Arn said. He pulled his notebook out of his pocket and rested it on his knees.

"But you already know my boy."

"I have never met him, Mrs. Randall—."

"Schwartz!" she snapped. "No one knows my married name around here. I took my grandfather's name on my mother's side. Figured no one would think of looking for me under Schwartz."

"I apologize," Arn said, digesting what she had just said. "But I *don't* know your son."

"Have you researched my late husband? Have you learned about Bo?"

Arn nodded.

"Then you know Pudgy, for he was just as… evil, just as crazy as his father the day my girl and I fled Custer."

Arn waited silently, knowing some people just need a moment to gather their thoughts. Especially when bad memories resurface. "Bo Randall was a man consumed by hatred. Even before we were married, he had a nasty streak. Foolish me… I thought he'd come out of it once we were a couple. But he didn't. Everything the man did was to fuel that hatred."

"I read his service record. He developed a loathing for officers. Probably as a result of him getting court martialed for black marketing in Vietnam."

Beth forced a laugh. "A hatred for officers was just an excuse. He hated everyone and everything after he got out of prison. If it wasn't officers, he would have come up with someone else to hate—cowboys or farmers or mechanics. Anything to justify his sick hostility."

She stopped and looked over at Arn. "And when officers were not the subject of his anger, he began hating me. Oh, I could take the beatings. Any farm girl like me has endured far more than Bo dished out. But when he started brainwashing Pudgy, things got even worse." She leaned closer to Arn. "Bo killed and buried a man in the forest outside Custer a few years before we split. I always suspected Bo took Pudgy along when he did it."

Arn looked at his notes. "Pudgy was... thirteen when you and Bo broke up. Have you ever had contact with him since you moved from Custer?"

Beth stood. "That is the reason I moved so suddenly from Seattle to here."

She walked to a writing desk and dropped the leaf. She reached into one of the pigeonholes and came away with a letter. After looking at it for a long moment, she handed it to Arn. "Read it if you think there's anything that'll help you."

Arn unfolded the one-page letter Pudgy had sent to his mother.

I'm doing good in the Army, Ma. Just in case you wondered. Going to enroll in college after this special school that the Army intend sending me to. I think the running will help me drop some weight. You might not even recognize me when you see me again. I apologize for siding with Pappy all those times he was mean to you. But at least I tried to protect Jen. Though now, I seem to have developed a dislike for officers. Like Pappy did, and I don't know if it's something he instilled in me, or if is because I had some bad dealings with officers in the Army myself. I hope you do well in Seattle, and I'll come see you soon.

Love you guys,

Pudgy.

Arn handed the letter back and she said, "Keep it. There might be something you can use to find him."

Arn noted the APO on envelope's the return address. "Did Pudgy serve in the Middle East or Europe?"

"Who knows," Beth said. "All I know is when I received that letter with his promise to come see me, I took Jen—that's my girl—we left that same night. Spent it in a motel in Tacoma huddled together. Jen was always so close to Pudgy, but even she got to be afraid of what he might do if he came visiting. Luckily, I found this place."

Arn looked around the tiny parlor with its paisley wallpaper and tattered area throw rugs and noted there were no photos hanging on the walls. Nothing to distract from the dreary atmosphere of the house. "Do you have any pictures of Pudgy?"

Clicking of the knitting needles grew faster. "When Bo kicked me out of the house, that *just* what he done—kicked me and Jen out. He allowed us to take one change of clothes. That was it. So, I have no photos of Pudgy."

"Pudgy enlisted in Sheridan."

"To hide it from Bo, no doubt," Beth said. "He was dead set against anything military and would have thrashed Pudgy if he knew he was enlisting."

"We found no record under Pudgy Randall."

"Pudgy's Christian name is Allen," Beth laughed. "Allen Randall. As if there was anything *Christian* about him after Bo worked his hatred on the boy."

Arn made note that photos were unavailable, something he had hoped to find when he spoke with Beth. "Is there anything that would distinguish Pudgy?"

Beth set her needles down and began curling more yard into a ball. "Look for someone dressed to the nines. That is the only positive thing that rubbed off from Bo—he was always insisted in dressing nicely since he was a youngster."

Arn circled *dressed well*. He had that note and Pudgy's given name to begin referencing once he got the information to Wagner. "What did he look like?"

Beth paused from her knitting and looked at Arn. "Good looking boy. He always looked younger than he was, just like his sister. Good genes, I always figured 'cause Bo held his age well. But anything distinguishing?" she shrugged. "Brown eyes. Brown hair. Heavy set, though he might have lost his baby fat by now."

"You mentioned he was close to your daughter."

"Was," Beth said. "Some years after we moved here, Jenifer thought that she'd like to meet up with her brother and see how he turned out. But after I told her some stories about her father—and how Pudgy was just like Bo—she came to her senses. But then, Jenifer always was smart. Always was too sharp for her own good. And in case you're wondering, I don't have any pictures of Jen, either."

Arn remained quiet as he often did. He found folks often told him things in their own time. Their own way. He remained silent long enough for her to say, "And I see you're wondering why I have no pictures of my children."

"It crossed my mind."

"As it would cross Pudgy's, if he ever found me." Beth picked up her needles again and looked at them for a moment. When Bo kicked us out of the house, he wouldn't let us take anything except that change of clothes. Certainly nothing sentimental like photos."

"And after you moved to Seattle?"

"I always was afraid that Pudgy would find me one day. And when he did, he would demand to know about his sister. I couldn't chance that he would find her. So I never kept any photos of her, even though she'd come home with a photo pack from school every year. Shame, a beautiful girl like that never even had a chance to date in school. Participate in sports." Beth leaned closer. "You think that was wrong, Mr. Anderson—keeping Jen so close to home so that her crazy brother wouldn't spot her if he managed to find us?"

Arn looked at Beth and thought how she was *just* as crazy as Bo and Pudgy, denying her daughter some of the life seasonings that young girl should encounter. It was, he finally concluded, what fear did to a body. "What became of Jenifer?"

Beth smiled wide. "Army. She grew up a tomboy so I suppose the Army suited her just fine. I was always so worried that her and Pudgy would run into one another someplace, but they never did. She did her twenty years and retired." Beth jabbed the air with her needles. "But, there is no need to know where she is. If you find her, Pudgy can find her. Just be satisfied that she is doing good in life without knowing *anything* about Pudgy that will help you."

45

A RN SOMEHOW ENDURED THE RIDE back to Seattle to catch his flight with only one big bug stuck under his collar. When Sven dropped him off at the United terminal, he said, "you still have five hours before your flight leaves," he winked. "I know where we could hook up with a couple babes."

Arn shook his head and thanked the old man for the offer. And for the trip to Olympia. "I can get a lot done over my phone while I wait for my flight."

"Suit yourself," Sven said as he swung his leg over the bike. He situated his pillow with the hole in it under his butt and settled down. "I'd say see you next time, but—at your age—there might not be a next time," and he roared off.

Arn entered the airport and made his way to the food court. He grabbed a Big Mac and

fries and picked a spot in the corner away from others and flipped open his phone. Ana Maria picked up on the first ring. "Tell me Beth was helpful?"

"Reluctantly at first," Arn said. "But she gave me Pudgy's name— Allen Randall. I need you to get with Sgt. Wagner. If he can cross reference that name with the Sheridan enlistment records, we can get a photo to pass around. Maybe we'll get lucky and Pudgy will be in the surveillance videos."

"Can't do that," Ana Maria said. "I'm off to the library to interview Ethan Ames. You'll have to call Wagner yourself."

"Thought you were interviewing him in his office?"

"He said there's some construction started yesterday that's so noisy we couldn't hear one another. I didn't want to go... just any place. The library has enough people around..."

Arn understood. Ana Maria was thinking self-preservation now, picking a meeting place with enough people that—if Doc or Jonah came near—she would have help. Or at least witnesses. "Keep me posted if you hear anything about Jonah or Doc. And watch your backside."

Ana Maria hesitated. "I will."

Arn detected something in Ana Maria's voice that he had grown to recognize as concern. "What problems have you had since I've been gone?"

"None."

"Bull," Arn said. "Is it Doc Henry?"

"Doc Henry *and* Jonah Barb," she said at last. "Oblanski still has had no luck finding either one. Danny woke up last thinking he heard someone at the front door and called the police, but they found no one. I gotta run and make a call before I meet with Ethan."

"Call who?"

"Mary Ann from up in Custer," Ana Maria said. "She says she just remembered some things she forgot before. I'll keep you posted."

Arn stuck his last fry into the tiny catchup cup as Gorilla Legs answered the phone. Arn could only describe her phone manners as a growl until, he identified himself. "Mr. Anderson," she said, softening her voice. If that were even possible. "Whatever can I do for you?"

"I'd like to speak with Chief Oblanski."

"He's in an important meeting," she said, "but I am certain he will wish to take *your* call. One moment."

Willie Nelson sang with Ray Charles softly in the phone until Chief Oblanski came online. "Did you learn anything from Beth Randall?" he asked.

Arn explained that Beth had told him Pudgy's proper name. "I had no luck calling Wagner. If you get hold of him, ask him to research Allen Randall's enlistment records. If we can find a photo of Pudgy—."

"You might be barking up the wrong tree there, pard'ner, if you're still thinking this Pudgy might be your suspect."

"How so?"

"Officers took a report this morning from Gold's Gym. Winger had his truck broken into and a whole toolbox stolen right there in the parking lot."

"How does that change the fact that Pudgy floated to the top of my suspect list?"

"I'll tell you how," Oblanski said. "Winger's tools were engraved by a marking pen so he could identify them. Engraved *S. H.*"

Samantha Holder's name popped into Arn's mind until Oblanski said., "It's for Winger's name," and Arn felt his heart sink. All this time, he had suspected Samantha of coldcocking him the night they were to meet, wielding a Craftsman wrench with her initials engraved. "Were they *Craftsman?*"

"They were," Oblanski said. "S. H. Steven Hayes. I got one call into Wagner already trying to locate Winger. He's got a meeting with Mike the Mauler when we find him. Now I *have* to run. I'm riding out with the deputies to meet with DCI. Some rancher found a dead body stuffed in his culvert."

Arn thought back to Bulldog. Had Danny brought in another of his old A.I.M. buddies to... talk with Doc Henry? If it was, Doc was becoming bolder. Less cautious in his killings. More likely now than he was when he worked an honest job to make his move on Ana Maria.

Arn dialed Ana Maria's number. It went straight to voice mail and he called Danny. He answered the phone out of breath. "I hate to admit it, but it's hard for this old man to hang a twelve-foot sheet of drywall on the ceiling without help."

"Then take a break," Arn said. He tossed the empty McDonald's sack in the trash and talked as he walked. "I need you to get a message to Ana Maria."

"Why not call her?"

"Because by now she's turned her ringer off while she conducted her interview with Ethan at the library." He told Danny about another dead body Oblanski was headed to. "You didn't con one of your other A.I.M. pards into trying to take out Doc Henry?"

"I didn't con Bulldog—."

"Just tell me," Arn pressed.

"No," Danny said.

"Then it's all the more reason she's alerted. Just go on over there—."

"Now you're authorizing me to take the truck?"

"This is more important than you getting a ticket for no DL. Just slip her a note under the door at the library room's she's at telling her Doc's about his work again, and suggest she get a police escort home."

"She's not gonna like you doting over her like this—."

"Just do it," Arn said. "Her safety might depend on it."

"Ok," Danny said. "I'll clean up real quick and drive on over."

———

Arn did his best not to worry about Ana Maria. He watched intently as men and women, families and single yuppies, walked—some ran— past him on their way to flights. Or missed flights altogether. Still, his thoughts returned to Ana Maria and the can of worms she might have opened with her coverage of the RSL and the veterans' deaths. Since the years that Arn had known her, Ana Maria had developed a sense of where danger lurked. She had avoided many circumstances in her reporting that might have had disastrous consequences for others less astute. But he'd also known her to throw caution to the stiff Wyoming wind when she thought a hot story was to be had.

He watched in amusement the people walking by and thought there were just too many variables that he couldn't get a grip on with these deaths. Jonah had been at the top of his suspect list with his radical zealots protesting at most of the VA facilities where the deaths had occurred

He had analyzed Samantha, also at VA centers, also traveling the area. But with Kane's man finding her tools were just as she claimed—*Snap-On*—she had slid down the suspect list and slid down even farther when Oblanski's officer took a report from Winger— aka Steven Hayes—of his tools of the brand that the attacker used against Arn.

And Pudgy. Allen Randall. Before his trip to interview Beth, Pudgy had been on the fringe—a weak enough suspect to be overshadowed by others—strong enough as a suspect to warrant Arn flying to Seattle and talking with Beth. *Father Knows Best*, Arn thought of the old television show. But in this case, *Mother Knows Best*. If Beth thought her son capable of murder, her instinct had told her what Pudgy might be capable of. Once Wagner obtained a photo of Allen Pudgy Randall and shared it with Kane to show to witnesses and compare with surveillance footage, Arn might have his killer.

Or not.

And amid all this was Doc Henry. There was no indication that he had anything to do with the deaths. Bulldog's murder—more than likely—but not the veterans' deaths. Doc wasn't about killing and terrorizing strange men. He was about killing and terrorizing women, and for now, it seemed his obsession with Ana Maria had brought him to town.

As Arn thought, he didn't know who he feared most going after Ana Maria—Doc Henry for his years of hatred, or Jonah Barb to silence her from exposing his RSL group. Danny called. "She wasn't at the library," he said. "She met with a nice-looking guy I'm guessing is Ethan Ames. They visited in a side room for over an hour and she left afterward."

"With him?"

"No. The librarian says Ana Maria left a few minutes before the guy did. He hung around looking at psychology books for sale in the book room before leaving. I tried calling her phone, but she must have forgotten to put the ringer back on."

"Dammit," Arn said, "I told her a dozen times it's not safe for her to keep her ringer off."

"She'll probably be home soon," Danny said. "She knows I'm making her favorite tonight—Welsh Rarebit."

"Ok," Arn said. "Take side streets home. Last thing you need is a ticket."

"You know it," Danny said and hung up.

46

ARN TRIED DOZING. HE DRAPED his hat over his eyes and, about the time that he actually thought he'd catch a nap, some urchin would run screaming by with the mom screaming even louder in hot pursuit. So when his phone vibrated in his pocket, he was fully awake as he flipped it open.

"Arn?" Ana Maria said, her voice strangely calm. Quiet. As if she were fighting to remain so. "You need to come back to Cheyenne."

"I'm waiting for my flight now." He checked his watch. "If it's not delayed, it leaves here in a little over three hours. Back in Cheyenne in six unless the Denver traffic's too nasty."

"I do not have six hours."

"What do you mean, you don't have six hours? You know I'm headed home, and you ought to be, too, if you want Danny's Welsh—."

"Arn!" And Maria snapped. "I'm telling you, in six hours I will be dead. Unless you get here in three."

Arn's gut churned as he recognized that voice, that angry yet pleading voice. Ana Maria needed help. And Arn was the only one to help her. "Ok," Arn said. "Breathe deeply and tell me with a yes or no—are you in danger right this instant?"

"Yes."

"Is someone holding you against your will?"

Yes."

"Are you in a position to tell me who?

There was a long pause and muffled voices over the phone before Ana Maria came back on, "not if I want to live through this night."

"Ok. Ok," Arn said, thinking quickly. "I'll charter a flight. Will that get me back in time?"

Muffled voices once again, and Arn could only imagine what condition Ana Maria was in right this moment. "Leave Seattle. Now. Talk with no one," muted voices. "Take no detours anywhere. Come straight to Cheyenne."

"Where?"

"When you arrive, call my phone number," Ana Maria said. "You will be told where to come. And Arn," she started sobbing, "do not deviate from your instructions," and the phone disconnected.

Arn grabbed his travel bag and ran to the information counter. He got directions to Business Air and ran across the terminal, stopping at the first kiosk he encountered. "I need to charter a flight."

The woman behind the counter leaned over and looked at a planner. "Where to?"

"Cheyenne, Wyoming."

"Oh my," she said. "That's a *loooong* way off. That will be pricy." She flipped a page. "And just when do you wish to fly out?"

"Now."

She grinned wide as she grabbed a phone and punched in numbers. "That *will* be expensive, indeed."

———

Arn didn't even know Honda made an airplane, let alone one that it flew above forty-thousand feet according to the pilot who seemed fascinated that someone would spend two-thousand dollars for a charter flight to someplace as remote as Wyoming. "There's cocktails in the fridge," the pilot called back and she laughed. "With what you're paying the company, we can afford for you to get knee-walking drunk at our expense."

"I'd just like some quiet time to think," he said and left the drink mixers alone while he dialed Oblanski's number. "I was just going to call you," the chief said, "and tell you about that croaker the rancher found in his culvert."

"Tell me later," Arn said, and hurriedly told Oblanski about his phone call from Ana Maria.

"She gave no hint as to who was holding her?"

"I got the distinct impression she was being monitored very closely. I shudder to think what would have happened if she said more than she was allowed."

"I'll put out a BOLO for her car—."

"Danny said her car was still parked at the library."

"Shit," Oblanski said. A beat. "Here's my plan—since you were warned not to contact the police, I'm going to call in every officer we have. Plainclothes. We only have a limited number of unmarked cars, but I'll authorize mileage for those who drive their own. I don't know just what to look for, and I'm relying on the experience of my officers to see when *something* is out of place that might lead us to her."

Arn checked his watch. The library had been closed for a couple hours. "Can you send a man over to talk with the librarian who saw Ana Maria there earlier? See if anyone followed her out to her car. And it might be a long shot, but could you send a TTY Denver Airport Police and ask them to run down Ethan Ames. He should just about be boarding his redeye for D. C. about now. He might remember something. Anything that he recalls from his interview with Ana Maria earlier."

"That I can do just as soon as we hang up," Oblanski said. "Think hard now, and tell me who *you* think took her?"

"Doc Henry would be at the very top of my list. I can see him taking her as a hostage to get me alone. I'd say he hates Ana Maria and me equally."

"I had a bad feeling about her broadcasts," Oblanski said. "I was afraid she'd stir up a hornet's nest with all that talk about the veterans' murders."

"Don't forget the RSL," Arn said. "Jonah Barb would be right under Doc on my suspect list. The way he's been sending her threatening emails. The dead cats. The slashed tires—."

"He's at the *bottom* of my list."

"The bottom? That man is about as snaky as they come."

"That man is about as *dead* as they come," Oblanski said, and Arn thought he heard the chief chuckle. "Colonel Barb was that body the rancher found in his culvert. The coroner thinks Jonah has been dead more than a week."

"That's impossible," Arn said. "He was emailing Ana Maria all this time.".

"Unless he wasn't the one sending the email," Oblanski said. "Unless someone else sent them."

"Doc Henry," Arn breathed, and mentally kicked himself in the keister. When Doc was actively luring unsuspecting women to their deaths in Colorado, he was not caught because of his profile origins on dating networks. The computer forensics officers never linked Doc to any of the victims, he hid his activities so well. It was old fashioned police work—and luck that Ana Maria acquired a cell phone to call Arn—that had solved the case and saved her. Even after Doc was caught, there was never any computer footprint to connect him to the other victims. "Was there by any chance a white rose atop the corpse?"

"Matter of fact, there was," Oblanski said. "Pretty wilted in this heat but it was there."

"Doc Henry," he whispered and his gut churned.

Arn thought deep, thought back to what he'd learned this last week with his interviews, his brief visits with people at the VA. "Oh, shit," he breathed.

"What is it?"

"If I'm right, Ana Maria is in *imminent* danger."

"From who?"

"When I know something more certain, I'll call," he said and closed his phone. "Shit," he whispered, as if the killer could hear him miles away.

47

A RN LANDED AT THE AIRPORT and tipped the pilot a hundred dollars for getting him quicker than he expected. *What the hell,* he thought. *What's another sawbuck as long as my credit card was maxed out anyway.*

Danny proudly sat behind the wheel of Arn's Olds ink the airport parking lot waiting for him when he landed. "Any word?"

"I called Oblanski an hour ago. And again, twenty minutes before we landed. Nothing. He has forty-odd officers combing the city looking for her. Got my gun?"

Danny reached in the glove box and handed Arn his Airweight .38. "You want me to drop myself off at home?"

"Not until I find out where I am supposed to go. Wherever it is, I might have you drop me off well away from the spot." Arn flipped his phone open. "Here goes."

Arn hit Ana Maria's number on speed dial. It rang. And rang. And rang. His gut started churning again, his mind racing: what has happened to Ana Maria that she won't—or can't—answer her cell phone. *Have I gotten here too late...*

Ana Maria came on the line. "Arn?"

"I'm here in Cheyenne. Where—."

"Just listen," she said, her voice breaking up. "You're to come to the VA Center. Park your car in the lot. You will be picked up and brought to my location. Are you at the airport?"

"I am."

"I am told you have but five minutes to get here," and the line went dead.

"Get to the VA," Arn said, already punching in Oblanski's number. "We only have five minutes tops."

"With your 442 I can halve that time."

Danny boiled the tires, smoke erupting from scorched rubber, the car's back-end fishtailing as he shot into traffic. "Ned. I've received another order."

"Hope it pays off," Oblanski said. "We haven't had any luck finding Ana Maria so far."

"The VA center. I've gotta be there in five minutes, so get word to your guys not to stop a gold Oldsmobile driving like hell."

"Five minutes doesn't give us enough time to meet you and fit you with a tracker."

"That's probably the idea," Arn said. "Whoever thought this out is one meticulous bastard." Arn told him his instructions were to wait for *someone* to pick him up at the VA. But take him where?

"Let me check the status of my units," Oblanski said. Arn clung tightly to the door handle as Danny slid around the corner onto Pershing. "I've got two officers in the vicinity," Oblanski said. "I'll keep them out of the VA compound. Set one up at each entrance and wait for you to come out. But how the hell will they know it's you?"

Arn thought as he rubbed his sweaty head. "I'll wear my Stetson. No one in their right mind wears a cowboy hat in this heat."

"And you still have no idea who is holding Ana Maria?"

"Not for certain. Have you tried pinging the cell tower?"

"AT&T tech are working on it, but she could be most anywhere in town. Locating someone just isn't that accurate to find out what building a cell is emitting signals," Oblanski said. ""But here's my plan—my officers will grab your tail when you're driven out, I've got the tactical team ready."

Danny ran through the light at the east entrance to the VA and headed for the parking lot. "Douse your lights," Arn said, "and motor over to the far parking lot real slow. I want whoever we're dealing with to see the car. And we might catch a break and see who the hell it is if he has to come all the way across the empty lot. Scoot down in the seat as soon as you park. I don't want you to be spotted. When we see who comes up to the car, you call Oblanski's number and tell him."

———

Arn jumped when the phone rang louder than Arn wished in the still night air. "My guys still haven't spotted you coming out of the compound," Oblanski said. "Are you sure Ana Maria said to come to the parking lot at the VA?" Oblanski said.

"That's what she was *told* to say."

"It's been nearly two hours."

Arn wiped sweat from his forehead with his bandana. The windows were rolled down in the Olds, and the humid air seemed to hang right over the old car. "Don't remind me. I'm getting more than a little worried."

"Keep me posted if you can," Oblanski said and hung up.

"What if it took us too long to get here?" Danny asked as he lay scrunched down in the driver's seat. "What if Ana Maria's been taken somewhere? Or worse?"

Danny didn't have to say aloud what Arn had been thinking since pulling in here and hearing nothing more. *Had it taken too long,* Arn had wondered. No, he finally concluded—it had not. Whoever held Ana Maria held her as a hostage to draw Arn in. The SOB was just being wary.

Arn caught movement in the parking lot and he griped his gun butt just as two mulie doe meandered across the lot towards the trees to the west.

Arn breathed out deeply and settled back in the seat.

When his phone rang.

"Arn," Ana Maria whispered into her phone. "Change of plans. Come into the main entrance."

"It's after hours. It's locked."

"No," she stammered. "It will be unlocked." Muted sounds coming from her end. "Come all the way down the hall until it tees. Go right. You'll receive more instructions."

Silence.

"Call Oblanski," Arn said. "I'm instructed to go inside."

"Maybe you'll be picked up out back."

"Maybe," Arn said. "Hold your hand over the dome light."

Arn rolled out of the car and avoided the streetlights over the parking lot, approaching the entrance in the shadows though he was certain he was being observed even now.

At the entrance to the VA, the automatic door failed to slide open and he worked his fingers between the doors, until one slid far enough he could get inside.

Once he got past the second set of sliding doors he paused, letting his eyes adjust to the darkened hallway. Off to his left, light filtered vaguely from down the hall from the Emergency Room, the waiting area outside the audio section and information desk cold. Dark. Empty, like Arn's gut had been these last hours since Ana Maria's first call.

He took the small revolver from his back pocket and held it beside his leg as he slowly made his way down the hallway, stopping now and again. Listening.

Silence but for noises coming from the ER.

When he reached the t-intersection, he peeked around the corner. "Take the hallway to the right," Ana Maria had told him, and he squinted. Light from an *EXIT* sign above a door was the only light in this part of the facility, the illuminating from that even growing dim as he entered the part of the center under construction.

He stopped and cocked an ear.

Had there been a noise coming from one of the empty side rooms… *whimpering*? *Sobbing*, loud in the quiet of the hallway?

He wiped the sweat from his palm and clutched the gun tighter while he inched his way toward the sound.

Stop! his instinct told him.

He put his ear to the wall. The sobbing he had heard before rose and fell just behind the door and he chanced a peek through the small square of door glass. Ana Maria sat in a chair. A rag—torn sheet perhaps—encircled her mouth, and zip ties secured her to the chair. Light from a house in back of the VA shone dimly through a window, illuminating Ana Maria's frightened eyes as she spotted him.

He opened the door and duckwalked inside the darkened room.
Paused.

His eyes still adjusting.

His ears attuned.

Her eyes widening. She tried moving her head, but the rag
prevented her, the whites of her frightened eyes warning him of...
what? He looked around the cluttered room, with the desks and file
cabinets stuffed there during the remodeling.

Once more he wiped sweat from his palm before gripping his gun
tightly and stood slowly. Four tall, metal filing cabinets stood an odd
angle against one another next to Ana Maria's chair, and desks had
been overturned atop one another across the room beside rows of
chairs.

He walked hunched over.

She tried screaming though the rag.

Arn reached for his knife to cut the zip ties when...

...a blur from behind the filing cabinets. A hand coming down on
his neck, and he dropped. Just like Winger had done that day in the
training room.

He fought consciousness. His gun skidded across the room.

In the darkness, he was only vaguely aware that a syringe of some
type stuck in his arm and he rolled away from it, his hand flailing,
slapping at the syringe, dropping to the floor.

His hand fell on a broken table leg. He lashed out and connected
with *someone* who fell against the filing cabinets. They toppled over
as Arn regained his wits enough, struggling to his feet, running out
the door.

Farther down the hallway a pile of two-by-fours sat stacked next to
sheets of plywood tipped against the wall.

With just enough room for Arn to hide.

Just long enough to shake off the effects of the blow.

And whatever had been stuck injected into his arm.

He wiggled between the wall and the plywood, keeping his face
down, covering his face from any shine. Any detection. *Hell to be a
Norwegian*, he thought. *If I was any whiter I'd have to fall into a fifty-
five gallon barrel of white-out. Just what I need when I'm trying to hide.*

His attacker stumbled out of the room and walked slowly down the hallway, checking open doors. Inside other filing cabinets stacked along one wall of the hallway.

The footsteps stopped beside the plywood.

Why the hell didn't I realize it was that bastard before, he thought as he continued holding his breath. *With Jonah dead over a week, there and how the killer* laid out *to Arn just who he was...* His lungs threatened to explode the longer he held his breath until...

The attacker resumed walking, searching, the shuffling steps on the sawdust-laden floor becoming fainter.

And stopped.

Arn shook his head as best he could within the confines of his small space, and his head began to clear.

Just as the effects of what he was injected with started to take effect.

He forced himself to remain conscious. Taking slow, quiet breaths. His attacker not knowing where his prey was hidden when...

...Arn's cell phone rang. And rang again. He fumbled to silence it. But too late for Arn.

"Thought you'd be dumb enough to keep your ringer on. Now climb on out of there. I don 't want this little gun of yours going off and making a ruckus. Now slip on out of there."

Arn crawled out on his elbows and knees and shook his head again. He tried standing, but he fell back against the wall, his vision blurred.

"No use standing up," Ethan said. "I didn't get as much Xylazine as I wanted before you swatted it away, but it's enough that you'll be drowsy until..."

Arn rubbed his eyes, Ethan's image blurring the longer Arn stared at him. "Ana Maria said you were on your way to D. C., but I knew better."

"Don't try to fool a psychologist," Ethan said. "I deal with some real *professional* liars trying to game the system. You didn't know a thing."

"Didn't I?" Arn rubbed his eyes. "I knew enough that the cops put out a BOLO on you. Ethan Ames—murderer of innocent veterans. The VA Slayer."

Arn tried standing but fell with his back against the wall. "You told me that you saw Jonah in the hallway the day Major Mills was found murdered here. If that were the case, Jonah would be alive then. But by that time, he was dead."

"Now you're clutching at limp straws," Ethan said. "Jonah's not dead. He just fled the area."

"So, the mighty Ethan Ames isn't all-knowing." Arn struggled to form words, drool dripping down one side of his mouth. If he could keep Ethan occupied long enough for the horse tranquilizer to wear off... "Jonah was found dead in a culvert at a ranch here. Probably killed by Doc Henry—."

"Now *that's* one crazy bastard. We were required to study his case in residency. But it doesn't prove you knew I killed those men."

Arn wiped the drool with his shirt sleeve, feeling more dripping down, his eyes becoming more blurred. "You told me *exactly* who you were when you gave me that profile: meticulous. Organized. Thinking they are more intelligent than everyone else in the room." Arn looked around the rubble, but there was nothing to use as a weapon. Even if he could focus on one. "Except you were not the most intelligent person—I found you out and now the law has, too."

"The only thing I didn't understand is why? Was it because of your father, or did you have bad run-ins with officers when you were in the military?"

"Who's to say I was *ever* in the military?"

"The verbiage you used now and again—*head* for restroom. *Affirmative. Negative.* A civilian just doesn't talk like that. And, you weren't the least concern ed with the Righteous Sword of the Lord protestors harming you. 'I can take care of them' is what you told me like you were... a Ranger?"

"Touché," Ethan said. "I will give you that and will remind myself not to slip up in the future."

"Believe me," Arn said, there will be no future for you once the law captures you."

"I doubt that," Ethan said, but his voice broke as if he believed Arn had alerted the law to him. "But to answer your question of why—because a man ought not to die before mysteries are explained to him—I can honestly say I hated officer even before I went into the Army. I can thank my dear nasty-ass pappy for instilling that into me."

"But why..."

"My old man wasn't much, but he was all I had. Mom didn't get along very well with him—guess she just couldn't take him ordering her around like he was still in the Army. So when she left for... Seattle is it... Pappy kind of educated me at home. Especially when I got accused of beating another kid and he pulled me out of school. The old man used to laugh at that—a high school dropout home-schooling his high school dropout of a kid."

"But... innocent officers. Never harmed you—."

"They were officers nonetheless. When I heard Pappy hung himself, I knew the thought of what Captain Sims and all the officers had done to him finally took its toll on the old man. And Pappy's hate within me just boiled over when I saw Sims that day in Sheridan."

Ethan sat atop the pile of lumber and covered Arn with the gun. "Captain Sims was the first one, but you already know that. I spotted him in the VA in Sheridan when I first landed this counseling gig with the VA. You could say I went off on the good Captain on impulse. Damn near got caught, too." He winked. "That's when I decided to think things out. Research the best way, the safest way to kill a man quickly. I didn't really find a fool proof way until I started counseling Johnny McGomerary once a week."

"The coke head?"

"I hate that term."

Arn thought back to what Johnny's dealer told the Denver investigators—Johnny's friend that he started selling to—was good looking. Well dressed. Everything Ethan was.

"That day I drove Johnny down to the VA in Denver and he stopped to make a buy, I met his dealer. I came back the next day to the same smokehouse and the man said he'd sell me all I wanted. As pure as I wanted, if I had the money. But all I needed was enough to OD those officers."

"So your sister isn't involved?"

"My sister?" Ethan said. "I don't even know *where* she is. Long grown and on her own by now, I figured. But when Ana Maria said you had a line on mom and was in route to interview her, well, you understand I couldn't take the chance that she'd tell you enough about me that you could hone in on me. Maybe provide you with some old photos that you could have aged them to look like I do now. And you'd recognize me. I couldn't take that chance, so I had to lure you here."

"But why *those* men?" Arn asked, shaking his head violently, trying to stay alert. Killing time. Feeling the effects of the Xylazine wear off ever so slowly. If only he had *enough* time.

"The only one besides Johnny I knew was Frank Mosby. He and I met while we were running a 10K. Guess I got so hooked on running in the Rangers I naturally *had* to hit the road most days back then."

The Rangers. Pudgy's special class he wrote about in his letter to Beth. Arn rubbed his neck and tried gathering his legs under him, but he fell onto his back. He grabbed the side of the plywood and sat up.

"You'll excuse me if I stunned the hell out of you—I have to take that class from Winger twice a year, only because I deal with violent veterans who might need controlling in my counseling work." He laughed. "I always thought it was ridiculous to have to attend until I saw how effective it was in knocking someone for a loop long enough to inject them with enough cocaine to kill a horse."

"Horse," Arn said, struggling to recall something about a horse… "Where did you get the tranquilizer?"

"An old friend," Ethan said. "He used to be in counseling after he came back from Iraq and after moving to Cheyenne. He and I were stationed at Ft. Sill for a time, and I told him what a decent place this was. That folks here needed traveling veterinarians. He had a hell of a time before I helped him down the straight and narrow and got him into college. And later, veterinarian school."

"Seth Barnes?"

Ethan nodded. "I didn't use the Xylazine but a couple times. Didn't need to. The stun was usually enough to put my man down and out long enough to give him the dose."

"That you gave in their veins and covered the injection site up with a Band-Aid?" Arn said, his thoughts clearing even though his coordination was still worse than a drunken weekend sailor.

Ethan laughed. "Pretty shrewd, don't cha think? Making it look like the old farts had just had a blood draw."

"And the ones under the tongue?"

Ethan shrugged. "Dudes get old... sometime it's hard to find a vein in the spur of the moment. When I had a man with collapsed veins, I simply injected under the tongue. Which I believe I will do to you."

"Now you're going to kill me?"

Ethan nodded. "You do have a grasp on your imminent future."

"That'll still leave Ana Maria—."

"No, it won't." He tapped his shirt pocket. "I have enough coke here to kill you both many times over. And when your friend, Chief Oblanski, finds you and Ana Maria together in a remote part of the VA with needles stuck in your arms, he'll just assume you two had your own private party."

Ethan stood and set the gun on the lumber pile as he dug into his shirt pocket to retrieve the syringe. He took the cap off the needle and pushed lightly on the plunger. "Took me a while to learn how to liquify this from the powder, but you might say I perfected it thanks to YouTube. He stepped toward Arn. "Say goodnight, Mr. Anderson."

Arn tried scooting back. HHe hit the wall. His hand groped in the dim light for something, anything that would be a weapon, his arm falling limp, useless to the floor.

Was that genuine sadness etched on Ethan's face as he advanced? *The Xylazine. Tranquilizer. Skewing my mind. Imagining things. Imagining...* a figure that threw himself over the pile of lumber and crashed into Ethan. The syringe dropped on the floor, rolling away as...

Ethan fumbled for the coke-filled syringe as he turned into the figure...

...too late. Danny—the hypodermic filled with Xylazine in his hand—impaled Ethan's neck with the needle, and pushed the plunger home.

Ethan backhanded Danny and he toppled over the lumber.

Arn groped for the syringe of cocaine Ethan had dropped, but he kicked Arn in the side, and he fell back against the wall.

Ethan clawed at the syringe dangling from his neck and jerked it out. He looked at Danny with an animal rage in his eyes. "You little bastard," he said looking for the gun in the dark. Failing to find it, he grabbed an old, worn Barlow knife from his pocket and opened a blade as he advanced on Danny. Steps *slowing. Slower. Legs buckling.* Ethan slashed the air with the blade, when he fell to the floor, a dazed and glassy look washing over his eyes as he lay immobile on his back, staring up at the ceiling.

Danny crawled back across the pile of lumber and kicked Ethan's syringe of coke away before grabbing Arn's gun form the pile of lumber. He pointed it at Ethan, but the gun was unnecessary—Ethan wouldn't be moving on his own any time soon.

Danny crawled to Arn and eased him flat onto the floor.

"What the hell…"

"Just lay there," Danny said as he tucked Arn's gun into his waistband. He looked at Ethan lying semi-conscious a few feet away. "I shot him in the neck with the stuff he intended shooting you up with. Horse tranquilizer if Ana Mari is correct."

"Ana Maria…"

Danny kept his hand on Arn's shoulder, talking quietly. "She's all right, I untied the rag long enough for her to tell me what was going on."

Arn rubbed his head, only slightly less foggy than before, and turned his head to look at Ethan.

"Looks like Ethan got just enough horse tranquilizer to make him drowsy," Danny kicked Ethan's leg. "This ought to keep him out at least long enough for Oblanski's men to find us."

"But Ana Maria…"

"I said she's fine." Danny punched numbers in his trac phone. "And you will be, too, as soon as the paramedics arrive."

48

ARN FOLLOWED CHIEF OBLANSKI INTO the interview room just as Mike the Mauler was beginning to start the interview. "Take a break from this one," Oblanski told him. "This is more a debriefing than an interrogation." He smiled at her. "I think Ana Maria's going to be a cooperative one."

"I hope to shout." Ana Maria rubbed gauze wrapped around her wrists covering the cuts from the zip ties. Bruising on each cheek showing where Ethan had tied the sheet tightly around her mouth that her makeup didn't quite hide, and a bruise showed on the side of her neck where he had stunned her.

"I tried to call you," Ana Maria told Arn.

"When?"

"After I finished interviewing Ethan. He caught up with me in the parking lot and wondered if I wanted to catch brunch before he flew out. While we were driving to the Village Inn, I got a call from Mary Ann in Custer. She'd remembered that Bo's middle name was Ames. I guess Ethan saw there was something wrong after I hung up and pulled into the park beside the Big Boy locomotive. I wasn't going to break down, but something about his threats to OD me on coke loosened my tongue."

Arn hit the table and pain shot up his arm from the injection site. "How could I have missed Ethan?" Arn said. "The running habit. A lover of horses. He even counseled Seth Barnes and later got the tranquilizer from him. Remember I said Seth refused to dime off his friend because he helped him and was a good listener? Who better to listen than a therapist?

"And some… simple things he said. Military verbiage: affirmative. Negative. Referred to a restroom as a head. Like he was used to talking that way. Like he'd been used to answering others in that manner, yet when I first met him, he denied being prior military. That alone should have set off red flags."

"I'm as much at fault," Wagner said. "I put off checking those enlistment files from Sheridan, and just a few hours ago got a photo of Ethan Allan Randall in my inbox. It showed a heavy-set kid of eighteen, but it was Ethan all right.

"And the dates… when I managed to cross reference them, all your suspects were at most of the VAs—Samantha and Winger. Jonah with his goofy bunch protesting. Blinded me to even consider other suspects."

"Speaking of Jonah Barb," Arn said. "What theories do you have as to his murder, Ned?"

Oblanski sipped on a Diet Coke. "Nothing that will hold water. Whoever killed him—I'm betting that Doc Henry did—strangled him with a belt and stuffed him in that culvert a week ago. Why he kept sending threatening emails and the cat and slashed tires to Ana Maria making it appear as if Jonah was responsible makes no sense. Does it to you?"

Ana Maria shook her head. "None. Except I'll still have to look over my shoulder for him."

"No leads on Doc?" Arn asked.

"Not yet. He never gave a notice at Mimi's. Just one night when he was supposed to cook, he just never showed. We went to his apartment he rented on the south side, and everything was still there except his computer."eHH

Someone knocked on the interview room door and Wagner answered it. Danny came in with paper plates and forks and a lemon meringue pie. "Figured we'd need some comfort food while we talk about how we ever missed Ethan."

When Danny laid a piece of pie in front of Oblanski, he paused. "I recall that last pie you made—."

"I didn't make this one," Danny said. "Didn't have time. Bought it ready-made from Shari's Pies."

Ana Maria nudged him. "With what you did last night, you deserve to take a break."

Danny rubbed his shoulder. "Don't have much choice. That Ethan is one strong SOB. When he tossed me over that the pile of lumber, I hit so hard I'm surprised I didn't break a shoulder."

"I bet you're glad that Xylazine you shot into Ethan took effect when it did," Arn said. "I know I am."

Danny passed out forks and napkins and sat at the small interrogation table. "I didn't know how much tranquilizer was left, or how much of a dose you got. When I untied Ana Maria's gag, she said you had knocked the needle and syringe away just as Ethan was injecting you before you ran off. She figured you didn't receive a full dose."

"All I know is that I'm grateful you were as sneaky as you were," Ana Maria said.

Danny shrugged. "There are *some* things I remember from 'Nam—like putting the sneak on an enemy."

Oblanski cautiously bit into the first piece, and a smile crossed his face. "I'm assuming there'll be a special TV presentation on all this," he asked Ana Maria.

She nodded and dabbed at her bruised mouth with a napkin. "DeAngelo said that—after he spent a fortune on Arn's trip to Seattle, not to mention reimbursing him for the charter flight back—there had *better* be something special. He agreed to an hour-long presentation, which is unheard of here."

"I'm hoping you leave out Winger and Samantha's non-involvement in the events," Arn said.

"Have you been brave enough to get hold of her?" Oblanski asked. "Hard to let a looker like that get away."

Arn finished his pie in three bites. He was famished after being monitored at the hospital all night form the effects of the Xylazine. In the room right next to Ethan. "I've left three messages with her secretary here and one each at Hot Springs and Sheridan. She hasn't returned my calls, and I'm not holding my breath she will." Arn shook his head. "Only one to blame is myself. If I hadn't suspected her—."

"You weren't alone," Ana Maria said and turned to Oblanski.

"When Arn brought up the possibility of two killers—one gruesome and sloppy, the other one meticulous—even *I* thought Sam might be a suspect, working with Pudgy. Especially when we discussed brother-sister serial killers, and what a beauty his sister was, though we had no pics. So when I saw Seth Barnes and Sam at dinner... I guess my suspicions got the better of me."

"I will graciously make it a point to meet with her," Oblanski said. "Tell her the reasons she was suspected. As I'll do with Winger Hayes."

"You gonna meet with Winger?" Wagner said. "Now what's he done?"

"It's what he *hasn't* done," Oblanski said. "When it looked like it was Winger's wrench that tried caving Arn's head in, The Mauler brought Winger in for interrogation. Damned near had him in tears. I think I owe him an explanation just to ease his mind that we're not bringing him back for round two with The Mauler."

"I'm just thankful all this is over," Ana Maria said. "Now I can go home and crash for about a week."

"Just make sure your house alarm is armed," Oblanski said. "Doc Henry's still out there. Somewhere."

———

The Mauler came out for a moment to get fresh coffee for the stenographer and two officers guarding him as well as for Ethan. Oblanski stared through the one-way glass into the interrogation. "He said this was the easiest interrogation he'd ever had. And the lengthiest. The Mauler figures this will clear up all the veteran-deaths here and in Wyoming and South Dakota."

Arn turned the volume up. "Now let's get to this sixth retired military officer," The Mauler asked. "When did you first make contact with him and...?

Arn flipped the volume control off. "Has Ethan said anything we don't already know?"

Oblanski looked at hen scratchings on a legal pad in front of him. "Hard to keep track, but Ethan confirmed much of what we already knew: he targeted officers because his father hated them and passed that hatred off to his son. He freely admitted he would have killed his mother to prevent us from discovering his identity if he would have known her address. But by the time he found her address in Seattle, the house was empty, and he searched for her since. That's what he intended doing when he lured you to the VA and had that syringe of Xylazine—get you doped up enough where you'd tell him Beth's address and not even care if you did."

"Did he come clean with attacking me?"

"He did," Oblanski answered, his arms crossed, watching the casual way in which Ethan answered The Mauler's questions. "He laughed about it, until he became serious and said he should have finished the job. As far as the tools, he stole the crescent wrench from Winger's toolbox hoping to set him up. Or set up Samantha as they have the same initials."

"Guess Ethan didn't know Sam is a *Snap-On* tool gal."

"Apparently," Oblanski said. "He said his secretary had learned from the 'gossip pool of secretaries' as he put it that Samantha and you were to go to dinner that night at Outback, and he let the air out of her tires right before she left her apartment the VA provides for her. 'I felt sorry for Anderson' he said, 'that Sam wasn't there to meet him So I did', and he laughed his fool head off."

Oblanski flipped the volume switch again. "Sure, I ran away from the old man when I was sixteen," Ethan said, and the stenographer tapped on her key machine. "Went to work at a ranch by Dayton until I turned eighteen—old enough to enlist there at the Army recruiting office in Sheridan. I was always going to come home and prod the old man. Wear my uniform. Maybe tell him I wanted to get into OCS. Become an officer. Just to piss him off." Ethan laughed. "Except before I went home on leave, he'd hung himself. Guess the damned officers finally pushed him over the edge."

Oblanski turned down the volume. "He also owned Brian Gibbs' murder. Ethan stopped at the Legion right after you left and had a beer with Brian Gibbs. He told him how you'd been in there looking for information, and he was worried that Gibbs might eventually get around to mentioning that Ethan was an ex-Ranger. 'Couldn't have that,' he told us. 'Someone might get around to looking for a former serviceman. And eventually narrow the search down further if they were looking for a Ranger," and he killed Gibbs after he locked the Legion up for the night."

"And he tossed the colonel wings beside the body?' Arn asked.

"Another thing I should have picked up on. That single colonel wing left beside Gibbs' body was bright. Shiny. Not like a pair that had been worn extensively during protests."

"I missed it, too," Oblanski said and turned up the speaker volume to the interrogation room.

The Mauler wrapped up his interview, the guards walking towards Ethan, the stenographer packing up her machine. "Thank you for your cooperation."

Ethan held up his hands as if in surrender. "No sense to lie. Besides, all this won't make a whit of difference. I'm crazy, don't you know."

"How so?" The Mauler asked.

"What sane man would kill military officers over something as flimsy as what his old man taught him? What judge won't look at my psych eval—whenever you get around to sending me to Evanston to see the state shrinks—and the ease with which I'm relating in all the details the deaths of my... victims and not determine I am a raving lunatic that deserves being locked up in your state mental institution."

"If I didn't know better," The Mauler said, "I'd say you're planning on gaming the system."

"Me?" Ethan feigned a hurt look as he held one hand over his heart. "Not hardly. But," he paused while the guards unchained him from the ring in the floor, "with the proper mental health treatment I could get better. Might heal enough that the shrinks in Evanston pronounce me... *cured*. If that happens, I'll get released to live a normal life. To function well in society. That day comes, I might even come back here," Ethan faced the one-way glass and cocked his finger like a mini-gun, "I might just look up my old friend Arn Anderson.

245

Epilogue

A RN PAUSED AT THE DOOR, his finger not quite touching the keypad on the house alarm before punching in the security code and arming the system. Snow had started early this year, as if often did in the high elevation of Cheyenne, and he carefully took off his wet boots before Dann-the-Clean-Nazi saw him tramping around the house.

"Where is everybody?" he called out.

"Sewing room," Danny shouted back.

As soon as Arn stepped into the room, he knew things were not right. Danny sat holding a plate with a half-eaten piece of chocolate cake, and Ana Maria sat transfixed at something in her lap. She looked up at Arn and handed him a dried and pressed white rose. "This came in the mail today."

"Doc," Arn said. "The son-of-a-bitch is still around." It had been two months since Doc had disappeared after killing Jonah Barb and Bulldog, though nothing could be directly tied to Doc. Oblanski had issued a five-state BOLO on him, and the DCI had followed up on every lead that came in to the Doc Henry Task Force tip line. There had been more *Doc leads* than those claiming to know where Jimmy Hoffa was panted. But thus far, all the sightings had been fruitless.

Ana Maria handed Arn a letter. "The flower came pressed inside this."

Arn opened the letter and read it twice:

Dearest Ana Maria,

If you are wondering just where I moved to, keep wondering. Neither the local law nor the state or federal boys have laid a glove on me. And they won't.

Now to the meat of the reason for my writing: I need you to understand what happened that time we first met online and later in person in Denver. I did not keep you with me to harm you permanently. I did not take you from that basement—and later when we fled Denver—to cause you any pain. I took you with me to be with me. And that is the reason for those threatening emails months ago. That was the reason for warning you with that dead cat thing (though now I admit it was pretty juvenile as was slashing your tires.) I warned you because I feared for your safety with the attention it would bring upon you. There was a killer out there—and believe me, I know killers—hunting veterans at local facilities.

I so wanted you to just stop your nightly specials. Take yourself out of harm's way. But you didn't. And by the time I realized you were taken and in imminent danger, it was too late for me to help you. Dr. Ames had already taken you, and I couldn't find you. That was the one time I was glad Anderson was alive—so that he could save my Ana Maria. When he came riding in on the white horse Olds of his I was actually grateful to him.

Just the thing that I envisioned when I worked so hard to gain parole. To save you myself.

We will meet again. That is a mathematical certainty. But you don't have to worry about looking over your shoulder, waiting for me to harm you. I won't.

I cannot say the same for Arn Anderson.

About the Author

C. M. WENDELBOE ENTERED THE law enforcement profession when he was discharged from the Marines as the Vietnam war was winding down.

In the 1970s, his career included assisting federal and tribal law enforcement agencies embroiled in conflicts with American Indian Movement activists in South Dakota.

He moved to Gillette, Wyoming, and found his niche, where he remained a sheriff's deputy for more than 25 years.

During his 38-year career in law enforcement he had served successful stints as police chief, policy adviser, and other supervisory roles for several agencies. Yet he always has felt most proud of "working the street." He was a patrol supervisor when he retired to pursue his true vocation as a fiction writer.

He writes the Spirit Road Mystery series; Bitter Wind Mystery series, Nelson Lane Frontier Mystery series, and the Tucker Ashley Western series.

CPSIA information can be obtained
at www.ICGtesting.com
Printed in the USA
FFHW020637141219
56835981-62518FF